Sunrise Over Savannah

"This is a beautiful story. Well written, deep characters, lots of drama, especially toward the end."

—Love Bytes (The Blog of Sid Love)

"Scotty Cade writes a remarkable story about love, forgiveness, and getting a second chance to live life to its fullest, as well as to love and be loved."

—Prism Book Alliance

Chasing the Horizon

"This was a lovely read… If you love romance, hot lovin' and walking contradictions…you will love *Chasing the Horizon*. Highly recommending."

—MM Good Book Reviews

"Mr. Cade wrote a wonderful story for Garner and Hawk… I would highly recommend this book and cannot wait to see what is in store for us next."

—The Novel Approach

An Unconventional Courtship

"I really liked this book and [am] interested in finding out what happens with the characters."

—Mrs. Condit & Friends Read Books

An Unconventional Union

"I enjoyed this one. It's a well-written love story between our two guys but has enough twists, sadness and pain to keep it from becoming sappy."

—Literary Nymphs Reviews

"Beautifully written with characters that live and breathe off of the written page, *An Unconventional Union* is one of my favorite books I've read this year."

—Top 2 Bottom Reviews

By SCOTTY CADE

Acting Out
Final Encore
The Mystery of Ruby Lode

Sunrise Over Savannah • Chasing the Horizon

An Unconventional Courtship
An Unconventional Union

LOVE SERIES
Bounty of Love
Foundation of Love
Treasure of Love
Wings of Love

Published by DREAMSPINNER PRESS
http://www.dreamspinnerpress.com

ACTING OUT

SCOTTY CADE

Dreamspinner Press

Published by
DREAMSPINNER PRESS

5032 Capital Circle SW, Suite 2, PMB# 279, Tallahassee, FL 32305-7886 USA
http://www.dreamspinnerpress.com/

Acting Out
© 2014 Scotty Cade.

Cover Art
© 2014 Reese Dante.
http://www.reesedante.com
Cover content is for illustrative purposes only and any person depicted on the cover is a model.

ISBN: 978-1-63216-111-6
Digital ISBN: 978-1-63216-112-3
Library of Congress Control Number: 2014944163
First Edition September 2014

Printed in the United States of America
∞
This paper meets the requirements of
ANSI/NISO Z39.48-1992 (Permanence of Paper).

To my loving husband, Kell, who continues to sacrifice his time so I can fulfill my dreams of writing. Writing takes me away from him and our business, and he always picks up the load. I love you!

Also, to my BNO boys on Martha's Vineyard. You have no idea how much book material you guys give me. There is a little part of each of you in all of my characters, and for that you will always live on in my revelry. Kell and I treasure your friendship more than you'll ever know.

FOREWORD

IN PREPARATION for this book, I spent hours upon hours doing research about the "Gay for Pay" porn industry. I forced myself to watch a lot of hot guys getting it on. But… that's a whole other story.

Sorry! I digress. Now where was I? Oh yeah. But—the more websites I stumbled upon, the more intrigued I became. I've never been a porn watcher, not because I'm too much of a prude, but simply because I never really got into it. But… with that said, I perused over two dozen sites, many of them "military type" sites, and I watched snippets of the free videos available to "looky loos" like me, and to be blatantly honest, it was pretty apparent to this novice that only a few held true to the myth of "straight" on "straight."

After narrowing it down to these few sites, because they seemed legitimate and because the guys did pre- and post-video interviews, I bought trial memberships and binge watched. What I saw was real "straight" guys having gay sex. Sure, they were having sex, but there was just no emotional connection between the men. They were going through the acts, doing any and everything, but there was no real lust or affection between them. And… that got the old wheels a-turning.

So I started previewing the many videos each of these sites had to offer, but more importantly, I listened intently to the interviews, where the guys talked about themselves and why they did what they did. I was amazed at the camaraderie between the men, all supporting one another and at the same time teasing one another, albeit mercifully. With each interview I learned more and more about what made these men tick. Much to my surprise, many of them were married with small children, and many had girlfriends. It was clear that they were doing what they had to do to put food on the table.

After gravitating to a couple of guys in particular, I watched every video for each of them—sometimes together, sometimes with other guys—and I instantly liked these two men and was drawn to them and their story. Or... at least what I could piece together from watching their interviews. They seemed open and honest and genuinely humble. These are the two men who inspired Eli and Hamish.

I hope you enjoy this story because I sacrificed a lot of hours watching gay porn for your reading enjoyment. ☺

XXOO

Scotty

CHAPTER ONE
CIRCUMSTANCE

FIRST SERGEANT Elijah Preston gripped the edge of the bathroom sink and stared at his hazy reflection in the mirror. The long hot shower had done nothing for his disposition, and he sighed as the unrecognizable image staring back summed up his life to a tee. His life had been unrecognizable for a while now. He had very little money, no real place to call home, no job, no real friends, and worst of all, he didn't see any of that changing in the foreseeable future.

He dropped his head in defeat and fixated on the cracked floor tiles under his bare feet. *I hate this fucking hellhole of a motel.* In a fit of frustration, Elijah ripped the tiny blow-dryer from the wall mount and pointed it at the foggy mirror. A blurry-edged circle appeared as his image slowly started to materialize. Under the harsh florescent lighting, his normally piercing hazel eyes appeared dull and lifeless. His sun-bleached skin looked dry, weather-beaten, and not at all like the smooth olive complexion he'd sported as a teenager.

IT HAD been exactly one month to the day since Elijah had been honorably discharged from the United States Marine Corps after serving one very long tour of duty. He'd signed on the dotted line right after high school graduation with the hopes of getting as far away from his alcoholic parents and his hometown of Berry, Kentucky, as he could, but also knowing it was the only chance he had of getting a good education and making something out of his life. His strategy had been to do the normal four years active duty, work hard, save as much money as he could, and then get a degree while he spent the next four years on reserve duty until his discharge. But his plan had been interrupted by the small print and one particular "unless needed" clause in his enlistment papers. Right after basic training, he'd been shipped overseas to Afghanistan and had spent almost his entire eight-year tour of duty there.

When he'd left Afghanistan, he'd also left behind everyone who'd mattered to him. After his grandmother died, he'd refused stateside visits, knowing that the people serving with him were more his family than those he'd left behind, and even Afghanistan was better than the hellhole he used to call home. He'd thought seriously about reenlisting but had decided against it, figuring it was time to stop running away and make a life for himself outside of the military.

Two weeks before his discharge, he'd been stationed at Marine Corps Base Quantico in Quantico, Virginia, with little to do but get his affairs in order, map out his future, and anticipate the life of a civilian. In doing so, he'd discovered that sometimes the best-laid plans fall apart.

RIGHT AFTER he'd enlisted, Elijah had opened a checking account at a small bank in Berry, and during his eight years overseas, via automatic deposit, he'd saved almost every penny he'd earned. Or so he thought. He'd put his mother's name on the account in case anything happened to him while he was overseas, and although his parents had been on the wagon at the time, during the last eight years, they'd helped themselves to every penny of his money.

She'd given him some tear-filled, cockamamie story about how she'd supposedly "invested" the money in a sure thing that had gone sour, but he'd known that, more than likely, they'd spent it all on vodka, cigarettes, and gambling. He'd kicked himself in the ass over and over for not having the bank statements electronically sent to him, but he'd never imagined, no matter how weak they were, they would steal from their only child. To add insult to injury, when he'd told them he was coming to get his truck, they'd confessed it had been in an accident and was no longer drivable.

So here he was after eight years in the USMC with nothing but his last paycheck and a certification in communications to show for his time served. For the last month he'd lived in this dive of a motel, pinched every penny, and searched the Internet day after day for a job in his field. He had no ties to anyone or anything, so location was no issue; he could relocate anywhere in the country. In the meantime, he also searched locally for anything that would help supplement what little money he had until he eventually found a job and moved.

ELIJAH HUNG his wet towel over the shower rod and stepped onto the soiled carpet of the small bedroom. The morning sun was beating through the dingy blue drapes barely covering the double windows, and the clock on top of the battered chest read 8:35. He fumbled through the drawers and retrieved his last pair of clean underwear, a worn T-shirt, and a pair of white socks. When he stepped into his briefs and attempted to pull them up, his finger went right through the thin cotton and the waistband separated from the rest of the underwear. "Motherfucker," he hissed.

He angrily tossed the underwear into the trash can in the corner of the room and stepped into his old blue jeans commando. After pulling the T-shirt over his head and slipping on his socks and shoes, he went back into the bathroom.

Elijah ran his forefinger around the edge of a small jar, getting the last bit of pomade and rubbing it in his hands before applying it to his light brown hair. "You've held off as long as you can, Eli," he mumbled, spiking his bangs and wishing the military cut would hurry up and grow out. "You need clothes."

With no other choice, Elijah called a cab to take him the four miles to the Walmart in nearby Dumfries and sat outside his motel room and waited. And waited. When the cab finally dropped him off in front of the store exactly ninety minutes later, Elijah asked the driver to pick him up in an hour, not wanting to pay the extra fee for making the guy wait.

Elijah rolled the shopping cart up and down the aisles of the men's department, trying to decide what to buy. After wearing nothing but uniforms for the last eight years, he was at a total loss for what was in style. Not that he was a stylish guy, but he needed something up-to-date so he wouldn't look like a hick if he did get a job interview. After much deliberation, he decided to start with the basics. Two pairs of khaki pants, two pairs of blue jeans, and two white cotton button-down shirts. He was staring at a table of colored T-shirts, trying to decide which colors to choose, when a middle-aged man stepped up beside him. "Definitely the green one," he said. "It'll look great with your eyes."

"Uh, thanks," Elijah said. "Kinda been a while since I bought anything new."

"Military?" the man asked.

"USMC," Elijah replied. "Last eight years."

The man smiled and nodded like he understood what Elijah was going through. "How long have you been out?"

"About a month," Elijah replied.

"Ah yes. I remember feeling the same way twenty years ago."

"Marine?" Elijah asked.

"Army man myself," the man responded. "But feeling like the civilian world left you behind is a universal sensation."

Looking at his watch, Elijah realized he was almost out of time. The minute the driver arrived at the store, he knew the meter would be clicking away. He put the green T-shirt in his cart along with a red one and a yellow one. "I hate to run, but I have a cab picking me up in fifteen, so I need to get a move on."

"No problem," the man said, nodding. "I totally understand. Good luck with the shopping," he added, turning and walking away without another word.

Elijah felt a slight stab of sadness. That man was literally the only person he'd had any semblance of a conversation with in the last few days, and he even understood a little of what Elijah was going through. He pushed the melancholy feeling to the back of his mind and focused on the rest of his shopping. The sportswear department for a couple of pairs of running shorts and tank tops, the underwear department for underwear and socks, and finally health and beauty aids for toothpaste, pomade, and deodorant. On the way to the register, he saw a display and felt instantly guilty but splurged anyway by tossing a bottle of Old Spice into his cart. *Gotta smell nice for the nonexistent ladies beating down my door.*

Elijah looked at his watch again as the automatic doors opened in front of him. *Right on time.* He scanned the parking lot and was relieved when he didn't see the cab sitting idle with the meter running. He took a seat on the bench in front of the store and waited.

Thirty minutes came and went and still no cab. He fished his phone out of his pocket and was about to hit redial when a voice said, "Where are you headed, son?"

Elijah looked up to see the middle-aged gentleman from the men's department standing in front of him. "The Seasons Motel," Elijah responded without hesitation.

"Come on," the man said with a gesture of his head. "I'm going right by there. I'll be glad to drop you off."

"Are you sure?" Elijah asked.

The man smiled. "Absolutely. I'm Royce, by the way."

"As in Rolls Royce?" Elijah asked with a smile while he gathered his bags.

"No such luck, but don't I wish." Royce chuckled.

"I'm Elijah. Elijah Preston, but my friends call me Eli."

My friends call me Eli. As soon as the words left his mouth, Elijah felt another stab of sadness. He no longer had any friends. Not really. Not here anyway.

"Good to meet you, Eli," Royce said, interrupting Eli's pity party.

Eli sucked it up and forced a smile. "I really appreciate the lift."

"Don't give it another thought," Royce responded. "I remember feeling very disjointed when I was discharged. But it gets better. I promise."

Eli offered a weak smile.

"What do you do?" Royce asked as they walked to his car.

"Nothing right now," Eli replied. "I'm looking for full-time work in my field, but I'd take anything at the moment to hold me over until I can find something more permanent."

"I see," Royce said as they reached his pickup truck. Eli heard the click of the locks, and when Royce climbed in he did the same.

Royce sat in the driver's seat looking forward and tapping his fingers on the steering wheel. Eli felt like there was something else the man wanted to say but for some reason was holding back.

Curious, Eli turned to face Royce. "If there's something you want to say, man, feel free," he said. "I'm not a sensitive guy."

Royce nodded but didn't say anything. He simply started the truck and pulled out of the parking lot.

Once they were on the highway, Royce cleared his throat, and Eli looked in his direction.

"I might have some work for you if you're interested," Royce said hesitantly.

Eli's ears perked up. "Hell yeah, I'm interested," he said without a second thought.

Royce reached into a little compartment on his dashboard, retrieved a business card, and handed it to Eli.

Eli took the card and read it from beginning to end.

Hotmilitaryguys.com

Check out the number one gay military porn site on the Internet.

100% authentic Marines, Soldiers, Fighter Pilots, and Sailors all waiting for you!

Royce Mackey, Proprietor—571-HOTGUYS

Eli read the card again to make sure he hadn't misread it the first time and offered it back to Royce, who was staring straight ahead at the highway. "Thanks for the offer, but I'm not gay, man," he said.

Royce accepted the card but didn't put it back into the compartment. "No problem, but for the record, none of my guys are gay," he said in a monotone voice.

"Are you serious?" Eli asked.

"Damn straight," Royce replied. "No pun intended," he added with a smile. "I may have a couple of bisexual guys in the mix, but ninety-nine percent of them are straight. Some are married, some engaged, and most of them have steady girlfriends. They all do it for the money."

Eli shook his head in disbelief. "You mean these supposed straight guys fuck other guys for money? On camera?"

Royce nodded. "Some do that, yeah, and others might just beat off alone for the camera. It's totally up to the guy to do what he feels comfortable with."

"You must pay a shitload of money," Eli said. "No pun intended."

"You're a good-looking man, Eli, and you've got a great body. You could make as much as ten thousand dollars a day, depending on how far you choose to go," Royce explained.

"Ten thousand dollars a day?" Eli repeated.

"Of course that's going all the way with several shoots in one day," Royce said. "But I guess it really doesn't matter if you're not interested."

Royce pulled up in front of Eli's motel and handed the card back to Eli. "Just keep this in case you change your mind. If you have any questions or just want to talk more, give me a call."

Eli didn't know why, but he took the card and slipped it into one of his shopping bags. "Thanks for the lift, Royce. I really appreciate it."

"Anytime," Royce responded. "And call if you have any questions."

Eli nodded out of politeness, gathered his bags, and slid out of the truck.

He walked toward his motel room and looked back when Royce tapped the horn a couple of times, then waved as he drove off.

Feeling a bit like he'd just been to the Twilight Zone, Eli dug the brass key out of his pocket and let himself into his motel room. While unpacking his bags, he came across the business card and thought about his encounter with Royce. He put the card on his bedside table and proceeded to remove all the tags from his new clothes and put everything away.

When he finished, it was nearing noon, and with his big chore for the morning complete, he sat down at his laptop to scan the want ads like he did every day. *At least this hellhole has Wi-Fi.* He fired up his computer and began his normal process of checking the online local newspaper and the local section of Craigslist for any temporary positions in his area, and then he hit the national search on Craigslist for anything permanent in his field. When he identified a potential position, he followed the instructions on the ad and submitted his resume electronically or via snail mail, whichever was preferred. Today, however, there wasn't a single new posting locally or even nationally that fit his qualifications. Discouraged, he sighed and shut his laptop, deciding there was nothing more he could do online. He called his career counselor at Quantico to see if there were any new developments, but as with his online search, he again came up empty.

Eli looked around his tiny room and in a fit of boredom turned the television on and channel surfed until he found the local news. He made himself a sandwich from the prepackaged lunchmeat in his fridge, kicked off his sneakers, and plopped down on the bed to eat his lunch and see what great things were happening in his little world of Dumfries, Virginia.

When the local news was over, Eli felt drained and wished he hadn't turned it on. He looked down at the paper plate on his lap and rearranged the crumbs covering the flower-patterned surface with his fingers. Eventually he put the empty dish on the bedside table, and Royce's business card caught his attention. Eli picked it up and read it again as if the words would somehow morph into something he could actually do. He rubbed the card between his fingers over and over until curiosity got the best of him. *It won't hurt to look.*

Eli opened his laptop, keyed in www.hotmilitaryguys.com, and waited as his Mac located the web site. When the site appeared, the banner on the home page featured a good-looking pilot in uniform up on a ladder next to some sort of aircraft. As Eli scrolled down the home page, he saw various military guys in seductive poses, their dog tags predominately displayed, some in uniform and some bare-chested with tattoos he recognized as very common USMC tats. Next he saw a warning that the site contained hardcore gay sexual situations and content, and a person must be eighteen years of age in order to continue, with an option to enter or leave the site right below it. Eli clicked enter.

The next page featured a large photo of a recruit of the week named Logan in the top half of his US Army uniform and naked from the waist down, his cock fully erect. Along the side of the screen were options for Live Chats, DVDs, Online Videos, Photo Galleries, Affiliated Sites, GIs, and About Us.

Eli clicked the About Us button and started reading.

Welcome to hotmilitaryguys.com, a site that was unknowingly in the making almost my entire life and created through my dreams. From as far back as I can remember, I've always been mesmerized and wholeheartedly attracted to men in military uniforms. That love turned into this web site, and today I can offer everyone who shares my dreams a way to explore and even get the opportunity to watch some of these guys act out your favorite fantasies.

Growing up in San Diego, I was always surrounded by men in uniform, and it was there, surrounded by these handsome and mostly willing men, that I first realized I was gay. There weren't as many gay bars as there are now, and the only other place we had to pick up men was adult bookstores, and trust me when I tell you I had my pick of any military man I wanted.

I quickly realized these hot and horny men would venture in after they struck out with the ladies, knowing they could stick their dick through a glory hole and always find a warm, welcoming mouth on the other side, and... most of the time that warm mouth was mine.

I eventually built up a roster and got to know these guys, built friendships with them, and earned their trust. Ultimately they stopped meeting me at the adult bookstore and started coming right to my own front door, knowing they could get what they wanted and slip out the back until the next time and never be outed by me.

As I got older and less promiscuous, I still longed to see hot military guys, so I came up with the idea for this site. I started talking to the guys I had good relationships with, and surprisingly they were along for the ride. I started hotmilitaryguys.com small but it quickly grew right along with the Internet. Ten years later I still have a thriving business.

So feel welcome to take the tour, look around the site, and sign up for a three-day trial.

Enjoy,

Royce Mackey

Proprietor, Director, and Lover of Men in Uniform

"Well I'll be," Eli whispered. "Royce is gay. I never would have pegged him for a homosexual."

Curious about the guys who were doing these things for Royce, Eli clicked on the *GIs* button and photos of guys in various stages of uniform or simply naked appeared below a row of buttons from A-Z. Eli clicked on the A button and a whole slew of photos of men whose names all started with the letter *A* filled the screen. All the guys were very handsome and well built and didn't look the least bit nervous or ashamed. He clicked on a guy named Adam, and a larger picture with a bio popped up. On the sidebar was a list of videos with thumbnail photos and a description of each video. When Eli clicked on one of the videos, a membership screen popped up, and he couldn't go any further unless he bought a membership to the site.

Still trying to determine how many men were into this sort of thing, he randomly clicked on the letter *J*. After counting at least thirty photos in that section alone, he randomly chose a guy named Jayden and clicked on his photo. When he scrolled down, Eli saw a similar list of thumbnail photos connected to videos, but one in particular was titled "Jayden Sheds his Uniform Solo" and had a Free button beside it. Eli clicked on the button, and a black screen opened up with a disclaimer that he couldn't read fast enough before the scene started.

The guy named Jayden was in full uniform, seated on a couch, with the sound of a girl moaning in the background, obviously from a straight porno playing out of sight. The guy was fondling himself through his trousers, and from the size of the bulge in his pants, building up quite an erection. The guy started slowly taking off his uniform, continuing to fondle himself, until he was naked except for his hat. He started to beat off, slowly at first, rubbing his abs, lifting his legs and rubbing his balls and asshole and then focusing on his dick again, picking up speed until he shot his load all over his stomach and chest. The scene ended with Jayden out of breath, his eyes closed and his body covered in his own release.

Eli stared at the screen in amazement. "I wonder how much that guy got paid to do that?" he mumbled. He continued to click on button after button, but unless you were a member, you didn't get more than a few photos and an occasional free snippet of some guy in a solo performance beating off. Deciding he'd seen enough to get an idea of what the site was all about, Eli closed his laptop, set it to the side, and lay back on his bed. He linked his fingers together, rested his joined hands on his chest, and closed his eyes. *I don't think I could ever do anything like that* was his last thought before he drifted off to sleep...

ELI WAS in his dress blues, sitting on a white leather couch, heart pumping frantically, and hands fidgeting in his lap. There were several cameras and bright lights pointing in his direction, and a flat-screen television was hanging on the wall right in front of him, starring a very large-chested woman going down on a Marine. On the table next to him was a bottle of lubricant and several neatly folded white towels. Someone yelled "Action!"

Eli stood, staring directly into the camera, and slid the release of his buckle to the left, pulling the woven cotton belt through until it was free. He slowly started to unbutton his coat, painstakingly, one brass button at a time. He let the coat slip off of his shoulders and tossed it onto the back of the couch before removing his white T-shirt and dropping it to the floor at his feet. He saw a flash out of the corner of his eye and turned to see his dog tags lying against his bare chest, reflecting the bright studio lights on the small monitor facing him. He quickly looked away, unable to watch what was unfolding right in front of him.

He sat on the edge of the couch and leaned over to untie his black patent-leather shoes, again focusing only on the camera. He pulled his left shoe off and then toed off his right, kicking them to the side before hooking his forefinger into the back of his sock. He peeled one off, then the other, and dropped them on top of his T-shirt.

He took a deep breath and stood, unhooking his trousers and stepping out of them, adding the pants to the top of the slowly accumulating pile of clothing.

A voice behind the camera yelled, "Cut," and a blurry face instructed him to sit back down, watch the video, stick his hand down his underwear, and start working on his erection.

The same voice yelled, "Action," and Eli sat down, leaned against the back of the couch, and slid his hand down his pants. He jumped to his feet in panic and disbelief when he realized his cock was gone.

ELI WOKE standing at the side of his bed, his heart pounding and his skin covered in a thin layer of sweat. He stuck his hand down his pants, and when he found his dick, he gripped it in relief. He sat on the edge of the bed and rested his head in his hands. *It was just a nightmare!*

CHAPTER TWO
REALITY

THE NEXT thirty days passed much in the same way the first had. Eli followed his routine of checking the papers and online sites for jobs daily and staying in close contact with his career counselor, and in addition, he'd started walking into town every day in the hopes he might see a Help Wanted sign in a window or come across someone in need of a day laborer. On his third day of venturing into town, the local hardware store had a large truck parked outside that was being unloaded by a puny high school kid. Eli went inside and offered to help. In the end he'd made fifty bucks for four hours of work and felt damned proud of himself. The physical labor had felt great and made Eli remember how much he missed working, only fueling his resolve to not give up. But in actuality he knew he was no closer to a real job than he'd been on the day of his discharge.

Seeing Royce's business card lying on the corner of his bedside table was a constant reminder of the man's bizarre offer, and Eli caught himself staring at it more than once a day. A couple of days after he'd met Royce, Eli had had enough and tossed the card into the trash, but late into the night, unable to sleep, he'd realized that however odd, the card had offered him a small sense of security. He'd hesitantly dug it out of the trash can, viewing it as a last resort, only if he became destitute. "Sometimes desperate times require desperate measures, and if you're hungry enough, Eli, you'll do anything," he'd said as he put the card in its original spot on the corner of the nightstand. He still didn't think he could do what he'd seen on that web site, but just knowing the card was there seemed to keep his feelings of desperation and hopelessness somewhat at bay.

It was one week into Eli's third month without a job, and he was experiencing one of those sleepless nights where he tossed and turned, worrying about how he was going to hold on. In a fit of frustration, he sat up, turned on the light. He stared at the blank television screen for a few minutes and then reached over for the remote, thinking a little mindless television might take his mind off his situation. In the dim lamplight, Eli once again saw Royce's card. Instead of picking up the remote, he picked up the card and held it for the longest time. *Can I really do this if it comes right down to the wire?*

Eli mentally ran over his finances in his head, something he did at least ten times a day. At best, if he pinched every penny, he only had enough money to survive for about two more weeks. *And then what, Eli?*

Deciding he wasn't ready to give in just yet, he wouldn't even think about the answer to that question. "Not yet, Eli," he told himself. "Tomorrow's another day." He put the card back in its place and hoped against hope that when the dark night turned to day, another opportunity would present itself.

The next week came and went with no new opportunities, and Eli's mood was quickly going from grim to hopeless. On Monday afternoon, after walking back from town in the pouring rain, again with no luck on the job front, Eli stepped into his dingy motel room soaked to the bone. He peeled out of his clothes and stood naked and shivering on the little square of linoleum just inside the door. He wrapped his arms around himself, forced his legs to step over the pile of wet clothing, and headed for the bathroom. Eli turned on the shower, closed the toilet seat, and sat, head in hands, while the water heated up.

He felt lifeless, drained, and ready to throw in the towel. He rubbed his hands over his face and wondered when this would all end. He realized that for the first time in his life, his pride and self-confidence were totally gone. They had dwindled away little by little with each rejection letter and every door slammed in his face and were not likely to return anytime soon. If he were to end it all now, would anyone miss him? Not likely. It would take months for the news to reach his buddies overseas, and his parents would only see his demise as a meal ticket lost, so the answer was one big fat no. Tears threatened the backs of his eyes, but he held them at bay.

When steam began to fill the tiny bathroom, he stepped into the shower. Mentally exhausted, he turned his back to the weak stream of hot water, leaned against the shower stall, and rested his head against his forearm.

The desperation that had threatened to derail him for the last few weeks finally won out, and Eli decided he had no more energy to fight it. He allowed the feeling of defeat to consume him, but he wouldn't allow the tears to fall. When he finished bathing, the water was barely warm, and he was weak and totally exhausted. He quickly rinsed off, and when he pulled the shower curtain back, he saw his naked reflection in the half-steamed-up mirror.

Through his swollen eyes, he stared at his upper body for the longest time without blinking. If he were forced to, he'd have to admit he was a handsome guy, in a rugged sort of way. His five-foot-eleven-inch frame was muscular and well defined from the last eight years as a Marine, and his deep hazel eyes had been called mesmerizing by more than a few girlfriends. His gaze drifted down to his groin. Having been in the military, he'd seen a lot of naked men, and he was above average in that department as well. *Fuck it, Eli! God gave you some looks, and the Marine Corps gave you a muscular body and your confidence, so stop wallowing in self-pity and do what you need to do.*

Eli stepped out of the shower with a new resolve. He dried off, put on a pair of shorts and a tank top, and sat on the edge of his bed. He picked up his cell phone with one hand and the business card with the other and held each in his hands for a few moments. *Shit or get off the pot, Eli.* He read the number and dialed.

Eli put the phone to his ear with a trembling hand and listened. One ring and then a second and he heard Royce's voice. "Eli. I'm so glad you called. I'd almost given up on you."

A nervous chuckle escaped Eli's lips. "That makes two of us," Eli said.

"Are you thinking of taking a trip to the wild side?" Royce asked wryly.

"Royce, I'm not sure what I'm thinking other than I'd like to know more."

"Acceptable answer," Royce said. "I tell you what. Why don't you let me come by and pick you up in about an hour? I made a couple Yankee pot roasts, and some of the guys are hanging around the house for dinner tonight. No pressure. I'll show you around and you can get a feel for the place."

"Tonight?" Eli asked, not sure he was quite ready to jump in with both feet. Then he realized he'd better *get* ready. He only had enough money to keep a roof over his head for a few more days. *And then what?* "Okay. Yeah," he replied. "I'll be ready."

"Oh and bring a swimsuit," Royce added. "Most nights after dinner we end up in the pool."

Eli didn't respond as he pictured a bunch of naked Marines sucking and fucking in a swimming pool. The hairs on the back of his neck instantly stood at attention.

"I can hear the wheels turning, Eli," Royce said. "Relax! I promise it's just swimming and water volleyball. No sex allowed in the pool."

Eli chuckled nervously, trying to cover up his embarrassment. "Yeah. Okay. Sounds like fun."

"Great. I'll see you in a bit," Royce said, and then the phone went dead.

Eli kept the phone to his ear long after Royce had disconnected, second-guessing his decision to make the call in the first place.

Lowering the phone to his side, he took a deep breath and tried to talk himself down. *Just check the place out and see what it's all about. You don't have to do anything you're not comfortable with.*

Eli went back into the bathroom and gave himself the once-over in the mirror. He ran a hand over his two-day-old beard and decided it was time for a shave. Afterward, he slapped a handful of Old Spice on his smooth, stubble-free face and for some odd reason took extra time styling his hair. Fumbling through his drawers, he decided on the green T-shirt Royce had suggested he buy, a pair of his new blue jeans, and his combat utility boots. When he was done, he stood in front of the mirror and smiled at his reflection. *I guess the pig is ready for slaughter.* He grabbed his swimming trunks and looked at his watch as he stepped out of his motel room. *Right on time.*

Relieved the rain had stopped, Eli took a seat on the little bench outside his door and fought the urge to run back into his room and lock the door behind him. *If worse comes to worst, you can just sleep in a cardboard box. You've slept in a lot worse in Afghanistan.*

Before Eli could contemplate that thought, Royce pulled into the parking lot. *Too late, Eli, your ride is here to take you to the abattoir.*

Royce must have spotted him because he pulled up right in front of his room and rolled down the window. "Don't look so scared, Eli. You're just coming for dinner and a little fun."

"It's the *fun* part that worries me," Eli said, half joking.

"Oh come on, Eli, no one's going to bite you," Royce said through a smile. "Unless you ask them to. Now get in."

Eli had to laugh at that one. He climbed into the truck and secured his seat belt.

Royce gave him one more look, then pulled out of the parking lot. "I was right," he said.

"About what?" Eli asked.

"That color does look great with your eyes."

"Oh, thanks," Eli said, looking down at the front of his T-shirt. "By the way, I gave the motel manager your name and told him if I wasn't back by midnight, I'd been kidnapped and to call the police."

Royce laughed out loud. "Good man. I'd expect nothing less from a Marine."

"Former Marine," Eli corrected.

"In my book, once a Marine, always a Marine," Royce said seriously. "In my experience, they don't make them any finer."

"In your line of work," Eli said with a slight grin, "I'm not sure how to take *finer*."

Royce briefly took his eyes off the road and cast a glance in Eli's direction. "Take it however you like," he said. "I sure hope that charm of yours comes across on video."

"Whoa," Eli protested. "I haven't agreed to do any video yet."

"I know… but you will," Royce assured him.

"You are a very confident man," Eli responded, focusing on the scenery outside his window.

"Not confidence," Royce replied. "Just experience."

"If you say so."

"Speaking of," Royce said. "You'll need a stage name."

Eli felt a chill run down his spine. "Why? I mean… I know why, but I haven't agreed to anything."

"It's best if you have one before I introduce you to the guys," Royce explained. "Less of a chance that someone slips up and calls you by your given name. Just think about it."

Eli didn't respond but stared out of the window, trying to get a bearing on where they were headed. Nothing looked familiar. "Where are we going?" he finally asked.

"I have a place in Montclair. On Lake Montclair to be exact," Royce explained.

Eli had heard the town mentioned on the television, but really knew nothing about it. "How far away is it?"

"We're almost there," Royce said as he slowed at a traffic light and stopped completely before he made a right turn on a red light. "Damn traffic cameras. I got a ticket in the mail last week for turning right on red without coming to a complete stop."

Eli nodded and craned his neck to read the street sign. "Country Club Drive, huh?" he said. "Sounds expensive."

"It was," Royce agreed as he made a few more turns and finally pulled the truck up to a security gate.

Eli watched as Royce punched in a code and the ornate gate slowly opened.

"We're here," he said, driving up a single-lane road.

"Is this your driveway?" Eli asked, taking in the scenery.

"Yeah. I know," Royce said, shaking his head. "I'm sure you think it's a little over the top, but I promise you, it came with the house."

Eli whistled. "It looks like whoever you bought the house from valued their privacy."

"Kind of makes you wonder what they were doing behind these gates."

"Hey, I'm the last one to judge, but I'll bet people say the same about you."

"Good point," Royce said as he rounded the next bend in the road and a massive house came into view.

"My God," Eli said. "You must be the Hugh Hefner of the gay porn industry."

Royce laughed. "Boy, don't I wish that were true."

"By the look of this house," Eli said, "it doesn't appear to be that far off."

Royce pulled up behind a string of cars ranging from BMWs to Corvettes, put the truck in park, and shut off the engine. "Look," he said. "Tonight is just about getting to know a few of the guys and hanging out. Nothing more."

Eli nodded and opened the door of the truck. He stopped just before he got out and looked over his shoulder. "Cal," he said.

Royce gave him a questioning look.

"My stage name," Eli added. "I want it to be Cal. Short for Calloway, my middle name."

"Nice," Royce said, flashing a knowing smile.

"Thanks. It was my mother's maiden name and one of the few things she gave me that didn't cost me dearly," Eli explained.

Royce frowned and then nodded at Eli. "Cal it is, then."

Eli slid off the seat, then turned and looked through the cab at Royce. "That still doesn't mean I've agreed to do anything."

"Okay, I get it," Royce replied. "You haven't agreed to do anything."

Eli nodded again and slammed the truck door. He walked around, stopped in front of the house, looked up, and whistled. "This is some place."

"Thanks," Royce said. "It serves the purpose."

Royce walked up to the massive double wooden doors, turned the brass doorknob, and pushed one side open. "Honey, I'm home," he yelled.

Eli followed Royce into the house and immediately smelled the aroma of pot roast, something he'd rarely smelled growing up unless he was visiting his grandmother. He looked around the two-story foyer with a freestanding stairway curving up to the second floor, then to the left and right. On the left was a massive dining room that could seat at least a dozen people, and to the right was some sort of set with lights and cameras everywhere, pointing at a king-size bed. Before Eli could comment, he heard a strong voice from somewhere else in the house yell, "We're in here, sweetheart."

Royce smiled and gestured with his head. "Come on."

Eli followed Royce past the stairs down a short hall that opened up into a gigantic room with very high ceilings. The back wall of the room was completely open to a covered patio that looked out over the lake. Eli was sure his eyes were as big as saucers and his mouth was hanging open, but he tried to keep cool and act like he'd seen houses like this every day of his life.

Eli looked around and was admiring the floor-to-ceiling stone fireplace when he heard Royce's voice. "What are you boys doing in my kitchen?" Royce asked with his hands on his hips, gazing across the room.

Turning, Eli saw two very good-looking and well-built guys, each standing at least six feet tall, at a stove behind a granite-covered island.

"I made cheesy mashed potatoes," one of the guys said.

"And just for some semblance of nutrition," the other guy said, "I roasted asparagus."

"Mashed potatoes *and* my baked macaroni?" Royce asked.

"What's your point?" the first guy asked, winking at Eli playfully. "I just finished working out, and I need to load up on carbs."

Eli smiled. It was obvious these guys had a comfortable relationship, whatever it was, and he chuckled at the banter.

Royce simply shook his head. "Well, at least get your asses over here and meet the newbie."

The first guy, dark hair in a military cut, very short on the sides and a little longer on top, came out with an extended hand. "Hey, man, I'm Rusty."

Eli accepted the firm handshake. "E—Cal," he corrected. "Good to meet you."

The other guy, who had longer blond hair, came around the island wiping his hands on a dishtowel and smiling. "Welcome to gay manor. I'm Gavin," he said right before Royce smacked him on the back of the head. "Ouch," he smirked, cowering but still extending his hand to Eli.

"Cal," Eli said nervously, "gay manor" echoing in his head but trying not to laugh at Royce's smack.

Gavin folded his arms across his chest. "Go ahead and laugh. Your turn's coming, man."

"Sorry," Eli said, figuring at some point that statement was probably going to hold true.

The four men stood in silence for a few seconds and Eli was the first to speak. "It smells really good in here."

All three men said, "Thanks," in unison, each one looking at the others with a surprised look on his face.

"So that's the way you want to play this?" Royce asked, looking at Rusty and Gavin.

"Fine. You get most of the credit," Gavin said.

"But," Rusty added, holding up his forefinger, "I'm taking all the credit for my cheddar, bacon, and cream cheese mashed potatoes."

Royce smirked and shook his head. "These guys kill me," he commented, winking at Eli. "Come on, let's let these ladies get back to destroying my kitchen while I show you around."

"Heyyy!" Rusty said. "You know we prefer Sally and Nancy when we're at the manor."

Eli couldn't help but laugh at that one, coming from these big, burly guys. "See you in a bit," he said to Gavin and Rusty.

"We'll be here," Rusty said. "And I hope you're hungry, dude."

"Very," Eli said.

"Good," Gavin added. "Great to meet you."

Eli followed Royce across the large room and walked out through the open rear wall to the covered patio. When they got to the rail Eli looked down and saw a lower level with a large kidney-shaped swimming pool, surrounded by pool decking with about a dozen lounge chairs spread here and there. To the left was a raised hot tub, nestled into boulders overlooking the pool with a waterfall spilling directly into the deep end. To the right was a thatched-roof tiki hut with a bar and stools. The scene was right out of a designer magazine.

Eli looked up, and through the trees was a full view of Lake Montclair. The evening sun was hanging low in the sky and reflecting orange and yellow ripples on the surface, and the sight reminded Eli of a calendar he'd once had of Lake Tahoe. "This is really beautiful," Eli said, taking in his surroundings.

Royce followed Eli's gaze. "Thanks. It's easy to take for granted sometimes when you see it every day."

"I can't imagine that," Eli replied.

The two men enjoyed the vistas in silence for a few seconds until they heard someone yell, "Fuck, not again."

"Follow me," Royce said, guiding Eli to a set of stairs that led to the lower level. When they got to the bottom of the stairs, he saw another covered patio much like the one upstairs. There were patio tables and chairs arranged in sitting areas and a couple of overstuffed chaise lounges for two. *I bet I can figure out what they use those chaise lounges for.*

The lower patio led to a big open game room. There were two pool tables, a foosball table, and an air hockey table in the middle of the room, with video games and pinball machines lining one wall and an oak bar lining the opposite wall. Eli counted five more guys hanging out down there, two sitting at the bar with beers in front of them watching a football game on the big screen over the bar, two playing pool, and one sitting on the air hockey table watching the pool game. All of the guys were equally as good-looking and muscular as Gavin and Rusty, but each of them had their own distinctive look.

Of the two guys seated at the bar, from what Eli could tell, one looked like he was much shorter than the other. The shorter man had dark brown hair cut very short and the other was a redhead. The two men playing pool were about his height; one had a shaved head and the other dark hair in a military cut. The last guy was very muscular but not overly so, with broad shoulders and jet black hair. He was at least six five. The two guys playing pool were playfully arguing over whether one of them could make a difficult shot, and the tall guy was putting in his two cents. As he bent over the pool table eyeing the shot, he was extremely animated, and his broad smile was both playful and warm. Eli instantly liked him.

"Hey, guys," Royce said. "I have someone I want you to meet."

The three men at the pool table stopped what they were doing and came over. The guys at the bar turned around on their seats and waved. When he got a good look at the taller of the two at the bar, Eli had the strongest feeling he knew the man from somewhere.

"This is Cal," Royce said. "He's checking us out."

The shorter guy was the first to speak. "I'm Matt, and I'm the only vertically challenged person in this club of giants. And this is Jayden," he added, gesturing to his friend.

Jayden! That's why I recognize this guy. I saw him jerking off on the web site.

Eli tried to not picture the guy with his hard cock in his hand and focused on the little man. He chuckled at his short joke and stuck out his hand. "Good to meet you, Matt." He nodded to Jayden. "You too, man."

The two guys with the pool cues introduced themselves as Logan and Pat, and the man with the warm smile walked up, wrapped his arms around Royce, and kissed him on the top of the head. "And this here is my boy Hamish," Royce said.

The other guys all booed in unison. "He's Royce's favorite," Logan shared.

"Yeah," Pat said. "The fair-haired child."

"Aw shucks, boss," Hamish said, smiling, his deep blue eyes twinkling with mischief. "Don't make the other guys hate me even more than they already do."

"That's impossible," Matt yelled, making all the guys laugh hysterically.

Hamish released his grip on Royce and offered his hand to Eli. "Welcome aboard, Cal," he said. Eli accepted the outstretched hand and shook it. "Don't let these guys fool you. They're all fighting one another to have hot sex with me on camera."

That statement drew even more boos and hisses from the others.

"Settle down, men," Hamish shouted to the guys. "You'll all get a turn to take a trip to wonderland." Hamish turned to Eli and winked. "Can I get you a beer, Cal?" he asked.

"Sure," Eli replied nervously.

"You ladies play nice," Royce said. "I'm going up to check on dinner. Give me about fifteen minutes and then bring your appetites and asses upstairs."

The guys rolled their eyes and nodded. "Yes, ma'am," they all said in unison.

Logan and Pat went back to the pool table to finish their game, and Eli watched Royce disappear down a hallway.

Hamish motioned with his head, and Eli followed him, taking a seat next to Matt and Jayden, who both turned back to face the flat-screen. Hamish walked around and pointed to the row of taps. "What's your poison?" he asked.

Eli scanned the brightly colored handles on the different taps. "Blue Moon will be fine."

"A man after my own heart," Hamish said, retrieving a frosted mug from a freezer under the bar. He held it under the tap and filled it with the icy cold brew.

"Ladies?" he asked, looking at Matt and Jayden.

They both slid their half-empty beer mugs across the bar and Hamish topped them off along with his own. He came back around the bar and took a seat next to Eli.

"So?" Hamish asked. "Where did he find you?"

"I'm sorry?" Eli said, not sure what Hamish meant.

"He picked me up at Dunkin' Donuts," Hamish admitted.

"The produce aisle at Wegman's Grocery Store for me," Jayden said, leaning around Matt.

"I have all of your sorry asses beat," Matt boasted. "He found me in the sporting goods department at Target."

"Snob," Hamish teased.

They were all staring at Eli, and he assumed they were waiting for his answer, so he fessed up. "In the men's department at Walmart."

"Yes!" Matt said, pumping his fist in the air. "Still the classiest dude here."

"Matt?" Jayden interrupted. "The last time I looked, Target is not Gucci."

"It's a hell of a lot better than Walmart, Dunkin' Donuts, or a grocery store," Matt argued.

"He's got a point," Hamish added.

Matt pumped his fist in the air again. "You bet your ass I do."

"Whatever," Jayden huffed.

Eli noticed a *Semper Fi* tattoo on Hamish's right tricep. "Active or discharged?" he asked, referring to the ink.

"Honorable discharge," Hamish said. "About two years now. You?"

"Same, but just about twelve weeks," Eli explained.

"What branch?" Matt asked.

Before Eli could answer, Hamish jumped in. "I'd bet my life he's all Marine."

They looked at Eli again, and he confirmed Hamish's suspicions. "He's right."

"I knew it," Hamish said. "I can smell a Marine a mile away."

Eli lifted his armpit and took a whiff. "Really? Then I need to change deodorants."

Everyone chuckled. "I think you smell just fine," Hamish said. "And if I'm not mistaken, I believe that fine aroma is Old Spice."

Eli nodded and smiled. "Right again. You do have a great nose. For Marines and aftershave," he added. He looked at Jayden and Matt. "What branch of the service were you guys in?"

"Army. Both of us," Matt said. "And Pat as well. We were all in the same company."

Jayden added, "But sorry to say, Logan was a navy man."

"I heard that," Logan yelled from the pool table.

"How in the hell did you hear that?" Hamish asked.

"You Marines may be able to smell one another, but us sailors have great hearing."

"Stop your bragging," Jayden quipped.

Logan pointed his pool stick at Jayden, but before he could say anything else they heard three thumps overhead.

"Playtime is over, guys," Hamish interrupted. "I think Mama is calling us to dinner."

Logan laid his cue on the pool table.

"To be continued," Pat said, doing the same.

Matt switched off the television and Eli followed the guys through the same hall Royce had disappeared through, which as he'd suspected, led to another set of stairs.

The guys picked up plates, got in line at the stove, and started to serve themselves.

"Don't be shy," Royce said, gesturing to the line. "It's every man for himself around here."

Eli picked up a plate and offered one to Royce.

"You better look out, Hamish," Matt said. "Looks like the newbie is after the favored position."

"I see that," Hamish agreed, winking at Eli. "Thanks for the warning. I'll be sure to stay on my toes."

Eli sat with the guys around a large, rustic oak dining table on the opposite end of the den and attacked his food with a vengeance. The potatoes and asparagus were amazing, but the pot roast melted in his mouth, and the baked macaroni was like none he'd ever had before. It had been a long time since he'd had a home-cooked meal, and he was determined to savor every bite.

Royce sat at the head of the table, and whether it was planned or not, Eli sat to his right and Hamish to his left. The other men fell in wherever there was an open spot, and the back and forth banter continued. While Eli ate, he listened as the guys teased one another endlessly, but he could also see a strong bond of camaraderie between them, much like his unit overseas.

The teasing and conversation flowed easily around the dinner table, during cleanup, where everyone pitched in, and then back downstairs to the game room. Things really got animated when Rusty brought out the tequila, salt, and lime and started pouring shots.

After a beer, a couple of glasses of wine with dinner, and a couple of tequila shots, Eli was feeling no pain. But even tipsy, he could see the genuine ease with which these guys interacted, and it made him really miss his best friends back in Afghanistan. He had to keep reminding himself that he'd never had sex with any of *his* buddies.

It was obvious the comfort level they shared went way beyond just friendship, and although he didn't know for sure, he suspected they had all been paired up at one time or another in some sort of a sexual encounter. That thought creeped him out a little because he knew that if Royce had his way, he would be thrown right into the mix.

When they returned to the game room, after they'd all done shots, Logan and Pat picked up the pool game where they'd left off. When Pat sank the eight ball, ending the game, Logan demanded a rematch.

Someone suggested wrestling, and before Eli knew it, furniture was being pushed out of the way and shirts and shoes were coming off.

Eli laughed in disbelief when the guys starting pulling money out of their pockets and laying it on the table. He had no idea whom to bet on, and even if he did, he wasn't spending his last few dollars on a wrestling match, so he retreated to the bar and took a seat facing the crowd. He leaned back, resting on his elbows, and observed Pat and Logan rolling around on the floor with the other men urging them on. The playfulness and touchy-feely interaction between the wrestlers and onlookers caught Eli's attention. Although the onlookers weren't groping one another like the wrestlers were, there wasn't the standard protocol for typical "guy" interaction. The onlookers were hanging all over one another, not in a sexual way, but in a comfortable and relaxed way. If he had done with any of them what he suspected they'd done with one another, would he feel the same and be right in the middle of the mix?

Eli sighed, leaned his head back, and closed his eyes. He knew he had to make a decision about how far he was going to go with this, if at all, and wondered if he could pull any of it off. After a little self-deliberation, he decided he could probably do the solo. That was just jerking off on camera, but he was certain few or none of these guys had stopped there. The solo was probably the starting point, and if he consented the rest would surely follow.

Eli's concentration was interrupted by the sound of a warm voice in his ear. "You okay?"

He opened his eyes to see Hamish standing next to him with a look of concern on his face.

"I'm okay," Eli responded over the sound of catcalls and hoots and hollers.

"Wanna take a walk?" Hamish said, gesturing to the door.

"Sure," Eli said. "But don't you want to see who wins?"

Hamish laughed out loud. "You don't actually think I'm stupid enough to bet on these pansies, do you?"

Eli chuckled when he heard Royce pulling for Pat. "Looks like he's pretty into it."

"Ya think?" Hamish teased. "Anytime Royce can watch two men rolling around on the floor and groping one another, he's *into it*. The only thing better would be if they were both in uniform. I never saw a man love a uniform as much as Royce. Come on," he said and slapped Eli on the back. "Let's find a little quiet."

Eli followed Hamish past the pool area and to a set of stairs and a brick path that led down to the lake. Once at the water's edge, Eli leaned on the dock railing and stared at the velvety blue sky. The crescent moon seemed to be dancing just above the lake, reflecting brightly off the dark water. Eli had to resist the urge to reach out and try to touch it.

"Beautiful, isn't it?" Hamish asked.

"Yeah," Eli replied. "It reminds me of my nights in Afghanistan. At night, the sky there was so dark, it made the moon look like it was inches away. It was almost like you could pluck it right out of the sky with your fingertips."

"I remember," Hamish whispered.

Surprised, Eli turned to Hamish. "You were in Afghanistan?"

Hamish nodded. "Kabul."

"Eggers?" Eli asked.

"No, KAIA. I was an AIS Specialist there."

Eli searched his brain to remember what AIS stood for. "Aviation Information Systems?" he asked with hesitancy.

"You got it. You?" Hamish asked.

"Communications," Eli said. "Wire chief to be exact."

Hamish nodded but didn't respond.

The two men stood in silence for a few minutes, gazing up at the night sky.

Hamish was the first to speak again. "Can I ask you a question?"

"Sure," Eli said, turning to him.

"What makes you want to get involved with our little X-rated family?" he asked.

Eli looked back at the moon but didn't hesitate. "Money," he said.

Hamish dipped his head. "Same as the rest of us, then."

"I sort of figured that," Eli admitted.

"Don't get me wrong," Hamish said. "There are a couple of guys here because they are exhibitionists and love the attention, but ninety-nine percent of us are in it for the money. Most guys have steady girlfriends or wives and kids to support, but they've fallen on hard times, and to be honest, it's damn good money. Easy money in fact."

Eli turned to Hamish again. "Now can I ask *you* something?"

Hamish nodded.

"Are you gay?"

Hamish chuckled.

"Not that I care what people do in the privacy of their own bedroom," Eli clarified.

"No. I'm not gay."

"Then how do you do it?" Eli asked, meeting Hamish's eyes.

Hamish broke the gaze and turned to look out over the water. "There's not really a short answer to that question," he said. "But the gist of it is that all us guys feel like we are in this together. We do what we have to do to support ourselves and our families. And we try to support one another."

"But to have sex with another guy," Eli said.

"Listen," Hamish added. "A blow job is a blow job, and a warm hole is a warm hole. Once you get over the taboo of having sex with another man, you realize that sex is sex, it's all the same, and you're home free."

"It's really hard to wrap my head around, but I'll take your word for it."

Hamish looked back at Eli. "Seriously, Cal, I felt the same way you did when Royce propositioned me. But once you get here and get to know the guys, it almost becomes like a club you want to be part of. Almost like the feeling of being a Marine, like being a part of something bigger than you. I know it sounds crazy, but that's how it was for me and for most of the other guys as well."

This time Eli turned away and stared out over the water as if he might find the answers out there.

Hamish continued, "Like I said, most guys are here because they can't find work and are doing what they have to do to support themselves and/or their families. I don't know about you, but I have to admire that dedication."

Eli thought about what Hamish said and decided he agreed. "I do too," he said.

"The guys here feel like we are all in this together, and it makes it easier on each and every one of us. In the end, we're all doing the same things for mostly the same reasons. You know?" Hamish said. "We have this unspoken agreement among us that no one should feel isolated and ashamed for doing what they have to do to take care of themselves or the people they love."

Eli glanced at Hamish again and their eyes met. "You get where I'm coming from?" Hamish asked.

"I do," Eli admitted. "I just don't know if I can do it."

"Of course you can," Hamish assured him. "If you want to. The biggest hurdle we all had to face was simply believing that having sex with another man doesn't make you gay."

Hamish paused, then spoke again. "I'm not gay, and I hate labels, but up until I joined this elite group of men, I hadn't even considered having sex with another man."

"And now?" Eli asked.

"It took me a couple of months to get comfortable with everything," Hamish said, looking up at the stars, "but if I was forced to stick a label on my back, I would categorize myself as a bisexual."

"Does that mean you enjoy it now?" Eli asked.

"Sometimes," Hamish admitted. "It's like a regular job. Some days you enjoy your work more than others, and sometimes you get along better with one coworker versus another. It's really no different. There are guys I enjoy being with more than others, but it's a job and you can't pick and choose. I mean, if I really went to Royce and said I will not do a scene with a certain guy, he wouldn't make me. But again, it's our unspoken code of ethics that keeps us all together."

"Wow!" Eli said, shaking his head. "I didn't see that coming."

Out of the corner of his eye, Eli saw Hamish change positions and then felt Hamish's hands kneading his tense shoulders.

"Relax, man," Hamish said. "You're as wound up as a Slinky."

Eli dropped his head and tried to loosen up a bit. He had to admit he was enjoying the human touch.

"Look, man," Hamish continued. "I've given you a lot to think about. Don't make any decisions right now. Sleep on it and feel free to ask me as many questions as you like."

"I do have one question, and it's kind of personal," Eli said.

Hamish chuckled. "It's okay, man. Anything. I can guarantee you, you're not the first to ask."

"What's it like to suck dick and take it up the ass?"

"Well! In my opinion, it depends on the person," Hamish said. "The 'sucking dick' part is pretty easy, but the 'taking it up the ass,' as you put it, that takes some getting used to. But again depending on the person, it can be very enjoyable. You just have to get over your mental hang-ups and take what pleasure you can get out of it. The more you do it, the easier it gets. I promise."

When Hamish gave Eli's shoulders one last squeeze and removed his hands, Eli secretly didn't want him to stop. Human contact was something he hadn't felt in such a long time, and the fact that it was coming from a guy didn't really matter. That thought surprised him, and he tucked it away for later dissection.

"We better get back up to the house to make sure those guys haven't killed each other yet," Hamish joked.

Eli laughed. "Thanks, man," he said. "I appreciate you taking the time to talk to me."

"My pleasure. And whatever you decide, you've got my support," Hamish said, pulling Eli into a bear hug.

CHAPTER THREE
DECISIONS

WHEN ELI and Hamish got back to the house, the guys were all lined up at the bar watching porn with a shot glass displayed in front of each of them, and a tequila bottle nearby. Royce had a video camera on his shoulder and was filming the interaction.

"Hey, guys," Gavin yelled when he saw them walk in. "Come join us. We're doing moan shots."

Eli looked at Hamish for clarification. Hamish rolled his eyes. "Every time the girl moans, the guy next in line has to do a shot."

Eli smiled. "That sounds like it could get dangerous," he said. "And what's with the camera?"

"Oh hell," Hamish said. "When the alcohol starts flowing, you never know what's gonna happen around here."

"Do you mean what I think you mean?" Eli asked.

"Maybe?" Hamish confirmed. "Look, man, these guys know each other very well and doing what we do day after day, you learn to separate sex from emotion. And to be completely honest, sex feels good. And when you can enjoy it without any emotions or baggage, it's even better."

"I'm not sure I'm quite ready for that yet," Eli said nervously.

"I get it," Hamish said. "Baby steps. How about I take you home, then?"

"Do you mind?" Eli asked.

Hamish shook his head. "Not at all. We have a little time before it gets crazy around here, so why don't we have one more drink before we go?"

Eli nodded and followed Hamish over to the bar, where he poured them each another beer.

"Come on, guys," Logan yelled. "Aren't you gonna join us?" Just then the girl moaned again and everyone laughed, pointing at Logan.

"No, thanks," Hamish said. "You know what tequila does to me."

"That's why we want you to join in," Matt said. "You give the best head."

Everyone roared in agreement.

Hamish turned to Eli and flashed an embarrassed smile. "I sure wish I knew who started that rumor."

"More importantly, is it true?" Eli asked.

"Probably."

Eli laughed. "Oookay. I guess you should own up to it, then."

"I know. It's a gift," Hamish teased. "But the guys think they're embarrassing me, so I let them have it."

"I do love how everything is so open around here," Eli said. "Is any topic off-limits?"

Hamish thought for a second. "None that I've come across. In fact these guys talk about everything from taking a dump, to douching, to brushing their teeth. If you do decide to become one of the guys, you'll learn there's only one unspoken rule."

"And that is?" Eli asked.

"You're clean inside and out and your breath is fresh," Hamish said.

Eli smacked the bar with the palm of his hand. "Damn, man! You've got to start warning me before you drop shit like this on me."

Hamish smiled. "Got it."

"So these guys have sex just for the fun of it?" Eli asked, gesturing to the row of men staring at the television screen.

"Sometimes," Hamish replied. "Some of the single guys have even said sex with a buddy is way less complicated than sex with a woman."

"How so?" Eli asked.

"Because with a woman, there are usually some type of strings attached and more than likely some sort of demands, which always leads to fallout."

"Good point," Eli agreed.

"But…," Hamish added, "if they do have sex for the fun of it and someone is around to film it, they still get paid, and it'll end up on Royce's site."

Eli tossed that around in his head for a moment. "That's a great lead-in to my next question. How much do you get paid?"

"I can't talk about specifics, because everyone is different based on the amount of time they've been with Royce, but what I can tell you is the further you go the more you get paid."

"Can you clarify that a little?" Eli asked.

Hamish smiled. "Well, for starters, you get paid a certain amount for a solo. Then you get paid more when you graduate to a mutual jerk-off. And then the really big bucks kick in when you start sucking and fucking."

Royce came over and put the camera on Eli and Hamish. "You look great on camera, Cal."

"Ah… shucks, Ms. Daisy," Eli said.

Royce smiled. "That kind of humor and charisma is exactly what I want to see come across on camera."

A loud moan followed by laughter made them all turn back to the guys. Royce again aimed the camera in their direction. "These ladies better start giving me some action or I'm going to bed," Royce complained. "Next time," he added, "I'm choosing the video, and I'm gonna make damn sure that bitch moans with every thrust."

Eli and Hamish both laughed.

"That reminds me," Royce said. He picked up the remote and pressed pause.

That drew a loud bunch of whines from the guys.

"Listen up," Royce said. "Who's available tomorrow for a few shoots?"

"My girlfriend's away on a business trip," Pat said. "So you've got me all weekend if you want me."

"Who else?" Royce asked.

"My wife left yesterday to see her mother," Gavin said. "So count me in."

"I'm in," Hamish said.

"Us too," Rusty and Jayden chimed in.

"Sorry, Royce," Matt said. "My girlfriend's gonna kick me to the curb if I don't spend the weekend with her. I'm on such a short leash these days."

Logan waved his hand. "Count me out too, man, sorry. I'm on reserve duty all weekend."

Eli saw Royce look in his direction and braced himself. "What about you, Mr. Calloway?"

Eli froze. He'd heard the question, but his damn mouth wouldn't work. He felt the blood draining out of his face, and his heart started to race.

"I don't think our friend is quite ready to make that commitment just yet," Hamish said, getting to his feet. "In fact, he had a few questions, so I promised to give him a lift home. I'm sure he'll be able to give you an answer soon."

Eli looked directly at Hamish, and he hoped his eyes conveyed the relief and sincere thanks he was feeling.

They must have, because Hamish smiled and nodded. "You ready?"

"Yes, sir," Eli responded.

"I'll see *you* in the morning, then," Royce said to Hamish. "I've got an entire weekend to fill with hot military guys, and I'd like to put you in as many spots as I can."

Royce dug in his pocket, withdrew an envelope, and handed it to Eli. "Here's an offer I put together and a standard contract for you to review. I hope this will help you make up your mind."

Eli accepted the envelope, shoved it in his back pocket, and waved at the others. "Good night, guys," he yelled, but the girl in the video had just moaned again and the shots were flowing.

"I'll tell them you said good-bye," Royce assured him.

"I promise I'll call you tomorrow," Eli said over his shoulder as he turned and followed Hamish to the door.

Hamish walked up to a black convertible BMW at the head of the line and held up his keys. The car chirped and the door locks popped.

"Nice ride," Eli said, opening the door and getting in.

"Thanks. Got it about a year ago. It's the one thing I splurged on."

Eli smiled. "Do I dare ask what paid for it?"

Hamish started the engine. "I think you already know the answer to that question."

"Yep," Eli responded. "Just checking."

"Where to?" Hamish asked.

"The Seasons Motel," Eli said, feeling a little embarrassed and looking out of the window to avoid eye contact with Hamish.

A million thoughts were going through his head, and the last thing Eli remembered was Hamish making his way down the single-lane driveway, stopping briefly at the gate while it opened, and then continuing through.

Eli jumped when Hamish laid a hand on his leg.

"Sorry, I didn't mean to startle you. I said your name but you didn't answer. Look, man. I can sense the internal struggles and almost hear the questions rolling around in your head," he said softly. "I was exactly where you are a couple of years ago. Do you want to talk about it?"

Eli just looked at Hamish's hand resting on his leg. Hamish instantly removed his hand and returned it to the steering wheel. "I'm sorry. Sometimes I forget I'm not around the guys. Anyway I just want to make sure you're okay."

"No!" Eli said. "Seriously. If I can't handle another man's hand resting on my leg, how am I supposed to…?"

"It's okay, Cal."

"No. Really," Eli insisted. "Please put it back."

Hamish put his hand back on Eli's leg, and Eli laid his trembling hand on top of Hamish's.

"Not life-shattering, huh?" Hamish asked.

Hamish spread his fingers wide, and when Eli's fingers fell between his, Hamish closed his again and they were linked together. "It's just touch, man. No different than if you were holding a girl's hand."

Eli stared at their joined hands for a few minutes and realized that Hamish was right. It was just human touch. And much to his surprise, it felt okay. He started to relax, and he settled into his thoughts. "Royce?" Eli asked. "Is he an okay guy?"

"The best!" Hamish replied. "Sure he likes his kinkiness and he loves watching us fuck one another, but he found me at the darkest time in my life, when I had nowhere else to turn. He gave me a job, a place to live, and a sense of self-worth again."

"By paying you to have sex with other guys?"

Hamish nodded. "Technically, I suppose that's right. At least in the beginning."

"And now?" Eli asked.

"Yes. I still have sex with guys for money. But now I do it because I genuinely love and respect most of these guys and I enjoy it. We look out for one another, and we have the closest thing to a family I've had in a long time."

Hamish paused and then sighed. "Look, man, like I said. If you get over the 'I'm having sex with a guy' thing, what's so bad about it? We make damn good money, it feels good, and we get our rocks off at the same time."

"What about right and wrong? Morals?" Eli asked.

"The way I see it," Hamish said, "every saint has a past and every sinner has a future. We bring a lot of joy to a lot of people."

"Gay people who watch porn?" Eli interrupted.

"Yeah, so what?" Hamish said, retrieving his hand and putting it back on the wheel. "Gay people have a right to be happy. Don't they?"

"But at someone else's expense?"

"Cal. No one is forcing you to do anything," Hamish said with a matter-of-fact tone to his voice. "This is all you, man. You can't pin this on anyone but yourself. Royce simply gave you an opportunity. It's totally up to you to take it or leave it."

"That's the fucking problem," Eli snapped. "I want to blame someone, anyone, for the fact that I'm desperate enough to do gay porn just to survive."

Hamish sighed. "Okay. Let's look at your other options."

"Not many of them, but I'm listening," Eli said.

"Do you have any friends or family you can call?"

"No," Eli whispered. "All my friends are still in Afghanistan, and as far as I'm concerned, fuck my family. They're the ones who got me into this situation."

"Oookay, moving on. How much money do you have?" Hamish asked.

"Not much. Enough for a couple more days at this dive of a no-tell motel."

Hamish shook his head. "Man… you're not giving me much to work with."

Silence loomed between them until Hamish spoke again. "What's happening on the job front?"

"Absolutely nothing," Eli said sadly. "I go online every day looking for something in my field and then hit the local stuff for anything to hold me over. But it's tough out there."

"What about Career Services?"

"I check in with them on a daily basis," Eli replied. "They're tired of hearing from me."

"Okay, look," Hamish said finally. "I can give you a roof over your head, so you don't have to be worried about being on the streets. But… that doesn't address the job or money issues."

Eli felt tears stabbing the backs of his eyes, but he held them at bay. He'd just met Hamish tonight and the guy had already taken him under his wing and offered him a place to stay.

Eli tentatively laid his hand on Hamish's leg. "I could never let you do that, but thank you for offering. For all you know, I could be a drug dealer or ax murderer."

Hamish chuckled. "I doubt it. You're a fellow Marine and Marines look out for one another."

"I'll figure something out," Eli said, giving Hamish's leg a quick squeeze before removing his hand. "A couple more questions and then I'm done. I promise."

"Shoot," Hamish said.

"Do you ever feel like you're a hooker and Royce is your pimp?"

Hamish threw his head back and laughed out loud. "I guess if you think about our relationship in those terms, you can make that case. But you can make that same case about almost any career choice if you try hard enough."

"I guess you're right," Eli conceded.

"Royce makes a lot of money off of our backs, literally," Hamish justified. "But in return he pays us very well, puts a roof over our head if we need one, always has a stocked bar and a shitload of food for his guys. He even rents a beach house every summer for our enjoyment and pays for all our expenses when we do remote shoots. Hell, just this year, we've already been to—" Hamish paused and listed on his fingertips. "—San Diego, Manhattan, Charleston, South Beach, and Key West."

"That's all well and good," Eli said. "But at what emotional cost?"

Hamish put his car in park. He turned to Eli and again rested his hand on Eli's leg. "Cal! Man! Everything has a cost. The big question is, are you willing to pay that cost?"

"That *is* the question," Eli agreed. "But why does it feel like if I do this, I'm selling my soul to the devil?"

"I wish I could tell you everything was going to be all right, but you know I can't do that. But... I will tell you that whatever decision you make, I'm sure it will be the right one for you."

"Thanks."

"Remember," Hamish said, digging a card out of his console and handing it to Eli, "my offer to give you a roof over your head is an open invitation, regardless of your decision. Feel free to call me if you have any other questions or you just want to talk things through."

"I don't know what to say," Eli replied, starting to choke up a little.

Hamish leaned over and placed a kiss on Eli's cheek. "Say nothing. Just do what's right for you. And look at the bright side. If you decide to give it a shot, you don't have to do it forever. Just long enough to get back on your feet."

Eli nodded, opened the car door and got out, then leaned his head back in. "Thanks for the lift and for the ear," he said, and closed the door.

He stood in the parking lot, watching the taillights of the BMW until they were no longer visible. He dug the key out of his blue jeans and let himself into his damp and dingy motel room. Eli turned on the lamp and looked around. *Hell. I'd let the entire Marine Corps fuck me if it meant I could check out of this place.*

After that realization, Eli was pretty sure what his decision was going to be. But when he settled in bed, opened the envelope Royce had given him, and read the pay scale, the deal was cemented.

Eli folded up the offer and the contract, slipped them back into the envelope, and placed the envelope on his bedside table. He lay on his back and looked up at the water-stained ceiling tiles above his bed. He studied one stain, which oddly enough reminded him of an erect penis, and wondered if he should take that discovery as a sign.

Mentally, Eli went over the offer he'd just read. He was guaranteed seven hundred dollars for his first solo and five hundred for every solo after that. The rate went up to a thousand dollars if he did a scene with one or more guys and they jerked each other off. In addition, he got a bonus of two hundred dollars if they all made out before and during the scene. The next scale jumped up to two thousand dollars if he did all of the above, plus gave and got head until everyone got off. The rate was three thousand dollars for a scene with one or more guys where everything was done, including giving and receiving anal intercourse. The offer allowed for as many as three scenes a day, unless otherwise agreed upon.

As Royce had said, the contract was indeed a simple one. It was a one-page document that basically stated when the scene or scenes were filmed the actor was eighteen years of age or older, was not coerced in any way, and did the scenes of his own free will. If he signed the document, he signed away all the rights to any and all scenes and gave R. Mackey Productions the rights to market, sell, distribute, and/or destroy any and all scenes without his permission.

I can make anywhere from seventeen hundred to nine thousand dollars a day, depending on how far I'm willing to go.

For a second his mind drifted off to what he could do with that kind of money. Then his rational mind fought for dominance. *But at what cost, Eli? Your self-worth? Your morals? Your pride?*

His mind was again flooded with "what-ifs?" What if one of his fellow Marines found out? The chances were slim, but if they did, they were looking at gay porn, so that answered that. If he did this, would it make him gay? Logically, he knew the answer was no, but there was nothing logical about his thought patterns at the moment, so he decided to put that one on the back burner for now. Next. If he did the solo, would he go further? If he decided to suck some guy's cock for more money, would he end up taking a dick up his ass too? He didn't think he could do either, but if he did, he knew after that there was no going back. *But going back to what, Eli? Where? Your life has always been a shithole. If anyone should find out, you have no one to embarrass but yourself, certainly not your drunken parents. And even if they did find out, they did plenty to embarrass you when you were growing up. And payback is a bitch!*

Eli had always credited the Marines for saving him from his family. It was in the Marine Corps where he learned right from wrong, not from his parents. *Right from wrong!* What would the Marine Corps think? *Wrong*, of course. But wouldn't that be a contradiction to everything they teach and preach? They had always taught him to get the job done, at whatever cost.

This internal struggle went on for another hour until his brain was about to explode. "Enough!" he said, turning to his side and punching the cheap foam pillow under his head. *Like Hamish said, you can always do this until you get a job and get back on your feet. You're not committing to a life of gay pornography.*

Eli realized his brain was fried, and he forced his mind to shut down. *I'll make a final decision in the morning when I'm thinking more clearly.* He turned off the light and closed his eyes.

CHAPTER FOUR
ACTION

ELI WOKE a little after eight o'clock. He rolled over and stretched. He'd slept remarkably well considering what was weighing on his mind. But for some reason he felt a certain level of resolve. Somewhere between wondering if he would end up gay and worrying about his friends seeing him jerking off, Eli had decided to throw caution to the wind and take the plunge. But only long enough to get back on his feet. And only the solo.

He felt lighter now that the decision was made, but he was suddenly anxious to get started. Eli sat up, threw back the covers, and swung his legs around, placing his bare feet firmly on the worn carpet. He dialed Royce's number, closed his eyes, and waited while the phone rang and rang.

"This better be good news," a sleepy voice said. "Do you know what time it is?"

Eli glanced at the clock. *Eight forty. What's he so cranky about?* "Sorry to wake you, Royce, but I figured you'd be up by now. But I think you'll like the reason."

"If you're calling to say yes," Royce agreed, "I will like the reason, and I'd say it was worth it."

"Then the answer is yes," Eli repeated nervously. "But only the solo."

"Good man," Royce said. "I'll be over to get you about ten o'clock. And, Eli?"

"Yes, sir?"

"Pack your things and check out of that god-awful motel. I have five empty bedrooms at the moment, and you can have your pick."

Eli sighed and thought for a minute.

"Relax, Cal. No strings attached," Royce said.

"With all due respect," Eli replied, "I think there are already strings attached, but I'll take you up on the offer anyway. I can't take this place another day."

"It's settled, then. I'll see you in a little over an hour."

"I'll be ready."

"Oh and don't forget your *uniforms*," Royce said wryly.

Eli rolled his eyes and chuckled. "I won't, Royce."

He hung up the phone, rubbed his eyes, and threw himself back on the bed. He stared at the stain on the ceiling tile again. "Well, penis. I've really gone and done it this time."

After showering, dressing, packing his clothes, and laying the hanging bag with the desired uniforms across his bed, Eli stood with his hands on his hips and looked around the tiny motel room. This was the last time he was going to walk across the soiled carpet. The last fitful night in the lumpy bed, the last shower in the moldy bathroom, and the last microwaved dinner. "Unless you really suck at jerking off," he mumbled. "Then you're back to square one."

There was a knock on the door and Eli jumped, his heart plummeting to his feet. *Oh God! This is it!*

He straightened his back and stood tall as he walked to the door.

"Is Mr. Willy ready for his close-up?" Royce asked, standing in the doorway wearing a broad smile.

"Oh for fuck's sake!" Eli responded nervously. "As ready as he's ever going to be, I guess."

Royce looked around. "I'll bet the owner of this place invented the short-term stay."

Eli threw Royce a questioning glance.

"You know, by the hour."

"Ohhh yeah," Eli chuckled. "You're probably right."

Royce reached for one of Eli's duffel bags. "Come on, man, let's get you out of this place."

Eli stopped him. "Let me get those. Besides, you'll probably be happier carrying the uniforms," he said, pointing to the hanging bag on the bed.

Royce winked at Eli. "Now you're just teasing me," he said.

Eli took one last look around. "I just need to stop at the office and give them my key."

"No problem, we'll stop on the way out."

DURING THE ride to the mansion, Eli stared out of the window, filled with apprehension. He continually rubbed his sweaty palms against his blue-jeans-covered thighs and tried to keep his left knee from bouncing.

"You're not on the way to the guillotine," Royce said, reaching over and squeezing Eli's left shoulder.

Eli turned to Royce and smiled weakly. "I know, just a little nervous is all."

"It'll be fine, son," Royce reassured. "It's just acting."

"That's what scares me," Eli said. "I tried out for a school play once, and the director told me I should stick to shop class."

Royce laughed. "It'll be just you, me, a still photographer, and the camera."

"Is that supposed to make me feel better?" Eli asked.

Royce was quiet for a moment. "I guess not."

Eli watched as Royce put on his blinker, pulled over to the side of the road, and slid the truck into park. When Royce turned to him and their eyes met, he had a look of concern on his face. "We can stop this right now, Eli," he said. "I don't want to force you into anything you're not comfortable with."

Eli held Royce's gaze until he heard the first cannon fire signaling an internal war was at hand. He focused his attention on a tiny crack in the windshield and braced himself for a struggle. He thought he'd already fought and won this war, but when his fingernails dug into his kneecaps, he realized it was still raging deep within him. *You can turn now and run or you can stand up and fight like a man until the end.*

The walls of the truck started closing in, and Eli was having trouble breathing. It was now or never. Eli struggled to fill his lungs with precious air, his resolve faltering with each intake until he was just about to wave the white flag of surrender. But somewhere in his core, his logical mind took over. *Stop! You have no other choice, Eli. You have no place to live and you're out of money. It's just sex. Stop being a pussy and just get the fucking job done.* Eli dug deep and found his voice. "No! I'm in."

"Look," Royce added, "if you're doing this because you need a roof over your head, take that out of the equation. You can stay at the mansion as long as you need to. I want you to be sure."

Eli suddenly turned his attention back to Royce. "Stop it, man!" he said. "Stop giving me a way out." Eli felt himself getting stronger with each word. "I need to get back on my feet, on my own, and this is a way to do it." Eli sat up straight and looked Royce in the eye. "I'm in."

"Okay," Royce said, putting the truck in drive again and easing back onto the highway.

WHEN THEY reached the house and walked into the foyer, the sitting room to the right was buzzing with activity. The lights were on, and the cameras were pointing at the bed where Logan and Gavin were seated, leaning against the headboard wearing T-shirts and gym shorts. When they saw Eli, they both smiled and waved, and Eli hesitantly returned the gesture.

"We're ready, boss," Rusty said to Royce, holding up a still camera.

"I'll be right there," Royce said. "Let me get Cal settled downstairs."

Eli's heart threatened to drop into his stomach again, but this time he fought the urge to panic. He calmly followed Royce down to the lower level and through one of the long hallways. "There are five bedrooms down here," Royce said, pointing down the corridor. "Take your pick and make yourself at home."

Royce held out the hanging bag, and Eli straightened his arm, still clinging to the duffel. Royce draped the bag over Eli's arm and smiled. "I have you scheduled for a twelve-thirty shoot, so be in your dress blues and upstairs by twelve fifteen."

"Yes, sir," Eli said with a nod. He watched Royce turn and walk away.

Then Royce stopped and looked over his shoulder. "Oh, and welcome home, son."

Eli flashed a weak smile. "Thanks, man. And thanks for the opportunity."

Walking down the hall, Eli peeked in each room and then moved on to the next. Each was very nicely appointed with either a queen- or king-size bed and private bathroom, and each was also fully equipped with an array of electronics and a flat-screen television. He decided on the room at the end of the hall, thinking it might be the quietest when the guys came over and the late-night partying started.

Eli dropped his duffels on the floor and laid the hanging bag on the bed, then went back and closed the door behind him. Focusing his attention on the hanging bag, he slowly moved the zipper down the length of the bag until the brass buttons on his uniform were shimmering in the overhead light. He hung the uniform on the back of the door and gave it the once-over. *Good as new, and it's a shame I'm about to disgrace everything it stands for.*

Eli shrugged off the feelings of dishonor and turned his attention to his duffels. He started unpacking each one, sorting things on the bed and putting them into dresser drawers. When he got to his black patent-leather dress shoes, he laid them on the bed with a pair of dark socks, a white T-shirt, and a pair of underwear. He took his toiletries into the bathroom, put everything away, and turned to the shower. The thing was four times larger than the shower in his motel room and had four showerheads, all pointing at various levels. There was a silver dispenser on the wall with four cylinders, each labeled with shampoo, conditioner, body wash, and shaving cream. *This guy doesn't miss a beat.*

Eli turned on the shower and closed the glass door. He stood in front of the huge mirror and stared at himself long and hard, as if the next time he saw his reflection, he would somehow be or even look different.

He slowly started unbuttoning his shirt, wondering what Royce was going to ask him to do. Would he be asked to do a striptease? If so, he surely wanted to be prepared. He tried to make a few seductive expressions, but they all ended up with him looking like he had gas. He started laughing so hard he was having trouble catching his breath. "I guess I'll wing it," he said to the mirror and finished stripping.

Stepping into the shower, Eli felt like he'd died and gone to heaven. The forceful jets massaged his entire body, and one of the jets was even positioned at his groin, giving him an almost instant erection. "Sorry, boy," he mumbled. "We've got to save the money-maker for the cameras."

Eli took his time showering, did a little manscaping, gave himself a close shave, rubbed some pomade through his hair, and then slapped some Old Spice on his face. He stepped back and looked at his trimmed, taut, and naked body in the mirror. *Not too shabby, Eli. Especially since you haven't been to a gym since your discharge. Gotta put on a show for the boys, you know!*

He fastened the last brass button on his uniform, locked his belt into place, and slipped on his white gloves. "Right on time," he said, looking at his watch. He picked up his hat and opened his bedroom door.

Exiting his room, Eli dipped his head to put on his hat and ran smack into Hamish. The impact forced a grunt out of each man, and Eli's hat went flying through the air. Before it could hit the ground, Hamish extended his long arm and caught it.

"Wow!" Hamish said, placing the hat on Eli's head. "Get a load of you."

Eli felt the blush as it crept up his face. "Hey, man," he said.

"Step back, Marine, and let me see if you pass inspection," Hamish ordered.

Eli smiled, stood at attention, and saluted. "Sir, yes, sir."

Hamish was wearing nothing but a pair of gym shorts, and Eli couldn't help but admire the man's well-defined body. From his broad shoulders and massive chest down to his six-pack abs and muscular legs, his body looked like that of one of the guys on the cover of *Men's Health Magazine*.

Damn, Eli thought, looking him up and down. *Even the man's bare feet are attractive.* Hamish gripped his hands behind his back and ran his eyes up and down Eli's uniformed body. "Exceptional," he finally said. "Now get a move on, Marine."

Eli smiled and did an about face. He took a step and jumped in surprise when Hamish's hand landed smack on his ass in a stinging slap.

Eli looked over his shoulder in surprise, and Hamish was smiling broadly. "Go get 'em, tiger," he said, adding a wink.

Eli knew he had a silly grin on his face, but he couldn't help it. Having Hamish's approval somehow made him feel better.

When Eli made it to the top of the stairs, Royce was waiting for him, and he whistled and flashed a broad smile when he saw his latest protégé. "You look incredible," he said. "You ready for this?"

Eli thought for a second before he answered. "Yeah, I think I am," he answered, suddenly ready to tackle this thing head on.

"Good man," Royce said. "Follow me."

Eli followed Royce outside to the deck, where everything appeared to be set up and waiting for him. There were three sets of lights on tripods, a video camera waiting on a table, and a duct-tape X on the floor, positioned with a clear view of the lake in the background.

Rusty was there holding up some type of meter as lights flashed repeatedly. Eli gave him a questioning glance and then looked at Royce. "Hey, Cal," Rusty said. "I'll be taking the stills."

Royce nodded. "While I take the video, Rusty will be working around us doing still shots from a bunch of different angles."

"I see," Eli said.

"First, I'd like to start off with you in full dress," Royce said. "Let's get you over there against the deck railing and I'll shoot you in several positions. I'd like to get you seductively staring into the camera, but not forced. Just try and be natural, like you're looking at some hot chick you really want."

All sorts of expressions ran through Eli's mind, and it took all he had not to start laughing. He cleared his mind and focused on the camera. He imagined Royce as a hot blonde, and he tried to remember his best looks from when he was attempting to pick up women. Eli followed Royce's instructions, and it was relatively easy. He held the *attention* position as Royce moved the camera slowly up and down his body and Rusty clicked away with still shots. Next he was posed *at ease* with his hat by his side, held in the crook of his arm. And last they had him saluting. Throughout all the shots, he focused seductively on the camera. Royce and Rusty both encouraged him throughout the process and seemed pleased with the results.

Next Royce took him back through the house, up the freestanding stairway to the second floor, and through a set of double doors. "This is it," Royce said.

Eli took a quick look around the room. The walls were all beige, except for one, which was mirrored. The carpet and ceilings were also beige, and there was a lone black leather chair in the middle of the room and a flat-screen television hanging opposite the chair. The lights and cameras Eli was getting used to were positioned everywhere, in various locations. There was an adjoining bathroom to the right and a table in the left corner with what appeared to be a bottle of lube and several towels. *Déjà vu*, Eli thought, remembering his vivid dream.

"What type of girls do you like?" Royce asked.

"Wait. What?" Eli asked, thrown a little off-kilter by the question.

Royce laughed. "Girls? You know, blondes, brunettes, redheads? Do you like big tits or long hot legs?"

Eli still didn't get it.

"For the porn video," Royce offered.

"Ohhhh," Eli responded. "I don't really have a type." He thought for a moment. "But for this purpose, I think blondes with big tits and long legs will do just fine."

Royce handed the remote to Eli. "Here, why don't you search for what you want while I get set up."

Eli flipped through all the movie options and finally settled on one he had already seen on pay-per-view when he'd first been discharged.

This was all becoming so real now. Eli pushed a slight wave of panic down, and then he looked Royce in the eye with a new determination. "Bring it on, Royce. I'm tired of feeling apprehensive and nervous. You wanted me here? Well now you've got me. Let's get this show on the road."

Royce looked at Rusty, who'd followed them upstairs, and flashed a smile. "Tell me I don't know how to pick 'em."

Rusty smiled and nodded.

"What do you want me to do?" Eli asked.

"Take a seat and just look at the camera like it's the one doing the interview," Royce directed. "Just so you'll know the process, we'll film some and then cut, fading in and out as we change positions and various stages of dress. I'll edit the footage and then lay a music track on top of the video for the final product."

"'Kay," Eli said.

Royce put the camera on his shoulder and a red light turned to green. "Cal. First solo. Take one. Action."

"Folks, this here is Cal. He's our new recruit, just discharged from the Marine Corps."

Eli nodded and said, "Hey."

"How old are you, Cal?"

"I'm twenty-seven, sir," Eli responded.

"Cal and I just met a few days ago, and I was floored when he agreed to join our little family. What a find."

Eli smiled and winked into the camera. "The pleasure is all mine."

"I'm gonna stop talking to you now and let you get down to business," Royce said. "Make me proud, soldier."

"Sir, yes, sir!" Eli said as Rusty clicked shot after shot.

The green light on the camera turned back to red and Royce said, "Cut. Great job, man. You're a natural at this."

Eli rolled his eyes. "I don't know about that."

"Trust me," Royce replied. "I'm the professional. Now! Let's get you to stand in front of the mirror and look at the camera's reflection as you slowly and seductively remove your gloves, belt, and start to unbutton your coat. Since this part will have no voice track, I'll give you verbal instructions throughout without cutting the scene."

Eli positioned himself in front of the mirror and found Royce and the camera. He dipped his head slightly, never breaking eye contact with the camera.

"Action," Royce called.

Still focused solely on the camera and grinning slightly, Eli worked his left glove, one finger at a time, until it was off, and he dropped it to the floor. He did the same with the right and slowly moved both hands to his belt buckle, released the mechanism, and allowed the belt to drop to the floor as well. Next he undid each brass button, starting at the bottom and working his way up until his coat sprang open, exposing his white T-shirt underneath.

Eli heard Royce very quietly instructing him. "Slip the coat off your shoulders, walk over to the chair and drape it over the back, then come around and take a seat. Still looking up at the camera."

Eli did what he was told, leaning back into the chair and laying a hand over his crotch.

"Excellent," Royce said. "Give your cock a squeeze, then bend down and remove your shoes and socks, looking up at the camera every few seconds."

Eli not only squeezed his dick, but he brought his other hand up and rubbed it across his T-shirt clad chest, stopping to pinch one of his nipples. He leaned forward, smiled into the camera, and then slowly untied his shoestring and slipped off his right shoe. He looked up at the camera and then back down at his left shoe and repeated the process. Glancing up again, he lifted his left foot and slowly peeled off his sock and did the same with the right.

Eli heard Royce again and followed more directions. He released his pants, giving the camera a glimpse of his gray boxer briefs. Then he brought his T-shirt halfway up his chest and rubbed his abs as he slowly slid his hands into his underwear and fondled himself.

Royce then positioned himself next to the television and calmly instructed Eli to pull his T-shirt over his head, exposing his dog tags and the eagle tattoo across his chest. He was told to then step out of his pants and relax back into the chair. Eli could now clearly see the big-titted blonde on the screen, and she was taking a pounding like a champ. The video was already having an effect on his cock, and Eli was amazed at how comfortable he felt, buck-ass naked in front of total strangers with a camera pointing directly at him. In fact, if he were being honest with himself, he was actually getting into it.

"Man, that's a pretty cock," Royce commented. "How big is that thing anyway?"

Eli wrapped his fingers around his length and squeezed. "Oh about eight inches or so, I guess."

"Eight inches of cocksure pretty," Royce added.

Eli lay back in the chair and worked his cock slowly, sliding one hand up and down his length while cupping his balls with the other. The last thing he heard before he totally lost himself in the video was Royce telling him that when he came to do it on his chest and abs.

Eli was caught somewhere in the middle of reality and fantasy, but the more he stroked himself, the further he receded into the fantasy playing out on the screen in front of him. He moved one hand behind his head, stretched his legs out, and closed his eyes. He worked his erection, enjoying the sensation, until he felt his balls start to draw up inside of him. With one long, seductive moan, he came in three huge spurts. The first release landed right under his chin and ran down his neck. The second landed on his dog tags, which were resting right between his pectoral muscles, and the third covered his lower abs. He milked his cock until there was nothing left. He opened his eyes and stared at the camera and then saluted with a half smile.

"Cut," Royce said, tossing Eli a towel. Royce had a nondescript look on his face and Eli wasn't sure if he'd done good or failed miserably. "I think you've been holding out on me, Marine."

"How so?" Eli asked.

"In all my years," Royce said, his expression turning into an all-out smile, "I think I've only seen two other guys this comfortable in front of the camera on their first solo performance. One was Dante, whom you haven't met yet, but will, and the other was Hamish."

Eli sighed and was overcome with a small sense of pride. "It was surprisingly easy."

"I know, right," Royce agreed. "Working up to the act is always harder than the act itself."

Eli stood and looked down as he wiped his chest and abs.

"Why don't you hop into the shower, and in an hour or two, if you're up to it, we'll do another scene," Royce suggested. "And, Cal?"

Eli looked up and met Royce's gaze.

"You did really well. You're a natural at this."

"Thanks," Eli said. "I think."

Eli closed the bathroom door behind himself and leaned against it. He shut his eyes and sighed as he listened to Rusty and Royce raving about his performance. All sorts of emotions were running through him, but the strongest was relief. *You did it, Eli! You actually did it. And it looks like you're about to do it again.*

When Eli reemerged squeaky clean with a towel wrapped around his waist, he found that someone had folded his uniform and underwear and stacked his things on the leather chair. Rather than dress again just to walk down the stairs to his room, Eli grabbed his things, opened the double doors, and stepped out into the hall. He immediately heard Royce's voice followed by a roar of laughter. Eli walked down the hall to an open door and stopped. Royce was behind the camera again and Rusty was clicking away taking stills. Hamish, Gavin, and Jayden were propped up against the headboard side by side laughing and cutting up like they were having a great time.

They were all shirtless, Hamish and Gavin on each side of the bed in blue jeans and Jayden in the middle wearing a pair of shorts.

Hamish apparently saw Eli standing in the doorway and was the first to acknowledge him. "Cal! Come in?" he said. "You're gonna have to see this eventually."

Royce turned around quickly and made a gesture for him to enter the room.

Jayden waved his hand. "Step right up," he said. "For the best show in town."

All the guys laughed and Gavin punched Jayden in the arm.

Eli hesitantly took a few steps forward and stopped at the foot of the bed, not sure he was ready to see anything more than he'd just done.

"It's okay," Gavin said. "You don't have to get into bed with us. Unless you… want to?"

"I think I'll pass this time," Eli said, taking a step back. "But thanks for the offer."

Royce pointed to a chair next to the door. "Have a seat," he said.

"We're rolling," Royce said to the guys, which prompted Jayden to open his arms and rest them on Hamish's and Gavin's shoulders.

Eli watched intently as the scene opened with Jayden explaining that he hadn't come in that particular room before, but he'd certainly come in a similar situation. Royce asked him if he thought he could come again and Jayden replied, "More than likely."

The guys started a back and forth banter about who should come on whom, laughing and talking shit like they weren't about to have sex with one another.

Royce asked the guys if any of them had any particular ideas or fantasies about how the shoot should go. Hamish quickly looked over at Gavin and said, "Yeah, with him facedown in the pillow and ass up in the air."

Gavin leaned across Jayden and smacked Hamish on the chest. "We'll see who ends up facedown, Marine."

Before anyone could say anything else, Royce jumped in. "I think everyone is eventually going to be facedown and ass up, along with some good ass eating, cocksucking, and ass fucking. It's up to you guys to determine who gets what and when."

By this time, Eli noticed, all the guys had their hands down their pants and were fondling themselves, with porn wailing on the television.

Hamish looked down at Jayden, whose erection was already protruding through his shorts. "Is this gonna be a race to the starting line?"

"Then you guys would lose, 'cause I was there ten minutes ago," Jayden admitted, undoing his belt and slipping out of his shorts.

"I'm partway there," Hamish said, unzipping his jeans and pulling out his erection.

"I'm getting there, but it's a bit warm in here," Gavin offered, peeling out of his jeans.

Eli looked away for a second when he realized Gavin wasn't wearing any underwear, but he quickly looked back, curiosity getting the best of him, wanting to see how he compared in size. *If I'm gonna enter this game, I guess I need to size up the competition.*

It struck Eli as funny how one minute he was nervous and blushing about all of this sexual freedom, and now he was evaluating the other guys' assets. He knew that most men, especially in the service, checked other guys out if for no other reason than to see how they compared in size, but this was a *right in your face* comparison.

Gavin wasn't fully hard yet, so it was unfair to judge him, but Hamish…. He was as hard as a flagpole, and what a sight that thing was. If he had to guess, Hamish had him by at least an inch in length, and had the girth to go with it. Eli wasn't a pencil dick by any means, but Hamish had him beat on both measures. Jayden was now in his underwear, but Eli could plainly see he was hung as well. Not as hung as he or Hamish, but holding his own.

Eli suddenly thought this whole scene was like a train wreck. You didn't want to watch, but you couldn't look away. He'd known of a couple of closeted gay men in Afghanistan, but he'd never seen them having sex and had never had a desire to, up until now. *What has gotten into you, Eli?*

Seconds later Hamish was out of his jeans, Jayden was kicking out of his underwear, and all three of them were naked and playing with themselves.

"Looks like you're ready," Jayden said to Hamish, bending over and without hesitation taking Hamish's erection in his mouth and moving his head up and down.

Hamish was lying back with his eyes closed while Jayden knelt over him, working his cock. In a split second, Gavin was under Jayden, taking his dick in his mouth, and suddenly Eli was having trouble keeping up with what was happening. He'd never been in a three-way, not even with women, and an awful lot of shit was going down very fast.

Then the dirty talk started. Hamish started guiding Jayden's head up and down while he told him to "suck that cock." Jayden and Gavin both moaned repeatedly with their mouths full, and Eli was glued to the scene in front of him.

In a quick change of positions, Gavin was on Hamish's cock while Jayden sucked on one then the other of Hamish's nipples. In yet another change, Gavin relinquished Hamish's penis and knelt in front of Jayden, who was now jerking Hamish off and going down on Gavin.

Eli thought this was like a free-for-all, but he couldn't keep up with the position changes. The one thing that was clearly evident was the lack of any romance or feelings. This was all raw man-on-man sex, and none of the guys showed any sort of emotions. This was all about what felt good physically, and suddenly he understood what Hamish had meant about getting over the "sex with a man" thing and just enjoying the act. He wasn't sure he could do it, but he understood it better now.

At some point while Eli was daydreaming, Jayden and Hamish switched positions and ended up side by side, arms over each other's shoulders while Gavin went down on them one at a time, switching back and forth. Then Hamish was up on his knees in front of Jayden and Jayden took him in while Gavin continued to go down on Jayden.

Eli thought this was all very confusing, but the guys looked like it came naturally and seemed to be enjoying it. No one was ever ignored, and no one ever lay back and did nothing. Everyone's cock was either in someone else's mouth or hand at all times.

But it appeared that things were about to get a little more interesting.

The dirty talk picked up again and this time was followed by a lot of ass slapping. Gavin was now on his knees going down on Jayden, and Hamish was behind Gavin, riming him. Eli realized he must have had a strained look on his face because when his eyes briefly met Rusty's, the guy gave him a sympathetic look but quickly went back to snapping photos.

Eli knew what was eventually coming, but when Jayden slipped a condom on Hamish, he wasn't sure he was quite ready to witness it. He stood in an attempt to flee, but Royce intervened and rested a hand on his shoulder. "It's okay," he mouthed. "Stay."

Eli hesitated, then decided Royce was right to ask him to stay. These guys were doing this to support their families, get educations, get back on their feet like him, or for whatever their personal reasons were, and they didn't deserve to be looked down on for it.

He sat back down and realized he would have to give these men the respect they deserved. When he settled in again, Jayden was on his back with Gavin between his legs, and Gavin was on all fours with Hamish about to penetrate him. Hamish pushed in slowly, and Gavin said, "Easy" in between moans, but eventually took all of him.

The dirty talk started again, with Jayden commenting on how much better Gavin sucked when he had something up his ass and Gavin moaning right through it all. Eli watched intently, as Gavin really seemed to be enjoying having a dick up his ass. *Could that be pleasurable?* Once or twice a girl had stuck her finger up his ass while he was getting a blowjob, and it had felt pretty good, but a finger and a cock were two very different things.

"Fuck, yeah. Give it to me harder," Gavin said as Hamish picked up his pace. "Oh yeah! Fuck me, daddy. Harder, man. Harder."

"You like that?" Hamish asked Gavin as he rammed in and out of him. "Take that big dick," he continued.

As the trash talk went on, Hamish pulled out of Gavin and straddled Jayden, who'd moved down to the corner of the bed. Gavin switched positions and knelt between Hamish's legs. He went down on him while Hamish seated himself on Jayden.

Hamish threw his head back and closed his eyes as he started slowly moving up and down Jayden's length. Small sounds that could only be described as whimpers started to escape Hamish's lips, and Eli put his hand in front of his crotch when he felt his erection building. As if sensing Eli's arousal, Hamish opened his eyes and locked on to Eli's.

Eli wanted to look away, but he couldn't. Hamish's deep blue eyes mesmerized him and bored right into him. Hamish flashed a million-dollar smile and winked at Eli.

By now Eli was rock hard, and it took every bit of willpower he had not to reach under his towel and begin stroking himself. He couldn't believe he was having this reaction to guys having sex. Eli looked around, and it was apparent Rusty and Royce were both hard, so maybe it was just the testosterone in the room. But whatever it was, it was damned hot.

Hamish threw his head back again and closed his eyes, riding Jayden like a bucking bronco. Eli had a flash of Hamish riding him the same way, his tight hole surrounding Eli's cock as he slowly moved up and down, and that vision almost sent Eli over the edge.

The next move had Jayden on his back with his legs in the air and Gavin sliding into him. Hamish was positioned at Jayden's head and had his dick in Jayden's mouth, fucking his face.

At first, Jayden didn't seem to enjoy Gavin's dick up his ass as much as Gavin had seemed to enjoy Hamish's, but eventually Jayden got into it, and before long he was begging for it harder and deeper like Gavin had earlier, and it appeared that Gavin was happy to oblige.

Hamish threw his head back and roared as he came on Jayden's face and neck. Seconds later, Gavin convulsed, pulled out, and blew his load on Jayden's chest. Jayden wasn't far behind and came with such force he covered his neck and shoulders with his own release. The three guys collapsed alongside one another and tried to catch their breath.

Royce yelled, "Cut," and the guys burst into laughter.

"Was that enough dirty talk, ass slapping, ass licking, fucking, and sucking for you, boss?" Gavin asked.

"Hell yeah," Royce replied. "Nice job. Now get cleaned up so we can finish the scene."

Eli watched as all three guys hopped up and ran into the bathroom together, Hamish giving him a smile and another wink as he passed by.

"So?" Royce asked. "What did you think?"

Eli shook his head. "I'm not sure what I think, Royce," he said honestly.

Royce put the camera down. "Do you think you could ever *do* any of those things?" he asked.

"I don't know the answer to that either," Eli replied. "I've never even kissed another guy, let alone any of that other stuff."

"Well," Royce said, "that's how you make the big bucks."

"I'll keep that in mind."

Before Eli had time to think about Royce's questions, the bathroom door opened and the guys came out one by one, laughing and slapping each other on the ass. They had apparently all showered together, and when Eli thought about it, after what they'd just done to one another, a shower was nothing. Hamish and Gavin put their jeans back on and Jayden his shorts, and they climbed back in bed in their original positions.

"Rolling," Royce said, and the guys settled down.

"That was fucking amazing, soldiers," Royce said for the take. "How was it from your end?"

All three guys smiled. "Jayden's some good ass pussy," Gavin teased. He looked at Hamish. "And you give the best head."

Hamish rolled his eyes and smiled. "That's what I keep hearing."

Royce chuckled at the lighthearted teasing. "Well, boys, I can't wait to do this again. Thanks for coming with me."

"My pleasure," Hamish said.

"Anytime," Gavin and Jayden said in unison.

Eli stood. "Nice job, guys."

Eli received several thanks before Royce said, "You're next. Why don't you get changed into your fatigues for the next shoot?"

"Same room?" Eli asked.

"No, let's use the one next door," Royce said. "It has a bed instead of a chair."

Eli nodded and left the room, making his way back down to the basement. He put his dress blues away, took a quick shower, and changed into his fatigues. He checked himself one last time in the mirror and slapped his cap on his head.

He opened his door and, much to his surprise, Hamish was staring back at him. His hand was in the air like he was about to knock.

"Hamish!" Eli said.

"Hey, man. Can I come in for a minute?"

"Sure, but Royce is waiting for me upstairs to do one more shoot," Eli explained.

"Yeah. About that," Hamish said. "The boss asked me to tell you not to rush. He's gonna be delayed about fifteen minutes."

Eli stepped back into the room. "Oh, thanks, I appreciate the heads-up, then."

Hamish bounced from one foot to the other. "Uh, I was headed down here anyway. You know, to see if you were okay. That was a hell of a lot to absorb for your first day."

Eli smiled appreciatively. "That's nice of you, Hamish. It was a lot. But I'm still standing."

"Good to hear," Hamish said as he sat on the edge of the bed and patted the spot next to him. "Sit down for a second. Will ya?"

Eli did what was asked of him, sat down next to Hamish, and gave him a questioning glance.

Hamish looked like he was trying to figure out how to say something and not really succeeding.

"Hamish, if there's something you need to say, please just come out with it," Eli said.

"I... I wanted to tell you not to let it bother you. It happens to the best of us," Hamish explained.

"What happens to the best of us?"

"I saw your erection under the towel during our shoot," Hamish mumbled. "I just wanted you to know it doesn't make you gay. It's just all the raw sex and testosterone in the room, and it happens to all of us."

Eli felt the blush creeping up his face and looked at the floor. "Thanks for saying that," he said. "I mean, I haven't even kissed a man before, and suddenly I was watching everything unfold in front of me, and I guess I got caught up in the fantasy."

"Seriously, Cal," Hamish said, standing and starting to nervously pace. "It does happen to all of us, but that was a little too much for you to see so soon. Man, we're all straight, but after doing this for a while, gay, straight, bisexual, it all blurs the lines and you just have sex. You might prefer it with a woman, but you get used to it with guys, and then either sex works fine if the one you prefer isn't around."

Hamish sat back down. "I just don't want you to make any decisions based on what you saw today. Don't let it scare you. If you want to do more, take it a little at a time until you are totally comfortable and then move on if you're so inclined."

"I appreciate the words of wisdom, and believe me, Hamish, they help more than you know," Eli said. "Like I said, I've never even kissed another guy. How can I even think about doing some of the things I just saw?"

As if in slow motion, Eli saw Hamish lean in. Felt Hamish's hand cup the back of his neck, and somewhere in the back of his mind, Eli thought, *Holy shit! He's gonna kiss me.* Then he felt warm, crushing lips pressing against his own. *Stop this, Eli! Pull away!* But for some unknown reason he didn't stop it. He didn't pull away. Instead he closed his eyes like a teenage girl being kissed for the first time. Something about being held tightly in place by Hamish's large hand at the base of his neck and the forcefulness of the kiss caught Eli off guard, and he suddenly had the urge to see it through.

Eli felt the fingers of Hamish's other hand on his face and then running through his hair, and he instinctively tilted his head to give Hamish better access. When Hamish's tongue sought entry against his lips, Eli, without conscious thought, not only opened for him but also sought entry of his own. He tasted Hamish as their tongues fought for dominance, and when the kiss finally ended and Hamish pulled away,

Eli pictured the famous kiss between Scarlet O'Hara and Rhett Butler, and he suddenly realized he'd been royally kissed.

Hamish got to his feet and looked down at Eli with a satisfied smile. "Now you can scratch that one off of your list." Without another word, he turned and left the room.

Eli stayed seated on the edge of the bed and pressed his fingertip to his lips. He'd just been kissed by a man, and damned if he not only didn't mind it, he even liked it. It felt different from a woman's kiss. There was something raw and masculine behind it. Not like the soft, gentle kiss of a woman, but forceful and rugged. *Fuck! Like I didn't have enough shit going on in my head already.*

Eli stood and paced a little, running his hands through his hair, and then eventually negotiated the halls and stairway to his next shoot. Hamish had left him in a foggy haze of disillusion, and he knew he had to get himself under control before he reached his destination. Eli did what the Marine Corps had taught him to do, and that was to push the crap to the back of his mind and focus on the task at hand.

When he reached his destination, Eli stopped in the doorway and looked in. This room was different from the last, an actual bedroom furnished like any other bedroom except for the lights and cameras.

Royce and Rusty were there setting up, so Eli entered. As with the other rooms, this room also had an adjoining bathroom and plenty of lube, towels, and a bowl full of foil-wrapped condoms. But unlike the other room, on the bedside table was an array of dildos in various sizes and one other thing that Eli didn't recognize.

"It's a butt plug," Royce said, apparently watching Eli examine the collection.

Eli raised an eyebrow.

Royce chuckled. "Sometimes guys use it to stay hard during a shoot."

Eli nodded, but didn't respond. He didn't quite know how to respond to that one.

"We're going to go a little further with this shoot," Royce said. "If you're up to it."

Eli raised his eyebrow again. *This day is just getting better and better*, he thought sarcastically.

Royce hesitated and Eli knew this wasn't going to be good. "I thought we'd do a little butt action."

"What kind of butt action?" Eli asked hesitantly.

"How far are you willing to go?" Royce said.

Eli shook his head. "I don't think I'm quite ready for anything that serious yet."

"We don't need penetration," Royce clarified, "but maybe just a little teasing."

"Teasing?" Eli asked.

"Do you trust me?" Royce asked.

Eli thought for a few seconds. Royce hadn't lied to him as far as he knew. Hadn't made him do anything he wasn't comfortable with. Had given him an opportunity and put a roof over his head. He thought he trusted him. As much as he could someone he'd known for such a short time. But instead of expressing that sentiment, he said, "I want to, Royce. I really want to."

Royce smiled. "Then trust me until I give you reason not to. How about that?"

Eli nodded hesitantly.

"Look, Cal," Royce continued. "It's my job to push you to your limits without asking you to do anything you don't want to do. Just allow me to guide you through the scene, and if I ask you to do anything you're uncomfortable with, say cut and we'll stop. Agreed?"

"Agreed," Eli replied, picking up the remote control and flipping through his porn options like an old pro.

He found a three-way with two guys and a girl and fast-forwarded through the limited foreplay to the down and dirty. A blonde-headed woman was taking it doggy style from one of the guys while blowing the other guy kneeling in front of her. The scene looked oddly familiar, and he realized it was one of the positions Gavin, Jayden, and Hamish had been in during their scene.

Royce threw the camera over his shoulder and looked around the room. "Let's get you lying back on the bed with your legs stretched out and your feet crossed at the ankles and we'll do the opening," he instructed.

Eli lay back, stretched out, linked his fingers across his stomach, and crossed his boot-clad feet as he'd been instructed.

"Rolling," Royce said. "Everyone. You guys remember Cal."

Eli nodded to the camera and smiled.

"Good to have your handsome mug with us for your second solo, soldier. And so relaxed too."

If they only knew, Eli thought. But instead he flashed a broad smile, knowing he could pull off this part easily. "Good to be back. And why not be comfortable in a place like this?"

"Maybe because you're about to jerk off on camera, among other things," Royce said.

"Been there. Done that," Eli said through a smirk. "Except for the 'among other things,'" he added with a chuckle.

"Let's not keep the good folks at home waiting. Time to get this party started," Royce instructed.

"I'm ready when you are, boss."

"All righty, then." Royce gave Eli his next move. "Start unbuttoning your shirt slowly and pull it open all the way when you're done."

Eli looked directly into the camera and followed Royce's directions. As he released each button, he focused on looking as seductive as he thought he could. When the shirt was free, he pulled it open and exposed his bare chest.

"Now slip your hand down the front of your pants and start fondling yourself until you get hard."

Between the video and his hand, Eli was stiff in no time. He followed Royce's directions to the tee and released the front of his pants, exposing his briefs and the massive erection protruding through the thin, black cotton briefs he'd put on. He slid his pants down to his knees and fondled his balls while slowly stroking his hard-on, up and down, stopping, squeezing, and stroking again.

As per instructions, Eli slid his shirt off his shoulders and tossed it aside. He then crossed each foot over the opposite knee, one at a time, and slowly untied and removed his boots and gray crew socks, looking up to the camera every now and then, licking his lips and flashing a sly smile.

He rose up, slid his pants down, kicked out of them, and tossed them aside. Eli relaxed again and lay spread-eagled, while he continued to play with himself. He reached for the lube bottle and slowly squeezed, dripping lube over the top of his cock.

"Bend your knees, pull your feet back, and run your hand under your balls and circle your asshole," Royce whispered.

Eli felt a flash of hesitancy but did as he was told. He slipped his hand down under his balls and ran his middle finger around his opening very slowly, never breaking eye contact with the camera. To his surprise, it felt pretty good.

Royce hesitated, then asked, "Do you feel okay slipping your finger in a little?"

Eli remembered that woman's finger up his ass and it had felt okay, but he'd never actually fingered himself. *What the hell?* he thought.

He continued to tease his opening a few more times and then gently slipped his middle finger inside the tight ring. It was an odd sensation, but not altogether bad. *Time to put on a show, Eli.*

Eli started slowly moving his finger in and out, coaxing a moan out of his pursed lips. He closed his eyes and shifted his head from side to side while stroking his cock and fingering himself. It actually felt pretty good. Each time his finger penetrated his asshole, his penis jumped, and he thought it odd how the two were so connected.

"Now get up on your knees and turn around with your ass to the camera," Royce directed.

Eli hesitated only for a second. "What the fuck," he said under his breath.

"Now play with your asshole," Royce instructed.

Eli got up to his knees and repositioned himself as Royce had instructed. He was now up on his knees, bent over, with the top of his head in the pillow supporting his upper body. He had one hand on his erection and the other circling his hole. He suddenly wished that somehow his parents could see him now.

"Run your finger up and down the crack of your ass, stopping at your balls and then at your asshole," Royce guided.

Eli followed instructions, and lo and behold, it felt really good too. The pressure against his ass and balls was sending his cock into a tailspin, and he was about to come.

"Cut!" Eli said.

Royce looked around the camera. "Are you okay?"

"Yeah," Eli said. "I'm about to come, though."

"Oh, that," Royce teased. "You know that's the point, right?"

"Very funny," Eli responded.

Royce readjusted a camera on a tripod aiming at his ass and got down to his knees, aiming his handheld between Eli and the bed, right at Eli's dick. "Go for it," he said. "Rolling."

Eli stroked his cock as he played with his asshole. The sensation was overwhelming, and his balls were withdrawing. Eli released a guttural moan as he rode the wave that was his orgasm. The first spasm consumed his body, with his release hitting him in the face, the second and third spasms dotting the sheets beneath him.

Eli milked his penis until there was nothing left inside and then rolled over on his back, trying to catch his breath.

"Excellent," Royce said. "Lick your top lip."

Eli did and tasted his own warm come as it clung to his skin. He brought his tongue back into his mouth, savored the flavor, swallowed, and then smiled seductively.

"Cut!" Royce said. "Incredible. Like I said, you're a natural."

Eli smiled, feeling rather proud of himself.

"How about we close out with you naked and just like you are, sitting against the headboard?"

"Fine by me," Eli said, getting into position, making sure not to lie in his own now cold, wet come.

"Rolling," Royce intoned. Then in a more sprightly tone, he asked, "So, Mr. Cal, how was that?"

"Incredible!" Eli said with a smile and actually meaning it. "That was really hot."

"If *you* thought it was hot, imagine what the folks at home are gonna think."

"I hope they enjoy it half as much as I did," Eli responded.

"I'm sure they will, soldier. I'm sure they will."

Eli smiled directly into the camera, licked his upper lip again, and tilted his head to one side. "Uhm… uhm good."

Royce howled. "As usual, thanks for coming, my friend."

"Anytime," Eli said.

"Cut!" Royce yelled. "Eli, *you* are killing me."

"And surprising myself," Eli responded.

"Just keep doing what you're doing and you're gonna have a following in no time," Royce assured him.

"Is that a good thing?" Eli asked.

"Absolutely," Royce said. "When I start getting e-mails from viewers wanting to see more of you, you've made it big on my site."

"I'll remember that," Eli said.

Royce pointed to the bathroom. "You're done for the day, so help yourself to a shower if you like. I'll have your pay ready for you by the end of the day."

"Thanks," Eli said, adding up his day's pay: twelve hundred dollars for an hour's work. "Not bad!"

CHAPTER FIVE
EXPLORATION

INSTEAD OF showering, Eli went back down to his room and took a whore bath. While he washed what was left of the dried come off his lip and the lube off his ass and cock, he pushed back the feelings of embarrassment and, not really regret, but something like it. *There'll be time for reflection later. Just do what you need to do right now and keep remembering that none of this is permanent.*

He dressed in his workout clothes and headed for the gym. Royce had told him it was on the backside of the pool house, so he knew exactly where he was going. Making his way down the long hall, he saw Royce had set up shop in the bedroom two doors down from his. When he peeked in, he saw Rusty had traded in his camera for a condom and Pat was on his back with his legs up in the air, getting pounded. Gavin was taking stills, and as usual, Royce was behind the camera directing.

Eli ducked away quietly and made his way to the outside stairs and up to the pool area. He walked past the pool and hot tub and around to the back of the pool house and found the gym, right where it was supposed to be. The entire exterior was walled glass and looked out over the lake. He cupped his hands and looked through the glass, thinking the gym was enormous until he saw his reflection staring back at him and realized the rear wall was completely mirrored. He opened the door and was surprised to see a full workout room. Free weights lined one wall with incline, decline, and flat benches, a curling bench, and a dip machine. Various other machines took up the other side of the gym. There were a crunch machine, a butterfly machine, a rowing machine, and a varied array of chest press and leg press machines to boot.

Eli checked out the locker room and found a steam room and a sauna as well as showers and full bathroom facilities. *Nice!* he thought. *I can get very used to this.*

He picked up a neatly folded white towel off a stack on the counter and went back into the gym. He seated himself on the rowing machine and set it for fifteen hundred meters. *That should get the heart rate up.*

Eli was on his third set of decline bench presses and was struggling with the last rep, the bar almost resting on his chest, when he heard a voice.

"Need a spot?"

Eli looked up to see Hamish standing over him, his crotch positioned at Eli's head.

Eli nodded and Hamish assisted him with the last push.

"Sorry," Eli said once he had the bar secure on the rack. "I didn't hear anyone come in."

"I think you were grunting too loudly," Hamish teased.

"Fuck you," Eli said through a smile.

Hamish laughed. "Mind if I join you?"

Eli shook his head. "Not at all. As you just found out, I apparently need the help."

Hamish looked at the weights on the bar. It looked like he was mentally counting. "That's two hundred pounds, man. Which set were you on?"

"Third."

"How many reps?" Hamish asked.

"Twelve."

"Fuck, man, I can't even bench press that, and I've got—" Hamish looked Eli up and down. "—at least six inches and thirty pounds on you."

Eli wiped his face with his towel and blushed a little at the compliment. "Yeah, well, don't sweat it, you've got me beat in other areas."

Hamish flashed a sly grin. "I didn't know you noticed."

"How could I not have?" Eli asked. "That thing is huge."

"Thank you," Hamish said, bowing at the waist.

The two locked eyes for a few seconds until Eli looked away. "So we're gonna work out or not?" he asked.

"Yeah, man. Let's do it."

The two former Marines proceeded through their workout, laughing and teasing one another mercilessly. It turned out Hamish had a wicked sense of humor, and Eli fell right into the routine. He really enjoyed Hamish's company and the hysterical stories Hamish shared of his experiences with the guys and Royce. When they called it quits, Hamish suggested they hit the steam room for a little while.

"I didn't bring a suit," Eli said.

"Seriously, man," Hamish said. "We've already seen each other naked and in some very compromising positions. And why do we need a suit?"

"Wait! What?" Eli asked. "I saw you with Gavin and Jayden—"

"And I saw you in your fatigues with your ass up in the air rubbing your balls."

Fuck! Eli smiled awkwardly and felt a full-on blush creep up his face. "How?"

Hamish chuckled. "I was waiting to do a shoot next door, and just like you I moseyed on by and took a peek. And by the way, you have nothing to be ashamed of in the manhood department."

Damn if Eli didn't feel another blush coming on. *Fuck! That makes three times in the last hour.* "Thanks. I guess payback can be a bitch" was all he could think of to say.

"Listen, man. There are no secrets around here," Hamish told him. "Our dicks have been up each other's asses and we've come in one another's mouths, so we really have no reason to be shy when we're here."

That makes sense. "I guess you're right," Eli conceded. "What the fuck, let's hit the steam room."

The guys stripped down and settled side by side in the small room. For the first time since they'd started working out, silence loomed between them.

"Feel free. I imagine you have more questions for me," Hamish said.

Eli knew he had, but he hesitated before he spoke. "Yeah. I guess I do," he said a few seconds later. "So much has happened to me in the last few days, I feel like I'm caught in a tornado and spinning a little out of control. I mean... when I'm in front of the camera, I do what's asked of me with no hesitation, but when it's over I have to force myself not to second-guess everything. I can't imagine what tonight is going to be like when I finally crawl into bed alone with my thoughts."

Hamish reached over and put his hand on Eli's leg and squeezed. "It's going to be okay, man. We've all been where you are, and I promise you, it gets way easier."

Eli hesitantly rested his hand on top of Hamish's. For some odd reason he needed to have human contact. He wasn't sure what was happening to him, but his emotions were on a roller coaster, and he didn't like it one bit. "If you don't mind my asking, how did you get into all of this?" Eli finally said.

"I'm sure our stories are not too different," Hamish explained. "During my last two years in Afghanistan, my parents and my younger brother were in a boating accident, and my younger brother Joshua was the only one who survived."

Eli squeezed Hamish's hand. "I'm so sorry, man."

Hamish squeezed Eli's leg and withdrew his hand. Through the steam, Eli watched Hamish run his fingers through his hair, and Eli could clearly see the stress on Hamish's face. "Josh lost a leg and had multiple brain injuries. He was in a coma for a couple of months, and when he came out of it, he had to learn to do everything all over again. Luckily, he eventually recovered, but he was in the hospital for several months and in rehab for even longer. Shortly before I returned stateside, I found out that the money my parents left us had run out, and they were going to move Josh to some state-run facility. I was afraid his care was going to suffer, and I couldn't let that happen."

"That must have been so tough on you, being overseas when Josh was in such bad shape," Eli said.

"It was," Hamish said. "I think that was the hardest part. But when I got to Quantico for my last month, I tried to seek assistance from the Corps, but there was nothing they could actually do since he wasn't my child. One day I was off base having coffee at a Dunkin' Donuts trying to figure out what to do when Royce found me. He offered me a job, and I didn't hesitate for one second. I did everything I could do to make as much money as I could to get Josh the help he needed. And once Josh had fully recovered, I kept on doing it to put him through college. He's a senior this year with a three point nine grade point average."

Eli could hear the pride in Hamish's voice, and although he already liked the guy immensely, he now held him in even higher regard.

"I probably already know the answer to this question, but does Josh know what you sacrificed for him?" Eli asked.

"No," Hamish said, "and he never will."

Eli nodded.

"Listen, Cal—"

"Wait!" Eli interrupted. "My real name is Elijah... Eli Preston. I can't in good conscience have this kind of honest conversation with you and have you not know my real name. It just doesn't seem right."

Hamish laid his hand on Eli's leg again. "You have no idea how much I appreciate that, Eli. It's always as if we're living in some alternate universe here, going by aliases, and it makes you wonder sometimes what is real and what's not. You know in all the time I've been doing this, no one has ever asked me why, until you. And for the record, I'm Dawes... Dawes Turner." Hamish offered his hand for a shake. "Good to meet you, Eli."

Eli accepted the hand. "The pleasure's all mine, Dawes. And what a cool name."

"It was my mother's maiden name," Hamish said. "So where did Cal come from?"

"My middle name is Calloway," Eli explained. "Which just happens to be *my* mother's maiden name as well. And Hamish?"

"My grandfather's name."

Eli held his hand up. "Sorry, but you were about to say something when I interrupted you earlier."

"Oh! Only that I have one more year until Josh graduates, and I give this life up. I love Royce and I always will, but I've got a good education, and I want a real life somewhere with someone."

The two men remained silent for a long while.

"You want to tell me how you ended up here?" Hamish asked.

"After that story," Eli said, "how can I not?"

"You certainly don't have to if you're not comfortable," Hamish offered.

"No!" Eli said. "I want to."

Eli told Hamish the story about how his parents had blown all of his money and wrecked his truck and left him with nothing after eight years of hard work.

"Man," Hamish said. "That sucks."

"Yeah, it kinda does. But no use crying over spilled milk."

"I guess not. But," Hamish said, "it doesn't make it any easier to take either."

"I'm about as over it as I'm ever gonna get," Eli said, looking at his hands. "But I'm also over this steam. I'm about to shrivel up like a prune."

"Yeah, me too. Are you done with your shoots for the day?" Hamish asked.

"Yep. You?"

"I am," Hamish confirmed with a twinkle in his eye. "Why don't we get cleaned up, get out of here for a while, and find us a little trouble to get into?"

"I don't know about the 'getting into trouble' part," Eli said. "But I'd love to get out of here for a little while. My head is about to burst."

Hamish chuckled. "I remember the feeling." He slapped Eli on the leg. "Let's go before we fade away to nothing."

On the way back to his room to shower and change, Eli ran into Royce in the hall and officially got his first paycheck. "Perfect timing," he said, accepting the envelope.

"Heading out?" Royce asked.

Eli nodded. "Yeah. Hamish and I are gonna sneak out of here for a while."

"You boys have fun, and stay out of trouble."

ELI AND Hamish ended up at one of Hamish's favorite sports bars in Dumfries. It was still early, so the place was pretty empty. Eli hadn't said much on the drive, and now he was hunched over, resting his elbows on the bar and simply staring at the frosty mug of draft beer in front of him. Out of the corner of his eye, he saw Hamish studying him intently, so he turned and met his gaze.

"You okay?" Hamish asked.

"I guess, just got a lot on my mind."

"Talk to me, Eli. Sorry, can I call you Eli outside of work?"

Eli nodded. "Sure, man. You want me to call you Dawes?"

Hamish didn't hesitate. "Not that I don't want you using my real name, but I actually like Hamish. When I was little, my parents said I looked so much like my grandpa they used to call me Hamish Jr. and for some stupid reason, it makes me feel closer to them."

"That's not a stupid reason," Eli said, swirling his glass on the bar. "I think it's kinda nice."

Hamish smiled shyly. "Thanks, but enough about me. Tell me what's going on inside that head of yours."

Eli was silent for a long while. "I just don't know where to start."

"Okay, shall I play it all out for you?"

Eli smiled, very curious about what Hamish was going to come up with. "Shoot, man. This I gotta hear."

Hamish downed his beer and tapped the bar. The bartender walked over and drew another beer off the tap and placed it on a bar napkin in front of him. "Firstly," Hamish said, "I'm sure you're having a little buyer's remorse right about now. You're a straight former Marine who beat off on camera for money. Twice. And for gay men to boot."

Eli shook his head and opened his mouth to speak, but Hamish raised his hand to stop him. "No! Let me finish."

Eli closed his mouth and obliged.

"Thank you," Hamish said. "Next… you had your first man kiss, courtesy of yours truly, which, if I remember my first time correctly, freaked the hell out of me as well. And lastly you saw some pretty graphic man-on-man sex. How am I doing so far?"

Eli offered a weak grin. "So far so good."

"So you're thinking you got through today okay, but you know Royce is gonna keep trying to get you to do more. And you also know you won't make the big bucks unless you take the next step. And…

you're doubting if you can even handle what comes next if you decide to take the plunge."

Hamish paused, took a sip of his beer, and swallowed. "Now if all that isn't enough, you're worrying about fitting in with the other guys. If you do move forward and take the next step, will the guys accept you into their little band of brothers?"

After a quick look around, Hamish tapped his forefinger on the bar. "And lastly, you're *really* wondering what it feels like to have a dick in your mouth or one up your ass. Or probably both."

Hamish leaned back with a satisfied grin on his face and rested his arm on the back of his barstool.

Eli shook his head, downed what was left of his beer, and waved at the bartender. "I've got to give you credit, man. You hit the nail, or should I say *nails*, on the head."

Hamish nodded rather proudly. "Thank you. Okay so let me start with the easiest part, the guys."

The bartender walked over, and Hamish paused while the man filled Eli's mug and slid it across the bar right into Eli's open hand.

When they were again alone, Hamish leaned in and continued in a low voice. "Look, man. So many guys come in, jerk off in front of the camera, get their money, and we never see them again. I mean… we're cordial to them when they're at the house, but to be honest, a lot of those guys look down on the ones of us who take it to the next level. They all swear they're not queer and could never do the things we do. But in my opinion, most of them are just insecure and afraid they might like what we do a little too much, so they tuck their tails between their legs and run."

Eli instantly felt bad for Hamish and the other guys that anyone would judge them for doing what they had to do to survive.

"And Eli… I see the wheels turning again. Doing what we do doesn't make us queer."

"I know, you told me that already."

"But I don't think you're hearing me."

"I get what you're saying intellectually. About the act itself not making you queer," Eli shared. "But I grew up thinking that ass fucking and dick sucking were what made you queer." Eli stopped and shook his head. "Man. That sounds so horrible when I say it out loud."

Hamish offered a sympathetic smile. "I hate putting labels on anyone," he said, "but technically, most people define being gay as anyone who has relations with the same sex. And maybe that's true for the masses. However, in my opinion, being gay might be *what* you are, but it doesn't define *who* you are. To be completely honest, most guys come into this biz thinking they are most definitely straight, including myself, but most of us leave identifying as bisexual."

Eli cast a doubtful glance in Hamish's direction.

"Seriously," Hamish said. "Sex is sex. It's fun and it feels good. Let's face it, a pair of lips around your cock feels good no matter who they belong to, right? It's like I said before, lips are lips, and as crude as it sounds, a hole is a hole."

"I know we touched on this before, but do you really like having sex with guys?" Eli asked.

"Some more than others," Hamish explained. "Honestly, for me it's all about the chemistry. But my motto is 'always give 'em a good show.' We're getting paid to make people believe, and that's what I always strive to do."

"What about women?" Eli asked.

Hamish smiled. "What about them?"

"Do you still have sex with them?"

"Hell yeah! When I find a woman I'm attracted to and she offers."

"So here's one for you," Eli said. "Have you ever had sex with a guy when you weren't getting paid for it?"

"No! But," Hamish said, holding up a finger, "it's not because I wouldn't. It's because I never met a guy I felt an emotional connection to. 'Emotional connection' not to be confused with 'chemistry.' Now don't get me wrong, I love the guys at the mansion and enjoy having sex with most of them, but I could never see myself being with any of them long-term."

"Is that your goal?" Eli asked.

"Absolutely. When this is all over, I want a normal life with someone I love."

"Would you get into a long-term relationship with a guy?"

Eli could see Hamish mulling over the question, and then he spoke. "If you would have asked me that two years ago, I would have said hell no!"

"And now?" Eli asked.

"If I met the right guy and everything was there? I would."

At first Eli was shocked by Hamish's answer, but then the more he thought about it, the more he realized he really wasn't that shocked. Hamish seemed very comfortable in his own skin and knew exactly who he was. Why would Eli expect anything less?

"Like I said, Eli, I hate labels," Hamish reiterated. "I've learned a lot about myself since I joined Royce and the guys. I no longer look at things as black and white, and I like it that way. I'm secure enough with my own sexuality that when I meet the right person, it won't matter what sex they are."

Eli held up his beer mug. Hamish tapped his against it and both men took a sip.

"So to set your mind at ease where the guys are concerned," Hamish continued. "To become one of us, you just have to share our code of ethics. We're all in this together, we *all* do it all, and no one judges the other. In return, we don't judge the guys who decide this is not for them. It's that simple."

"To put it bluntly," Eli said, "I'll be accepted if I suck a dick and take one up my ass?"

Hamish shook his head and took another sip of his beer. "No. You'll be *accepted* as long as you don't judge. But… you'll be one of *us* if you end up doing what we do."

"I stand corrected," Eli said. "Although I don't understand the difference."

"You will," Hamish replied.

"So," Eli asked. "What *does* it feel like to take a dick up your ass?"

Hamish choked and spit a mouthful of beer across the bar. The bartender ran over, handed him a stack of napkins, and wiped down the bar.

Eli tried to stifle his laughter as Hamish wiped his mouth, chin, and neck, then wadded up the napkins and threw them at him. "Give a guy a little warning before you pop a question like that, will ya?"

Eli caught the ball of napkins midair and dropped it on the bar. "Sorry."

"To answer your question, it hurts like a motherfucker the first time," Hamish admitted. "And... a few times after that. But once you've adjusted, it can be quite pleasurable. The prostate is an amazing thing, and when it's brushed up against, it sends pleasure coursing through your body in waves. It's amazing how the cock and ass are so connected."

"It just doesn't seem natural," Eli said, shaking his head.

"Why is it any different than the vagina?" Hamish asked.

"For starters, the vagina was made for that."

Hamish laughed. "Come on, Eli, think about it. The vagina was made for procreating. It brings pleasure and has a purpose. The ass was made for eliminating waste. It brings pleasure and has a purpose. How are they any different?"

"Damn, I hate it when you make a good point," Eli teased.

"It's society that says anal sex isn't natural. Do you think it's okay to fuck a girl up the ass if she asks for it?"

"Hell yeah," Eli said.

"Then why is it not okay to fuck a guy up the ass? And before you answer that, remember women have no prostate to rub against, so they get a lot less pleasure than we do."

"Man! My head is whirling," Eli said.

"Look! If and when you decide that you're going to take the next step, I'll take you to the sex store and buy you a dildo. We've all practiced with one. It makes it much easier when you do the real thing."

"I'll keep that in mind," Eli said, rolling his eyes.

"Let me just go right into the sucking dick thing before you catch me off guard again," Hamish teased.

"Very funny," Eli said. "But please do. I'm on the edge of my seat."

Hamish smirked. "Okay so... sucking dick takes a little getting used to. It's foreign at first, but if you relax your throat it's much easier, and the gag reflex lessens."

"Oh Jesus," Eli hissed. "My goose is cooked. I have a horrible gag reflex."

Hamish laughed. "You can find ways to fake it, like fisting the base of the erection with your hand and just working the top with your mouth or moving your hand up and down awhile to tease the head, but if you really want to do it right, you've got to learn to deep throat. The best way is to approach it as if you were swallowing the cock. Take it to the back of your throat and swallow. It takes a little getting used to, but you'll get it eventually. And trust me. If you don't, these guys will let you know."

"Jesus," Eli said again. "I can't believe we're having this conversation. And now I'm gonna be judged on my performance?"

"Relax, they'll give you a grace period, but after that, look the hell out!"

"Oh, thanks!"

The two men sipped their beer in silence for a few minutes, and then Hamish spoke again. "Are you seriously considering going to the next level?"

"I don't know what the hell I'm considering," Eli said. "I've got to admit, though, you've piqued my interest, and now I'm curious to see if I could take it or not. I know that's where the big bucks are, and I do need to get back on my feet, so yeah. I guess I am."

Hamish downed his beer and dug in his pocket and threw a twenty on the bar. "Finish your beer and let's get out of here."

"Where to?" Eli asked, holding his beer mug to his lips and then taking a sip.

"The sex store," Hamish said.

Now it was Eli's turn to spit beer across the bar.

"What goes around, comes around," Hamish teased, handing Eli a stack of napkins.

HAMISH PULLED into the parking lot of the Adam and Eve adult superstore. Eli nervously pulled his hoodie up over his head as he got out of the car.

Hamish held the door for him, and Eli walked in with Hamish on his heels.

"Hi, Hamish," the bubbly blonde behind the counter said in a flirty tone while she batted her eyelashes wildly. "What can I *do* for you today?"

Please, God. Please, God. Don't let him say I need a dildo, Eli prayed.

"Oh hey, Bambi. My friend here needs a dildo," Hamish said rather nonchalantly.

Eli felt the blush crawling up his face as the blonde walked over. He offered her a weak smile from under his hoodie.

"What size?" she asked.

Eli looked at Hamish at a loss for words.

"He's just starting out, so nothing too big."

"I have just the thing," Bambi said, continuing to bat her lashes at Hamish. "It's a twofer. A small and a medium size in one box."

"Sounds perfect," Hamish agreed. "Give him a vibrator and a butt plug too, you know, to help stretch things out a little."

Eli cowered. *Just strike me down now, God, and spare me the embarrassment.*

It was obvious that Hamish was really enjoying this, and Eli was none too happy about it. "Can we just get the stuff and get out of here?" he hissed through closed teeth.

"Do you need any lube or condoms?" Hamish asked, leaning over the counter, winking and flirting with Bambi.

"No!" Eli said. "That will be it."

Eli paid Bambi, took the brown paper bag off the counter, and ran out of the front door as fast as he could. He stood at the car door, resting his head on the roof while he waited for Hamish to come out. Before Hamish exited, Eli heard the vehicle's door locks pop open, and he quickly got in and closed the door.

A few minutes later Hamish climbed in the car with bright red lipstick smeared all over his face. When he saw Eli looking at him, he smiled. "She likes me," he said, reaching for a tissue and cleaning his face.

Eli just grunted.

"And... I'm sorry," Hamish confessed. "That was mean."

"That *was* mean," Eli agreed.

"In my defense," Hamish said, grabbing the steering wheel, "she knows what I do and loves gay porn. By the way, she said you're really cute and she can't wait for your first video."

"A woman?" Eli asked.

"Sure," Hamish said. "There are a lot of women who like man-on-man sex."

"Oh God, I don't think I'll ever understand all of this."

"Sure you will," Hamish said.

"What in the hell have I gotten myself into?"

"Come on, Eli," Hamish teased. "She's harmless. Just likes a little man-on-man action." He started the car and pulled out of the parking lot. "Since I was such a dick back there, how about you let me make it up to you by cooking you dinner?"

"Fine!" Eli said in his curtest voice. "But it better be good."

"I'm an excellent cook. You'll see."

AS IT turned out, Hamish lived in the same neighborhood as Royce, almost directly across the lake, and although his house was much smaller, it was not any less impressive.

"Wow!" Eli said, looking around. "This is incredible."

Hamish smiled. "Thanks. I'm close enough to work, but not too close. If you get my drift."

Eli nodded.

Hamish dropped his keys on a credenza in the entry hall and kicked off his shoes. "Let me check the fridge, and I'll see what our options are. Make yourself at home."

Out of courtesy Eli took his shoes off as well and then walked around the living room admiring all the furnishings and accessories. He stopped when a photo caught his eye. He picked it up and admired what looked like a very happy family on vacation.

Hamish walked in carrying two beer glasses with frothy heads. "That's me, my mom, and my little brother Josh on our first trip to the Grand Canyon," he said, handing Eli the glass. "Your Blue Moon, sir."

"Thanks," Eli said, accepting the glass, silently wishing he had childhood memories and photographs. "Looks like you were having a lot of fun."

"It *was* fun."

Eli studied the photograph. There was a very attractive woman leaning against a car with a toddler in one arm and her other arm draped over the shoulder of a boy standing next to her. It was apparent from the broad smile, jet-black hair, and blue eyes that the boy was a young Hamish. "A pretty big age difference between you two, huh?"

"Yeah, after my mother had me, they tried for years to have more children, but it never happened. They eventually gave up and spoiled me rotten. But surprisingly, when my mother was forty-three years old, she got pregnant again. I think they called it a change of life pregnancy. I'm so grateful she did or I wouldn't have Josh, and I'd be all alone in this world."

Like me, Eli thought. But before he could focus on his pity party too long, the wheels in his head started turning. *I wonder if Hamish ever resents Josh for what he had to do to take care of him?*

Hamish tilted his head and studied Eli. "I know what you're probably thinking. And... if I'm right, the answer is not for a second."

Hamish pulled a cigar out of his top pocket and gestured for Eli to follow him out onto the balcony. "It's a Cuban."

"I'm right behind you," Eli said excitedly. "I haven't had a Cuban cigar since I was in Afghanistan."

"In your dreams," Hamish said, putting his beer down on the railing.

Eli gave him a quizzical look.

"Right behind me. Get it? That's a joke we use in the house all the time."

"Oh," Eli said. "Now I get it. Very funny."

Hamish rolled his eyes. "You know Royce is going to push for that, right?"

"Push for what?" Eli asked.

"Us doing a scene together," Hamish said, clipping off the end of the cigar, bringing it to his mouth, and lighting the end.

"Oh? I never gave that any thought," Eli said, knowing he was telling a little white lie.

Hamish took a puff off of the cigar and handed it to Eli. "Am I that hard on the eyes?"

Unfortunately Eli was in the middle of a draw when Hamish spoke. His eyes got wide and he stopped inhaling to say, "No—that's not what I—" Suddenly he started coughing as smoke went down the wrong way. He coughed for at least thirty seconds, Hamish slapping him on the back continuously. Just before he was able to speak, he raised his hand for Hamish to stop smacking him. "Enough. Thanks. I'm okay."

Hamish stopped his assault but was smiling from ear to ear. "Smoke much?" he asked.

"Ha-ha!" Eli choked out. "Hamish! I didn't mean you were...."

"Unattractive and undesirable?" Hamish asked.

"No! Just the opposite," Eli said. "I think you're a really good-looking man. But I also appreciate you taking me under your wing, and I sort of consider you a friend now. It just seems like it might be a little weird to have sex with a friend."

"Might be at that," Hamish agreed. "Wouldn't know. I had sex with most of the guys before I got to know them, so you're right. It might have been awkward if it had been the other way around."

"Do you spend a lot of time with the other guys?" Eli asked, handing the cigar back to Hamish.

"Not outside of work," Hamish replied. "I mean... none of them have been here. That is work." He gestured across the lake. "This is home. And I try and keep it that way."

"But you brought *me* here?"

"Yeah, that surprised me too," Hamish admitted. "Maybe it's like you said. We're becoming friends first."

"Either way, thanks for trusting me enough to bring me to your home."

Hamish nodded and handed the cigar back to Eli.

They passed the cigar back and forth, enjoying a comfortable silence. Eli was still sorting through his thoughts, and it seemed that Hamish was giving him the time to do so. They were both leaning over the railing looking out onto the lake when Hamish finally spoke. "You're wrong, you know," he said.

Eli turned to face him and took a sip of his beer. "About what?"

"Joshua. I don't regret a solitary thing I've done, or had to do, to take care of him. In fact, I would do it all over again exactly the same way if I had to."

Eli felt a lump developing in his throat, and he swallowed it back down. When he thought he could speak without his voice cracking, he laid his hand on Hamish's forearm. "That's so damned admirable, man. Joshua is a very lucky guy to have you as a brother. I hope he knows it."

"I'm the lucky one," Hamish corrected. "He's a great kid, and he's gonna make something of himself."

"Because of you," Eli added.

"Maybe a little," Hamish said. "But he's putting in the time and doing the work."

"Growing up I would have given my right arm to have someone care about me the way you care about Joshua," Eli confided.

Hamish stubbed out the cigar on the railing and draped an arm across Eli's shoulder. "I'm sorry, man," he said, resting his forehead against the side of Eli's head. "That must have sucked."

Surprisingly, Eli didn't tense up or even attempt to move. He accepted Hamish's consolation and took a little comfort in the fact that someone cared. "Yeah, well," he said, "I'm sure many had it worse than me. I normally try not to worry about the what-ifs."

"That's probably best," Hamish said. "But if you ever want to talk about it, I'm here."

"Thanks. But it won't change anything."

Hamish placed a soft kiss to the side of Eli's head. "Doesn't matter. Sometimes it just helps to talk about it. How about some dinner, then?"

"Sounds good to me."

"I've got two steaks coming up to room temperature and potatoes already in the oven," Hamish said.

"What can I do to help?" Eli asked.

"I don't know about you, but I've had enough beer for one night. Why don't you go to the wine cellar and pick out a nice cabernet? At the bottom of the stairs, first door on the right."

"I'm not a great wine connoisseur, but I'll give it a shot."

Eli found the wine cellar and took his time looking at all the wines and the vintages stacked on wooden shelves. There must have been at least sixty bottles of wine filling the small space, and he had no idea which to choose. Then he decided that Hamish must like all of them if he bought them, so in the end, he decided on a bottle because he liked the label.

Eli climbed the stairs and found Hamish fumbling around in the kitchen. He walked over to the counter and saw that Hamish was cutting off the ends of a stack of asparagus while a pan of oil heated over the stove.

"Let me see," Hamish said, craning his neck to read the label of the wine bottle.

Eli held it in both hands and presented it to him like he'd seen it done on television. "Your wine, sir."

"The 2009 Martin Ray. Excellent choice," Hamish commended. "That's from the Stag's Leap district of Napa."

"Oookay," Eli said with no desire to pretend he knew anything about the Stag's Leap district, or any other district, of Napa.

Hamish gestured over his shoulder to a drawer next to the refrigerator. "Opener's in there and glasses are overhead."

Eli found the opener and didn't think he embarrassed himself too much during the opening process. He didn't pour the wine right away because he remembered something about nice wine having to breathe before you poured it, but he got two glasses and set them down next to the wine bottle. "I assume this has to breathe?"

"Probably for a little while," Hamish confirmed.

"So what else can I do?" Eli asked.

"Why don't you check the potatoes to see if they're getting close while I put the steaks on the grill," Hamish suggested. "Oh! How do you like your steak?"

"I prefer it medium to medium well," Eli said. "But I'll take it any way it comes. I'm not picky."

"I'll do my best," Hamish yelled over his shoulder as he pushed open a glass door that led to the deck and disappeared.

Eli checked the potatoes and found they weren't quite ready, so he moved over to the sizzling pan of asparagus on the stove and shook it by the handle. Convinced nothing was going to burn, he leaned back on the counter and looked around the small but very attractive and well-appointed kitchen. *Hamish has great taste*, he thought. Although he'd never been to Italy, Eli imagined Hamish's kitchen looked like an authentic Tuscan kitchen. The walls and ceiling were hues of mustards and gold, the cabinets were a rich, dark mahogany, and the backsplash was made up of brightly colored ceramic tiles. There was an arch over the six-burner stove and stainless steel appliances finishing everything off.

"About seven minutes on each side and we'll be set," Hamish said, returning with an empty platter in one hand and an egg timer in the other.

"Probably about fifteen in here as well," Eli replied.

Hamish gestured to the wine bottle with his head. "How about we sample that wine, then?"

Eli filled the glasses half-full, handed one to Hamish, and tapped this glass against Hamish's. "Cheers, and thanks for all this by the way."

"Anytime," Hamish said, swirling the wine around in his glass and taking a sip.

Eli followed Hamish's actions and tasted the deeply colored red liquid. Although he didn't know much about wine, Eli knew when something tasted good, and this tasted very good. "This is like drinking velvet," he said.

"It *is* nice," Hamish agreed.

Eli took another sip and licked his lips. "If this is what fine wine tastes like, I think I'm gonna *have* to take my career to the next step."

Hamish gave him a questioning glance.

"Because I'm gonna need money to support my new addiction."

Hamish laughed. "I'm glad you like it."

Eli held up his glass. "How much is this stuff anyway?"

"Oh, about fifty bucks a bottle if you were to buy this vintage now," Hamish explained. "But I bought a few of these a couple years back when I started my wine cellar, and I think I paid about twenty dollars a bottle."

"So now I see the trick," Eli said. "Buy cheaper vintages now and age them yourself versus buying them already aged. Makes sense."

"Bingo," Hamish said, tapping their glasses together again.

The egg timer dinged and Hamish spun on his heels. "Duty calls," he said over his shoulder.

"I'll start to get things ready in here."

WITH THEIR bellies full, Eli and Hamish were sitting side by side on the couch, their socked feet propped up on the coffee table, watching the New Orleans Saints play the Dallas Cowboys. Eli was focused on the game, but when he looked over at Hamish, the man was resting his head on the back of the couch with his eyes closed. Thinking he was dozing, Eli took full advantage of the opportunity and really studied his new friend.

Trying to take Hamish's advice and make an attempt to get over the man-on-man thing and not look at things as black and white, Eli realized he hadn't been blowing smoke up Hamish's ass when he told him he thought he was a good-looking man. In fact, resting like this, Hamish's features were more relaxed, and if possible, he was even more handsome.

"You fantasizing about using that dildo on me?" Hamish said, peeking through one eye.

"What? No!" Eli said, feeling like he'd been caught with his hand in the cookie jar.

"Well fuck you very much!" Hamish said, closing his eye again.

Fuck! "I didn't mean it like that," Eli said. "I just…."

"Just what?" Hamish asked playfully.

Eli didn't know what to say. "I'm so busted," he finally mumbled.

"Relax, man. I'm just teasing you. But I could feel you staring at me."

"Sorry, I thought you were dozing," Eli said.

"Apparently," Hamish said, still not moving.

"You just looked so… so tranquil I couldn't help it," Eli explained. "Do you know how much your features soften when you're relaxed?"

"All part of my master plan to get you under my spell," Hamish said.

"Is it now?" Eli asked.

Hamish cocked one eye open again. "Is it working?"

"I'll let you know," Eli teased.

Hamish raised his head and looked at Eli. "Speaking of that stuff we bought. You gonna try it on for size anytime soon?"

Eli tilted his head and thought for a second. "I think I'm working my way up to it. I really want—no, need to get out of this hole I'm in."

"By letting someone into yours?" Hamish asked with a grin.

"You're a real comedian," Eli said.

Hamish dipped his head in Eli's direction. "Thanks. Seriously, when you get ready, let me know and I can offer you a few pointers?"

"Sure! Anything that'll make the initial breach easier," Eli said with a nervous chuckle.

Hamish reached over to the end table and retrieved a pen and pad from the drawer. "You're gonna want to take notes."

Eli listened and took notes as Hamish shared all his secrets for preparing for anal intercourse. By the time Hamish dropped him off at the mansion a couple of hours later, Eli's head was again spinning from information overload.

Eli got out of the car and leaned over the passenger door. "Thanks for everything, man. I'll figure out how to thank you one of these days."

"No thanks needed," Hamish said. "Now go to work."

Eli turned and walked toward the house.

"You got your notes, right?" Hamish hollered as Eli climbed the stairs with his brown paper bag full of sex toys.

Eli waved him off. "Yes, daddy."

"Have fun, then, junior," Hamish yelled as he drove off.

Eli stepped into the foyer and immediately heard loud music, occasional clapping, and a lot of laughter coming up from the basement. He took the inside stairs to the lower level, which allowed him to get to his bedroom unnoticed, but curiosity got the best of him, and he peeked into the game room. Pat and Gavin and two other guys he didn't recognize were sitting on the bar, buck-ass naked, all sporting serious erections. Rusty and Jayden were across the room with rings, tossing them at the four men, trying to get a ringer. Every time one of the guys ended up with a ring on his cock, everyone took a shot. As usual,

Royce was in the thick of things, cheering them on with the camera over his shoulder.

Eli chuckled and shook his head in disbelief as he slipped away, not quite ready to end up on a bar, naked, with guys tossing rings at his dick for tequila. Eli shut his bedroom door and locked it, kicked off his shoes, and turned on the television to drown out some of the noise. Comfortably sitting cross-legged in the middle of his bed, he opened the brown paper bag and examined his new toys. As he unwrapped the packages, he brought back to mind what he remembered about Hamish's instructions: "If it were me and it was a couple of years ago, I'd start with that butt plug. It's smaller than the vibrator and the dildos and will help get you ready. Put a little lube on the thing and slip it in. It's gonna sting a little when you get to the widest part, but once it's in, the discomfort won't last too long. I'd wear it around a full day before you try anything else."

"I can't believe I'm supposed to walk around all day with a butt plug up my ass," Eli said to himself, taking a closer look at the oddly shaped rubber toy. Then he looked at the vibrator. *Since I've at least seen one of these, maybe I'll give it a whirl first. It seems less invasive.*

Eli sighed and closed his eyes. "No time like the present I guess," he whispered, unwrapping the battery-operated toy. *Oh shit. Batteries?* He quickly emptied the contents of the bag into the middle of the bed, and luckily a pack of *AA* batteries fell out. "Thank you, Hamish," he said, loading the batteries into the vibrator and then stripping.

Lying naked in the middle of his bed with his new toys spread out on either side of him, Eli retrieved a bottle of lube from his bedside table and picked up the remote control. *I'm sure Royce must have used this room for filming before, so maybe there's a leftover video in the DVD player.*

Eli pressed the Play button on the universal remote, and the firm ass of a brunette appeared on the screen. The shot was taken from behind, and she was kneeling between the legs of some guy and her head was going up and down. When the shot panned around to the left, Eli saw that she was going down on a burly guy while she fucked him with a vibrator.

"No way," he whispered. "This is way too much of a coincidence." Not putting it past Royce, Eli glanced around the room, half expecting to find a camera pointing on him from behind a picture or a lamp, but he saw nothing. Eli shrugged. *I guess it is a coincidence.* He turned the knob on the base to the right and the vibrator came to life; he turned it again and it sped up to the next speed. He turned it one more time and it whirled into high gear. He'd seen vibrators before, but he'd never used one or had one used on him. He had a pretty good idea what to do, though.

Eli coated his cock with an ample amount of lube, rubbed a little on the vibrator and his balls and ass, and leaned back to start the show. In the video, the guy was moaning continuously and gyrating his hips as the vibrator slid in and out of him in unison with the brunette's mouth working his dick. Eli hesitantly pressed the vibrator to his balls and moved it around a bit, getting a feel for the thing while he stroked his cock. The sensation was odd, but to his surprise, very pleasant. The vibration against his balls made his penis jerk involuntarily as he fisted himself and moved his hand up and down his length.

Staring at the screen without blinking and starting to get into the scene before him, Eli released himself, slid the vibrator up, and steadied it on the sensitive underside of the head of his cock. His penis jerked again and filled almost to capacity. He moved the toy up and down his length, now lying erect against his stomach, with one hand, while massaging his balls with the other. Occasionally he allowed his hand to slip farther down, circle his opening, and tease a little before moving back up to his balls. His nerve endings were on edge and heightened as the vibrating toy almost took on a life of its own, roaming all over his groin area.

"Jesus," Eli hissed. *This feels fucking amazing. I don't think I've ever been this hard.*

Eli guided the vibrator down and held it against his opening. His cock jerked several more times as if begging for attention, so he fisted it again and started moving his hand slowly. Wanting better access and wanting to feel more, Eli spread his knees farther apart and pulled back his legs. He guided the tip of the vibrator to his opening and gently pushed in. His initial reaction was to push back against the foreign object, but he restrained himself. The nerve endings surrounding his opening were tingling and begging for more attention. The combination of the vibrations against his ass and his hand moving up and down his dick had him on the verge of release. He slowed his hand, gripped the base of his erection, and gave himself a minute to recover. But much to his surprise his ass was still begging for more. He pushed the tip of the vibrator farther inside, pausing when he felt resistance, and held it there. His ass seemed to eventually relax around the vibrator and almost welcome the intrusion.

His pending release subsiding for the time being, Eli gripped his length again and started to move his hand up and down. He withdrew the tip of the vibrator from his ass, circled the sensitive skin surrounding it, and pushed back in, ever so lightly. As the tip of the vibrator entered him, his cock jerked again. He massaged the swollen head while he eased the vibrator in farther and realized more than ever how the two separate organs felt like one. Needing to push in a little farther, Eli felt another bit of resistance. He knew he must be pressing against the tight muscle guarding his opening and withdrew. Enjoying the sensations consuming him, Eli pumped his length as he pushed the tip of the vibrator in and out. He was close again and decided to give the vibrator one last attempt. When he felt the resistance this time, instead of withdrawing, he applied more pressure and forced the tip inside. "Fuck!" he cried, squeezing his eyes shut and throwing his head back so hard it slammed against the headboard. He immediately saw stars and withdrew the vibrator. His ass felt like it was literally on fire, burning and stinging to the point of bringing tears to his eyes. His erection instantly faded and he was left with a limp dick in his hands and an aching asshole.

"That went well," Eli whispered, suddenly remembering Hamish's words. *"Start with the butt plug. It's smaller and will help get you ready."*

When the burning in his ass subsided, Eli picked up the butt plug, applied some lube, and positioned it against his opening. He slowly pushed in and stopped when he felt resistance.

Here we go again. Eli withdrew and pushed in a few more times, and finally the butt plug slipped in past the muscle and seated. It hurt like hell, but nothing like the vibrator, and the discomfort quickly subsided. Eli sighed, lay back, and closed his eyes, relaxing and letting his body adjust. When he heard another moan out of the television, he cocked one eye open to see the burly guy behind the brunette, giving it to her from the rear. Eli rose upright to his knees and stared at the television. The combination of the butt plug up his ass and the scene playing out in front of him made Eli instantly hard again. He fisted himself once more and started pumping. The feeling of the plug against his prostate had him gyrating and moving his hips back and forth, wiggling and pumping into his hand. It took less than a minute before Eli was at the point of no return. "Fuuuuck!" he cried, his ass gripping the butt plug as he shot his load. The first round landed on the comforter at the foot of the bed and the remaining spasms dotted the sheets in front of him.

He allowed himself to fall backward on the bed, kicking his legs out in front of him and wincing when his ass hit the mattress, jostling the butt plug. His heart was still racing and his body was covered with goose bumps.

Jesus! That was intense!

When he was able to get to his feet, Eli took a few steps toward the bathroom and stopped. Every time the butt plug rubbed against his prostate, his dick jumped and he felt a wave of pleasure course through him. With each step, the sensation threw him a little off balance, and he thought he must look like he had some type of disability. *And I'm supposed to walk around here all day tomorrow with this in my ass? I think not.*

He cleaned himself up, wiggling here and there, trying to get used to the sensations going on inside of him. When he was through, he carried a towel back to the bed and wiped his release from the comforter and sheets and cleaned the vibrator. He then hurled the towel into the bathroom, climbed back in bed, and shut off the television. He could hear sounds of the guys still partying, but he drifted right off to sleep.

THE NEXT morning Eli woke lying on his belly with a raging hard-on caught between his stomach and the sheets. When he rolled over, a wave of pleasure coursed through him and goose bumps again covered his body. *The butt plug.* He needed to pee and have some coffee before he could try to process anything else. He climbed out of bed, spastically walked to the bathroom, and stood in front of the toilet. He painfully forced his erection to point downward, and when he started peeing, he sprayed all over everything in a two-foot area. *Jesus, Eli!*

His erection subsided some and he pulled toilet paper from the roll and bent down to clean up the mess he'd made. Another wave of pleasure consumed him, and his dick jumped and rose to attention. "Fuck!" he said. "I can't go through this all day."

Eli put on his gym shorts and carefully made his way up the stairs and to the kitchen. He was extremely happy when he saw the kitchen empty, indicating that no one was up yet. He loaded the Keurig with a pod and waited for his coffee to brew. A minute later, with his coffee in hand, Eli headed back to the stairway, twitching involuntarily every few steps but trying very hard not to spill his coffee.

Unfortunately, he ran into Royce in the hall and his morning went downhill from there.

"Cal, I'm glad you're up," Royce said. "Come and talk to me for a few minutes while I make my coffee."

"I'm just heading back to my—" Eli said, but Royce interrupted him.

"Oh come on. It'll only take a minute."

Eli smiled weakly and turned around, heading for the kitchen and praying he could make it without incident.

"Eli?" Royce said.

Eli stopped and stood in the hallway, dreading what was surely coming next.

"Are you wearing a butt plug?"

You're gonna fucking pay for this, Hamish!

"Yes, sir," Eli admitted.

Royce slapped Eli on the ass and applied pressure to the plug, which sent more waves of pleasure through Eli's body. "Damnnnn!" Eli said, feeling like he might have just come in his shorts. He looked down and saw a wet spot on the front and silently cursed himself.

"Good boy," Royce said, apparently not noticing the mishap. "I hope this means what I think this means."

"If you give me a couple of minutes," Eli said, covering the front of his shorts, "I'll be right back and we can talk."

"Sure," Royce said. "Eli?"

"Yes, sir?"

"Change your shorts, will you?" Royce said with a hearty laugh.

Totally embarrassed and feeling very exposed, Eli closed his eyes and bowed his head. "Yes, sir."

"Hurry back, son," Royce said. "We have business to talk about."

Eli turned and headed back to his room, mumbling the entire way. *This thing is coming out as soon as I get back to my room. Hamish, you're going to pay and pay big.*

A few minutes later, Eli padded into the kitchen barefoot, carrying a cold cup of coffee and wearing jeans and a T-shirt.

Royce was seated at the island sipping his tea.

"I can see you smiling behind that cup," Eli said. "What's so funny at this time of the morning?"

"Oh, nothing," Royce replied. "Just in a good mood is all."

"Oh?" Eli asked sarcastically.

Royce lowered his teacup. "Got a lot of great footage last night," he said. "I tell ya. It's so easy to get an orgy going around here. All you have to do is get a whole bunch of horny guys all liquored up and relaxed, and voila! An orgy. You should have stayed when you peeked in."

"Does anything go on around here that you don't know about?" Eli asked, surprised that Royce had seen him last night.

"Not much," Royce said. "But enough about me. Let's talk about you. How was your night with Hamish?"

"It was pretty low-key except for the sex store and instructions on what to do with a butt plug," Eli said. "But he's a really nice guy."

"You two becoming fast friends?"

"I think we are," Eli said, putting another pod in the Keurig.

"I'd love to shoot a scene with the two of you," Royce said. "What would you think about that?"

"I'd probably rather not," Eli said. "I think it would be pretty awkward since we've become friends."

"We can get into that later," Royce said. "Let's talk about your next move."

Eli climbed on the stool across from Royce and waited.

"I'd like you to do a scene with a guy named Quaid," Royce explained. "He was one of my top guys a couple of years ago, but he got married and moved away. He e-mailed me yesterday that he was going to be in town for the day and wanted to pick up some extra cash. He saw your first solo and asked specifically for you."

"You mean I'm live?" Eli asked in surprise.

"Went live yesterday," Royce said. "And the response has been incredible. Most e-mails for a newbie's solo in many years."

Eli was shocked and proud. "Wow. I didn't even know it was live."

"Normally I wait a week or so to give you time to back out if you want to," Royce explained. "But you seemed to be having no reservations, so I went with it. I hope you don't mind."

"No. I guess not," Eli said, trying to hide the shock in his voice.

"So what do you say about Quaid?"

Eli took a sip of his coffee and lowered the mug. "How much do I have to do?"

"I think you're ready to go for a little jerking each other off and blowing each other."

Just hearing the words made Eli nervous. "I haven't done anything like this before, Royce. I may suck at it."

"That's the beauty of my site," Royce explained. "Guys want to see first times, good or bad. I won't force you to do anything you're not comfortable with, but I think you should give it a try."

Eli thought about it and decided *what the fuck*. "Okay. What time?"

Royce glanced at his watch. "He'll be here in about thirty minutes."

"Thirty minutes! Jesus, Royce. How about a little warning next time?"

Royce laughed. "I didn't want to give you too much time to think about it and talk yourself out of it."

"Good point," Eli said. "I'll get cleaned up. Where should I meet you?"

"We'll use the suite upstairs where you did your last solo."

"Got it," Eli said, turning and moving toward the hallway.

"It's gonna be okay, Eli," Royce yelled. "And wear a T-shirt and sweats."

Eli didn't feel like it was going to be okay, but he'd made the decision to take his life in this direction, and he was sticking with it. He stopped, looked over his shoulder, and nodded.

Twenty-five minutes later, showered and looking his best, Eli climbed the stairs and stopped at the top landing. He could hear voices coming out of the suite and the now familiar sound of porn in the background. Not wanting to seem scared or intimidated in front of an experienced guy, Eli took a deep breath, straightened his shoulders, and walked in with a smile on his face.

Quaid was already on the bed, wearing nothing but a T-shirt and his underwear and having a conversation with Royce, who was seated on the edge of the bed. Eli's first impression was that he was a good-looking man. His hair was a dark blond, and his eyes were a light blue. He looked nicely built, at least what Eli could see through his tight T-shirt, and his legs were pretty muscular as well.

They both looked up and stopped talking when Eli walked into the room. Royce stood. "Quaid, meet Cal."

Quaid jumped up and shook Eli's hand.

"You guys climb in bed and lean back against the headboard," Royce instructed.

Both men did what was asked of them and waited.

"You ready?" Royce asked.

"Yep," Quaid said.

Eli nodded, not sure he could speak without his voice sounding shaky.

"Rolling," Royce said. "Cal, Quaid, thank you guys for taking the time to stop in and do a hot little scene for me and our viewers. Quaid, it's so good to have you back, man."

"Yep," Quaid said once more. And again, Eli just nodded and gave Royce his camera smile.

"Cal, you looked scared to death," Royce said.

Eli hesitated, took a deep breath, then admitted, "I haven't done this before, so yeah, I'm a little nervous."

"I tell you what, then," Royce said. "I'm just gonna have you guys jerk off and see where that takes us."

Eli looked over at Quaid, who already had his hand down his underpants, and saw his erection was starting to show through his shorts.

Damned if he's gonna show me up. Eli stuck his hand down his sweat pants, got to work, and before long he was getting as hard as a rock.

"Quaid, I know you've been chomping at the bit to get a hold of this newbie. How are you feeling right now?"

"I got this," he said.

Royce laughed. "You got this, huh? Okay, then," he said, moving around to get a closer shot. "You both are looking great from my end."

Quaid winked into the camera, leaned forward, took his shirt off, and flung it across the room. Eli followed his lead and threw his to the floor.

"Can you guys scoot a little closer together?" Royce asked. Quaid gave Eli a questioning glance and Eli nodded his approval. The two guys shimmied over until their shoulders were touching.

"Is that okay?" Royce asked.

Quaid smiled and looked over at Eli. "Oh yeah."

"Cal?" Royce asked.

"I'm good."

Quaid slid his underwear down and kicked them off, and Eli finally saw what the guy'd been hiding under his boxers.

"What do you think, Cal?" Royce asked.

"Looks like it's a lot to handle," Eli said, gazing at Quaid's package.

Quaid continued playing with himself, getting harder and harder, and Eli couldn't seem to take his eyes off him.

"Cal?" Royce asked. "You told me you've never been with a guy before, right?"

Eli nodded. "Never."

Royce continued. "How do you feel about reaching over there and jacking Quaid a little bit? Can you do that?"

"I can certainly try."

Eli released his cock and prayed his hand didn't start to tremble when he slipped it out of his sweat pants. He focused, reached over, and took Quaid in his hand. The sensation was odd, but not unfamiliar. He'd never held another man's penis in his hand, but it felt very similar to his. Quaid had a little more girth, but Eli had about an inch in length on him, which made him feel a bit better.

Eli gripped Quaid tightly and began to move his hand up and down, massaging and squeezing it like he would his own. Without warning, Quaid reached over and slipped his hand down Eli's sweats and grabbed his cock. Eli did his best to pretend he wasn't freaking out, but man, he was freaking out.

"That's not so bad, is it?" Royce asked.

"I'm not sure, but I don't think so," Eli said truthfully.

"Does it feel weird?" Royce asked.

"Yeah it does."

"Why don't you go ahead and take your sweats off, Cal?" Royce instructed.

Eli released Quaid's dick, slid his sweats down, and kicked them off.

Quaid took Eli's cock again, so Eli reached over and did the same. Quaid went one step further and started running his other hand over Eli's chest and abs. The sensation felt good, but the fact that a guy was doing it freaked Eli out again. He closed his eyes and tried to picture that big-titted blonde from the porn video he'd watched during his first shoot, but when he opened his eyes again, Quaid was still there.

Needing to regroup, Eli moved his hand from Quaid's erection and rested it behind his head, but Quaid continued to jack him off. Eli closed his eyes and pretended to be enjoying it while he tried to calm himself down and remember everything Hamish had told him to do.

Suddenly Eli's cock was surrounded by a warm, wet mouth. *Holy shit, Quaid's going down on me! And... it feels pretty damn good.* Eli had known this was going to happen, but for some reason the reality hadn't hit him until now. Before he knew it, a string of moans escaped his mouth, and he bit his bottom lip. Eli couldn't help himself; he opened one eye and took a peek at Quaid working over his length.

"How's that feel, Cal?" Royce asked in a hushed tone. "Is he doing a good job?"

"Hell yeah," Eli said before he even had time to prepare an answer.

Without even realizing what he was doing, Eli's hand moved to Quaid's back and started caressing it, making little circles with his fingers on the soft skin. When Quaid took Eli all the way down to the hilt, Eli shivered and another moan escaped his lips.

Quaid withdrew and Eli heard Royce's voice again. "Cal? Do you think you can return the favor?"

Eli tried to hide the panic he was feeling and nodded in agreement to buy himself some time. *This is it, Eli. No turning back now. Fuck it! You've come this far; you might as well go for it.*

Eli leaned forward, reached over, and took Quaid's penis in his hand again. He kissed Quaid's chest and stomach while rubbing Quaid's length. Eli took a deep breath, closed his eyes, and took Quaid into his mouth. Much to his surprise, Quaid's cock didn't taste like anything. It had no flavor. Eli wasn't sure what he was expecting, but he expected some kind of taste.

Eli pushed the stupid taste dilemma to the back of his mind and focused on the task at hand. He'd decided he didn't want to be known as the worst cocksucker in the house, so he'd better do himself proud. He started to move up and down on Quaid, and each time he went down too far, he gagged and had to come back up again. Quaid was a big boy, and no matter how much Eli tried to relax his throat like Hamish had explained, it just wasn't happening.

Quaid whimpered, and Eli decided he should take that as encouragement. He tried to take him in farther. But each time he gagged again. *Fuck! I can do this.*

Quaid's hand moved to Eli's head, guiding him up and down as his fingers caressed Eli's hair.

Eli fisted Quaid's cock and focused his tongue on the smooth skin under the head like he'd seen in some of Royce's other videos. The maneuver must have worked because after a few minutes, Quaid starting sliding his legs up and down the bed and moaning loudly, thrusting up into Eli's mouth.

"I'm getting close," Quaid whispered. "Let me work on you for a while."

Quaid guided Eli onto his back again and took his still semierect penis into his mouth. Quaid was using just the right amount of pressure and suction, and it was driving Eli insane. Eli threw his head back and closed his eyes, overwhelmed by the sensations coursing through his body. "Oh God!"

Suddenly Eli felt the waves of orgasm approaching. "I'm gonna come," he cried.

Quaid released Eli from his mouth and pumped his cock as Eli arched his back and shot the first of his load all over Quaid's face. Eli fisted the sheets as wave after wave coursed through him, covering Quaid's face and his own stomach with his release. Eli once again felt Quaid's warm mouth on him, licking him and milking him of whatever was left.

Quaid wiped Eli's come off of his face with his fingers and sucked each one of them clean before he licked Eli's stomach clean as well.

Eli's heart was still racing when Quaid lay back on the bed and began stroking himself. Eli leaned up on one elbow and once again took Quaid into his mouth. He tried to mimic what Quaid had just done to him, combining the right amount of suction and pressure, and whether he actually succeeded or Quaid was just so close he didn't know, but within minutes Quaid shouted, "I'm coming."

Eli backed off and Quaid took himself in hand and jerked two or three more times. Then he was shooting his load all over his stomach and chest.

Both men collapsed against the pillows and tried to catch their breath.

"Great job, guys," Royce said. "How was it, Cal?"

Eli shook his head. "I don't know, man, the jury's still out on all of this for me."

"Did you have fun?" Royce asked.

"Yeah," Eli said truthfully, looking over and smiling at Quaid. "Did *you*, Quaid?"

"Hell yeah," Quaid said, leaning up and kissing Eli right on the lips.

Eli laughed and playfully shoved him back against the pillow.

"Well, boys, that's all I can ask for. Thanks for coming." He paused for a beat, then said, "Cut!"

"Good job, man," Quaid said, looking over at Eli. "You're gonna be okay doing this."

"Don't know about that," Eli said. "But thanks."

Quaid looked toward the door and Eli followed his gaze.

"Hamish!" Quaid said, jumping out of the bed still naked and wrapping his arms around the big guy. "Man, you look great."

Quaid is right, Eli thought. *Hamish does look great.* Eli imagined the man never had as much as a bad hair day. He was in a royal blue golf shirt, which made his eyes look even bluer, and it was obvious that said eyes lit up even more at the sight of Quaid. Eli could tell these guys had some type of connection, and oddly the thought bothered him a little. He got out of bed, pulled on his sweats and T-shirt, and said hello to Hamish.

"How's it going, man?" Hamish asked, shaking Eli's hand. "I didn't know you had a shoot with Quaid."

"Okay and... nor did I," Eli admitted. "Royce sort of sprang it on me this morning."

Hamish looked at Royce and flashed a knowing grin. "Some things never change," he said.

"By the way," Eli said. "Your ass is grass later, mister."

Hamish gave him a questioning look.

"Later," Eli said dryly. "So you guys know each other, huh?" Eli looked between Quaid and Hamish.

"Yeah," Quaid said. "We go way back. Hamish was my protégé."

"Yeah," Hamish agreed. "He took me under his wing and helped me navigate the biz."

Eli quickly figured that Quaid had done the same things for Hamish that Hamish was doing for him, and for some reason that warmed him. He made a note to not be as hard on Hamish later as he'd first planned.

"You guys get situated," Royce said. "I need to have a few words with Cal."

Royce put his arm over Eli's shoulder and walked him into the hall. "How was it?" Royce asked.

"Not too bad," Eli admitted. "Certainly not as bad as I had imagined."

"Good to hear 'cause I have one more shoot for you," Royce said.

Eli cocked an eyebrow.

"With Gavin," Royce said. "And this one requires some fucking."

"Whoa!" Eli said. "I'm not ready to have a dick up my ass yet."

"No!" Royce said. "I know that. I want you to fuck Gavin."

A little relieved but still on edge, Eli said, "I don't know, Royce. This is an awful lot awful fast."

"I know. I'm sorry," Royce said. "But Bristol chickened out on me, and Gavin is downstairs, and I can't get another guy on such short notice."

"What about Quaid or Hamish?" Eli asked.

"Quaid has to leave right after his and Hamish's shoot, and as you know, Hamish and Gavin were just in a shoot together, so I can't do that again too soon."

"I don't know, Royce."

"It's okay if you're not ready," Royce said. "I just hate to send Gavin home. I know he needs the money."

Oh man, Eli thought. *Talk about playing the trump card.*

"Fine," Eli said. "Give me twenty to get cleaned up." He turned to leave, stopped, and looked over his shoulder. "And... what do you want me to wear this time?"

Royce smiled. "Wear that green T-shirt I told you to buy and a pair of jeans. And thanks, Eli. There will be a bonus in it for you."

Eli rolled his eyes, something he'd been doing a lot since he moved into this place. "There better be," he said.

On the way back to his room, Eli tried to tally up today's pay. *One thousand for the last shoot and two thousand for the next, plus a bonus; I should be able to afford a decent car by the end of the week.*

ELI SHOWERED, brushed his teeth, and combed his hair for the second time in an hour, dressed, and headed back upstairs. On the way to his shoot, he passed in front of the door where he'd left Hamish and Quaid and paused. And after he did, for some reason he wished he hadn't. Seeing Quaid fucking Hamish sparked something in him that he didn't quite understand. It wasn't exactly jealousy but it felt like something along those lines. *Snap out of it, Eli. What in the hell is going on with you?*

After careful consideration he thought what bothered him more than seeing them together was the fact that Hamish really seemed to be getting into it. But he remembered Hamish's words. "Always give them a good show!"

Man! I don't think I'll ever understand what's real and what's not while I'm stationed here in wonderland.

Eli watched as Quaid buried his cock deep inside of Hamish, pulled out, and slid in again, over and over. Hamish was a beautiful sight to behold. His muscular legs were in the air and his strong hands were gripping Quaid's thighs as he took the pounding like a man. Eli decided right then and there, friends or no friends, that if he was going to lose his virginity, and it looked like it was heading that direction, he wanted to lose it to Hamish. If Hamish agreed, that is. Eli moved on, still unsettled but resolved to talk to Royce about it after his next shoot.

When Eli got to the next suite, Gavin was alone in the room, sitting on the foot of the bed. He was dressed pretty much like Eli in jeans and T-shirt but had a concerned look on his face.

"Hey," Gavin said when he saw Eli standing in the door. "Thanks for stepping in, man. I can really use the money. I hope this isn't too much for you to handle."

Eli smiled. "I guess you'll be the judge of that, based on how well I perform."

"I'm sure you'll do fine, man. Royce tells me you're a natural at all of this."

Eli laughed. "Yeah. That's something to add to my résumé."

Gavin smiled. "Tell me about it. You wanna get comfortable?"

"Sure," Eli said, hopping on to the bed and resting his back against the headboard.

Gavin scooted up and sat next to him and looked at his watch. "We've got another couple of minutes. Anything you want to practice?"

Eli thought for a second. "Today's been a day of firsts already, but I'm a little skittish about kissing."

"That's one of my specialties," Gavin said with a smile. "Tongue or no tongue?"

"Hell. I don't know," Eli said.

"Well, if you don't want tongue," Gavin explained, "you can make it look like you're using tongue and not have to actually do it. May I?"

Eli nodded, and Gavin put his hand behind Eli's head and pulled him in closer. He brought their faces together and gently brushed his lips against Eli's and withdrew. "That's how we start," he said.

Then he covered Eli's lips with his mouth slightly open and made movements like a fish, opening and closing his mouth on top of Eli's without inserting his tongue into Eli's mouth.

He withdrew again. "If you kiss with an open mouth making fish movements, it appears that you're using tongue, and it looks more intimate than it really is.

"And this is the big kahuna," Gavin said just before he dove in tongue and all. Eli opened to him, wanting to experience it all, and just pretended he was kissing a woman. It was really no different except for the added masculine force he'd experienced when Hamish had kissed him.

Their kiss was interrupted when Royce walked into the room and cleared his throat. "I thought you boys were supposed to save that shit for the camera."

"We were just practicing," Gavin explained with a slight grin.

"Sure you were, you little minx," Royce said to Gavin. He looked at Eli. "He does that with all the newbies."

Eli stared at Gavin, and Gavin offered him a sly smile. "Thanks a lot," Eli said sarcastically.

"Anytime," Gavin replied.

"You boys ready?" Royce asked.

"As ready as I'll ever be?" Eli said.

"Go for it," Gavin said.

"Rolling!"

"So, Eli?" Royce said. "What's up, man?"

"Same ole, same ole," Eli said.

"You're getting to be a permanent fixture around here," Royce said. "In less than a week, you've done two solos, your first man-on-man with some dick sucking, and now you're moving on to the big-boy stuff. You ready for this?"

Eli gave the camera a hesitant smile. "Ready as I'll ever be. I guess."

"Well today," Royce explained, "I've paired you up with an old-timer—"

"Hey!" Gavin said. "I prefer veteran."

Eli reached over and patted Gavin's leg. "It's okay, man, I know better."

Royce rolled his eyes. "Okay, *veteran.* Not old-timer," he corrected. "Anyway I think you guys will be a good match. So I'm gonna leave the two of you alone to get acquainted, but after what I walked in on earlier, I don't think that'll take too long. I'll be back in a few to check on you."

Royce left the room and Eli and Gavin both looked straight ahead, staring at the television without saying a word. Eli didn't really know Gavin very well except for meeting him the first night he came over to the mansion and seeing him in that shoot on his first day of work.

The silence was deafening so Eli spoke. "You like porn?" he said, referring to the television.

"Not really," Gavin said quickly. "So how did you get into this?"

"Like most of you, I guess," Eli said. "I was in the men's department at Walmart when he found me."

"Royce pulled up alongside *me* at a red light and gave me his card. And here I am three years later," Gavin said. "Royce is a good guy, by the way. He won't do you wrong."

"Good to hear," Eli said. "So, you're a veteran, huh?"

Gavin nodded. "Yeah. You want me to take the lead?"

"That would be great since this is only my second shoot with a live body."

"All right," Gavin said. "I'm not one for small talk so let's get this show on the road."

Gavin pulled his T-shirt over his head and Eli did the same. They both unbuttoned their jeans and slid their hands down their pants and started fondling themselves. After a couple of minutes, Gavin leaned over and took Eli into his mouth. Eli decided immediately that Gavin knew what he was doing. He moved his lips up and down with a subtle sucking that was driving Eli crazy. Eli stretched out, brought his arms up behind his head, and rested them on the back of the bed. He was instantly hard and was seriously getting into it.

Gavin took a breather and stroked Eli's dick with his hand. "Okay so far?"

"Better than okay," Eli said.

When Gavin started up again, Eli found himself thrusting up into Gavin's mouth in unison with his movements. A few minutes later, Gavin stopped again long enough to rip off his jeans and Eli took advantage of the lull and did the same.

Gavin got to his knees and went down on Eli again, tormenting his cock with his masterful actions.

Eli hesitantly reached over and took Gavin's penis in hand and stroked it while Gavin continued to swallow his cock up to the hilt.

Gavin released him, got up on his knees, and started stroking himself as Eli watched. Eli had thought the sight of another man beating off in front of him was going to be awkward, but Gavin's actions were causing Eli's heart rate to increase and there was just something about the action that wasn't awkward at all. Eli took himself in hand and worked his erection as Gavin started rubbing his leg, working his way up to Eli's balls and caressing them while Eli beat off.

Gavin once again took Eli into his mouth and started those tantalizing moves, sending Eli into another tailspin. Eli reached for Gavin's erection once more, gave it a squeeze, and started stroking. When Gavin released him, his lips covered Eli's in a heated kiss. Not counting the practice run, this was only the third time he'd been kissed by a man and the second time on camera. The kiss was deep and long and Gavin took Eli in hand again and stroked as they made out like teenagers.

When the kiss ended, Gavin changed positions and lay on his back, giving Eli an open invitation to his dick. Eli nervously got to his knees, bent over Gavin, and took him into his mouth. He rubbed Gavin's chest with his left hand as he took as much of him as he could without gagging. When Eli's jaw couldn't take any more, he again took Gavin in hand and stroked. He continued to work Gavin's cock as he stretched out next to the man. Now lying side by side, Gavin took Eli's penis and they jerked each other off.

At some point Royce had entered the room again, and Eli heard his voice giving directions. Gavin came back up on his knees and wrapped his lips around Eli's dick. He slid all the way down and then came back up again and circled the head with his tongue, teasing the tender underside. Eli placed his hand on the back of Gavin's head, threw back his own head, and moaned with pleasure, in return coaxing a moan from Gavin.

"You ready to try this?" Gavin asked when he released Eli.

"Hell, yeah," Eli responded, ready for anything at this point.

After preparing himself, Gavin got on all fours and offered his ass up to Eli. Eli slid a condom on, positioned himself behind Gavin, and slowly started to push in. It was the tightest hole Eli had ever fucked. He had to force himself in, and the sensation was glorious.

"Easy," Gavin said, using his hand to help guide Eli.

"Sorry," Eli said. "You tell me when to move."

Eli held his position while Gavin stroked himself. When Gavin gave him the go-ahead, Eli pushed in again slowly until he was balls to ass and was suddenly surrounded by a tight and warm sensation encompassing his cock. He pulled back out and pushed in again, deliberately, causing a whimper to escape Gavin's lips.

Picking up his speed gradually, Eli pounded Gavin's ass, just like he'd seen Quaid doing to Hamish. And to his credit, Gavin took every lick like a man. With each forward thrust Gavin let out a guttural growl, which drove Eli to dig deeper and deeper.

"Fuck me, daddy," Gavin cried. "Don't be afraid."

Eli pumped harder and dug deeper as Gavin pleaded for it until Gavin was thrashing in front of him. Eli heard Royce tell him to get on his back and let Gavin straddle him, and within moments Gavin was on top of him riding his dick like a pony. Eli reached up and took Gavin's erection in hand and starting jerking him while Gavin rode him hard.

Eli vaguely heard Royce again instruct them to change positions, and Gavin ended up on his back with his left leg in the air and Eli kneeling at his opening. Eli slowly inserted his cock into Gavin again, and Gavin's head went back as he whimpered loudly, grabbing his own dick and pumping feverishly. Eli stared down at Gavin, his face contorting with each thrust, and he realized he liked this position the best. No matter how casual this sex was, he wanted some type of a connection, and looking into someone's eyes gave him that.

Eli then gripped Gavin's legs and threw them over his shoulders as he pounded away. Gavin held on to himself and stroked in unison with the beating his ass was taking. Without warning, Gavin let out a long cry and came all over his chest and stomach. The sight of Gavin coming with a dick up his ass just about pushed Eli over the edge, but he was able to pull out in time, remove the condom, and blow his load all over Gavin. "Oh my God" was all Eli could say as the first spurt hit Gavin in the face and spurt after spurt covered Gavin's chest.

Eli leaned back on his hands and struggled to catch his breath, but Gavin didn't even attempt to move. When he could breathe again, Eli sat back up and leaned over Gavin and covered his lips with his own, tasting the remnants of his own orgasm.

"Cut!" Royce said. "Cal? You okay?"

Eli nodded but didn't speak.

"You boys get cleaned up and then come back in for the closing."

When Gavin and Eli got to the bathroom, Gavin stopped him and turned him around so they were eye to eye.

"Seriously, man? Are you okay?"

"I'm good," Eli confessed. "I'm sure it's gonna hit me later, but for now I'm good." He placed a kiss on Gavin's lips. "But thanks for asking."

"Hey, man," Gavin said, "we're all in this together and you've already proven to me that you're one of us."

Eli pulled him in for a hug. "I appreciate that, man."

When they finished cleaning up, they hopped back on the bed and sat naked, leaning against the headboard.

"Rolling," Royce said. "Dayam, Cal. You are one wild fucker." He looked at Gavin. "How'd he do?"

"He was good," Gavin said. "Real good. Exceptional in fact."

Royce pointed at Eli. "Like I said before, Cal, you're a natural."

"Thanks," Eli said, flashing that now infamous smile at the camera.

"I hope we're gonna be seeing a lot more of you, son," Royce said.

"We'll see," Eli responded.

"I guess that's a wrap, then," Royce said. "Guys, as always, thanks for coming. And Cut!" Royce lowered the camera and grinned at them. "Another incredible job, guys. And you," he added, pointing at Eli again. "Are you sure you haven't done this before?"

"Positive," Eli responded, climbing out of bed and putting his jeans back on.

"Thanks again for doing this, man," Gavin said, slipping on his jeans and then holding out his hand. "I won't forget it."

Eli shook Gavin's hand. "No problem. Glad I could help. Uh, Royce, can I talk to you for a minute outside?"

"Stay, guys. I'm outta here anyway," Gavin said, pulling his T-shirt over his head.

"What's up?" Royce said, fiddling with his camera.

"About that shoot with Hamish," Eli said. "On second thought, it might be fun. In fact, I think I'm ready to go all the way."

Royce stopped what he was doing and put his camera down. "When?"

Eli laughed. "I need to ask Hamish first, but maybe tonight if he agrees and you're up for it."

"Count me in whenever," Royce said. "Do you want me to talk to him for you?"

"No!" Eli said, a little too anxiously. "I want to talk to him personally. And please don't mention it to him until I've had the chance to talk to him."

Royce nodded. "No problem. Just keep me posted and let me know as soon as you guys decide."

"Will do. Oh and, Royce. It's a beautiful day, do you mind if I hang out by the pool for a few hours?"

Royce waved him off. "Of course not, Eli. This is your home for as long as you want it to be, and you are welcome to use any part of it you like without having to ask."

"Thanks, Royce."

Eli walked back down to his room and threw himself on his bed. He closed his eyes and took a deep breath. *I just sucked a dick and fucked a guy and it wasn't disgusting. I kinda enjoyed it. Hamish was right. Once you get over the man-on-man part, it's not too bad and just feels good.*

So why do I feel like I should be more upset about it?

Eli answered his own question. *I guess 'cause you don't feel gay. And you still want to fuck women.*

Eli shrugged off the feeling, just grateful he wasn't having buyer's remorse. He hopped into the shower for the third time today, and when he got out, he saw the butt plug sitting on the counter. "I guess it's just you and me, kid," he said, looking at the oddly shaped piece of rubber. He combed his hair, picked up the butt plug, and headed into the bedroom. He dug through the drawer again and applied a little lube to himself and the plug, lay back on the bed, and worked it in until it was seated. It went in a little easier than it had last night, but it felt just as foreign. He sat up, prepared for the wave of pleasure, and rode it out before he stood. He practiced walking around his bedroom until he could move in normal strides without jerking spasms with each step.

Eli slipped on his swimsuit, grabbed a towel, an old *Men's Health Magazine* he'd found in the bathroom, and his cell phone, and set out to get a little sunshine. *I hope they have sunscreen by the pool.*

Walking through the game room and out the back door, Eli froze when he saw Hamish already lying in a chaise lounge by the pool. For a split second he was torn about whether he should venture out or go back to his room.

"It's now or never," Eli said to himself. "Suck it up and be a man." He chuckled when that thought conjured up several images from the last three hours.

Eli stuck the rolled-up magazine under his arm, wrapped the towel around his neck, and headed for the pool. As he got closer, Hamish saw him and waved him over. When Eli got to the other side of the pool he stopped. "Mind if I join you?"

"I was hoping you would," Hamish said. "Take a seat." He gestured to the lounge chair next to him. "Oh, and congratulations."

Eli figured he'd heard what had happened between him and Gavin but wanted to make sure. "For what?"

Hamish winked at him. "I see you got the butt plug in."

Eli ignored the statement but felt the blush as it crept up his face. He spread his towel over his chair, took a seat, and opened his magazine. "Fuck you," he finally said with a smirk.

"I thought we had decided against that," Hamish said. "But okay. If you insist."

"Very funny. Is it that obvious?"

"Relax," Hamish said. "Only to those of us who remember."

"I mean… I just spent the last twenty minutes walking around my room trying to get used to the damn thing so I could come out here and not walk like a spaz."

"You might need a wee bit more practice," Hamish teased.

"Fuck you," Eli said again.

Hamish laughed. "Speaking of fucking. I thought a lot about our conversation last night, and I changed my mind. I think it would be fun to do a shoot. I mean if you want to and don't think it would be too weird."

"Yes! I mean, no!" Eli said, surprised. "I don't think it would be too weird and yes, I'd like to do a shoot with you."

Hamish chuckled. "From what I hear, you had a pretty stellar day today. That's a lot to handle all at once. How're you holding up?"

"Surprisingly, I'm good. I mean I thought I would be regretting it all by now, but so far so good."

"I'm proud of you, man."

Eli blushed again, surprised at how much Hamish's words meant to him. "Thanks, Hamish. That means a lot coming from you."

"You earned it, E."

"Hey look," Eli said. "This is pretty awkward for me, but I trust you, and I was hoping you wouldn't mind being my first."

"Mind?" Hamish said. "Are you kidding? Hell the fuck yeah I'd like to pop that cherry."

"My man Hamish," Eli teased. "You really know how to woo a guy. Are you at least gonna buy me dinner first?"

"Thanks," Hamish said, blowing on his fingernails and rubbing them against his chest. "And if that's what it takes. But didn't I just do that last night?"

"Good point," Eli said. "Okay, so the only unanswered question is when?"

"How about now?" Hamish asked with a sparkle in his eye.

"What? No!" Eli said. "I've still got a little work to do to prepare myself, but how about tonight? Around seven o'clock maybe?"

"It's a date," Hamish said.

Eli called Royce from his cell phone and told him they were on for seven o'clock, and he could almost feel Royce's excitement through the phone.

Hamish and Eli spent the next few hours by the pool, bullshitting and getting to know each other better, laughing, teasing each other, and having a really good time. Hamish started pouring beers from the tap, and by four o'clock neither was feeling any pain.

When they decided they'd had enough sun, Hamish took to one of the upstairs bedrooms for a nap, and Eli set out to get himself ready. When he got back to his room, he pulled out his notes from the night before and lay back on his bed.

He read down the list and mentally checked off items completed: *butt plug for a day to loosen you up, drinks to help you relax, and experimenting with the vibrator.*

Next thing on his list was to start with the small dildo and work his way up to the big one. He saw a note scribbled in the margin that said "it helps to push out." The note also said if he couldn't get the big one in, he was supposed to sit over it, and right before he shot, he was supposed to impale himself on it and stretch the donut, so to speak. His last notation was regarding the code of ethics and said to always cleanse with a douche before the big event. *Where in the fuck am I gonna get a douche at this hour?*

Eli put that thought aside for now and laid his toys out on the bed with a great deal of determination. He yanked down his swimsuit and positioned himself on the bed, carefully removing the butt plug, noting it came out with a lot less pain than it had this morning. He decided to use the vibrator again to loosen himself up before he attempted to move on to the big guns. Within minutes he was hard as a rock, and his balls and asshole were tingling from the vibrations. Eli worked the tip of the vibrator in and out a few times until he felt the familiar resistance, took a deep breath, and pushed. Maybe it was the combination of the butt plug and the alcohol, but the tip of the vibrator glided right past the tight muscle and slipped in.

Feeling the stretch and a burning sensation, Eli winced and withdrew. He gave himself a few seconds to recover and pushed in again, this time a little farther. The burn was less painful, but the stretch turned into a stinging sensation. He kept repeating the process until he was working the device all the way in and back out again. If he'd thought his ass was vibrating earlier, this was registering as a full ten points on the Richter scale. Each time the gadget brushed against his prostate, Eli felt like he was going to come. At one point the sensation was so great, he held the vibrator in place and rode the waves of pleasure, sending him dangerously close to orgasm.

Eli hesitantly slid the mechanism from his ass, laid his head back, releasing a breath he hadn't realized he was holding, and closed his eyes. His ass was still tingling as the aftershocks coursed through his body. He picked up the small dildo and held it next to the vibrator to compare the size. After close examination, he determined the head of the dildo was larger, but the girth was only slightly wider around. *Piece of cake!*

Cock in hand, Eli positioned the dildo at his opening and pushed gently. He felt more resistance now, and the burn was beyond intense, but he kept working at it, pushing through the pain until it was bearable, retreating, giving it a couple of minutes, and then trying it again. He tried to remember everything Hamish had told him. *Relax and breathe.* Eli tried to relax his ass muscles and breathe as he stroked his length in unison with the movement of the dildo. But his ass just wouldn't give. Then Eli remembered what Hamish had said about pushing out. The combination of relaxing, breathing, and pushing out did the trick.

Eli came up off of the bed. "Fuck! Ow!" he cried as the head of the dildo slipped past his guardian muscle and lodged deep inside him. "Jesus!" he said as he threw his head back and closed his eyes. With the combination of the burn, the stinging from the stretch, and the pain in his gut, Eli opened his eyes to see his erection deflate right between his fingers.

He gave his body time to adjust, but the sensation was totally different from the vibrator. The dildo was very still, and more than anything, he just felt full. There was no stimulation against his prostate, and as his body relaxed around the intrusion, he decided he liked the vibrator much more. He turned the thing on and used it to get himself hard again and even ran it against the base of the dildo. Feeling the now vibrating dildo up his ass got him going, and within minutes he was hard again. Eli laid the vibrator at his side and gripped the base of the dildo. He slowly withdrew it, causing minor discomfort, and drove it in again. This time when the head of the dildo brushed against his prostate, it was like New Year's Eve. Noisemakers were sounding, fireworks were exploding, and he rode the effects until they passed. Wanting that feeling again, he moved the rubber dick in and out in short movements over and over again, brushing his prostate with each pass and sending his body into overload. When he could no longer handle the stimulation without coming, he withdrew the dildo and glanced over at the larger one lying by his side.

"In the famous words of my good friend Hamish, *I guess it's time to go for the gold*," he whispered.

Much to Eli's surprise, it didn't take sitting over the gold to get it in. He took his time, focused on relaxing, breathing and pushing out as Hamish had suggested, and with a little effort and minor discomfort, he was home free. The head and girth of this monster were bigger, but with dedication and patience, his ass gave way with less fuss than he'd expected.

Eli moved it around a little and then in and out to get a feel for the thing, but his main goal was to just get it in. One of the things Hamish had suggested was to come with one of these things up his ass, but after coming twice already today, he wanted to save up for the camera, so he passed on that experience for now.

Glancing at his watch, he saw it was already six fifteen, and he had to be ready to go at seven, so he cleaned and put everything away and then froze when he remembered what Hamish had told him about preparation and the douche. He hated to call Royce for help, but he would if he needed to. Eli leaned on the bathroom counter and stared at himself in the mirror quizzically. He felt like he was missing something. *Wait! This is a house where men have anal sex every day. There were condoms and lube in the bedside tables of every room I've been in so far. I bet if I look, I'll find what I need.*

Eli bent down and opened the cabinet under the sink, and lo and behold there was a case of disposable douches staring him right in the face. "Bingo!" he whispered.

After reading the instructions, Eli completed the task, showered, and dressed. Royce hadn't told him what to wear, so he settled on jeans and a golf shirt.

As he made his way to his deflowering, he shoved his hands in his pockets in an attempt to stop them from trembling. His heart was racing a mile a minute, and as he walked across the tile floor, his bare feet were suddenly cold. When he reached his destination, Hamish was reclining in the bed, hands behind his head, already stripped down to his underwear and watching porn on the television.

"Looks like someone's ready to go," Eli said nervously, stepping into the room and looking between Hamish and the television.

Hamish smiled. "How about you? Any second thoughts?"

"Nope. Other than being a little nervous, I think I'm good to go."

"How did it go with your preparation?" Hamish asked.

"Success," Eli said. "Even went for the gold."

"Good man," Hamish said, gesturing with his head and patting the spot next to him on the bed. "You wanna get out of all those clothes and join me?"

Eli nodded and pulled his shirt over his head. He slipped out of his jeans, climbed onto the bed, and scooted very close to Hamish.

Hamish wasted no time bringing Eli to him and covering Eli's lips with his own. When Eli felt Hamish's tongue, he opened to him.

"This is starting to be a habit with you, Cal," Royce said as he entered and saw the show had already started.

Hamish broke the kiss. "Sorry, Mama, all my fault. I was just trying to relax our boy before we got started."

"I see," Royce said. "You okay, Cal?"

Eli waved him off. "A little nervous, but I'm good."

"All righty, then," Royce said, hoisting the camera up over his shoulder. "Let's make it good, gentlemen," he added.

"We're gonna give the boys something to talk about. Aren't we, Cal?" Hamish said.

"I'll do my best," Eli replied, flashing a weak smile and trying to control his jitters. His heart rate was increasing, and now his palms were suddenly sweaty. "But I've seen that cock of yours in full regalia, and it's pretty damn impressive. I hope I can take it."

"You told me you took what we got you, and it's about the same size," Hamish whispered. "Just relax, breathe, and push out."

"Easy for you to—" Eli stopped talking when Royce interrupted.

"Ready, boys?"

Hamish and Eli looked at one another and nodded.

"Rolling," Royce said. "Good to see you again, Cal. And as always, my boy Hamish."

Eli and Hamish both smiled at the camera and nodded. Eli felt Hamish take his hand and hold on to it, the touch helping to calm his nerves a little.

Royce continued. "It's no secret that getting you two together has been my goal since I first met Cal, and now this is my lucky day."

"Maybe," Hamish said.

"Maybe not," Eli added.

"I'll be the judge of that," Royce continued. "Cal. So far our viewers have seen you in two steamy hot solos, but they haven't seen the man-on-man with Quaid, where you had your dick sucked by a guy for the first time and also sucked your first dick. And... the latest shoot where you plunged in with both feet, so to speak, and fucked Gavin. But they will very soon. Are you nervous about having a dick up your ass?"

Eli looked at Hamish. "Yeah, I am, to be honest. But I trust this guy, so it's all good."

Hamish gave the camera a sinister grin and patted Eli's leg. "And I promise I'll be gentle, Marine," he said and then added a wink.

Eli chuckled and rolled his eyes.

Royce cleared his throat. "It's no secret around here you guys have become fast friends in the short time Cal has been with us," he said. "Is that gonna be weird, fucking a friend?"

"I hope not," Eli said. "What do you think, Hamish?"

"I don't think so, but I guess we'll have to wait and see."

"Okay, then," Royce said. "Since both of you have your hands down your pants already, and Hamish looks like he's more than ready to go, I guess I'll leave you to it. No! Wait," Royce added. "Give us a peek of that thing, Hamish."

Hamish pulled his underwear down and flashed his fully erect cock.

"Jesus," Eli said, getting an up-close look at the thing.

"You sure picked a big one for your first time," Royce teased.

"Yeah," Eli said, winking at Hamish. "And don't think I'm not rethinking my decision right about now."

"Now, now," Hamish said, patting Eli's leg. "Size is simply a state of mind."

"And speaking of states," Eli teased, "that thing is the size of Texas."

Hamish winked at the camera and smiled.

"This should definitely be interesting," Royce said. "See you on the other end, boys. No pun intended, Cal."

Eli smiled weakly, and Hamish nodded at the camera again. Then they looked at one another and flashed a big smile.

Hamish released his dick and turned sideways. "Nice abs," he said to Eli, rubbing his six-pack. "How much do you work out?"

"A little bit," Eli responded, trying to control the shakiness in his voice.

Hamish leaned over and covered Eli's lips with his own. He cupped Eli's face with his left hand while he stroked himself with his right.

Eli reached up and laid a hand on Hamish's shoulder while continuing to fondle himself as well. He quickly realized he didn't need to keep stroking. His erection was already primed and ready for action.

Hamish's kisses were long and sensual, not like the staged kisses the guys sometimes did for the camera. Just a few minutes into the video, Eli felt like Hamish was actually making out with him, and not just for the camera. But again, Hamish's motto popped back into his mind. *Always give them a show.*

Hamish moved down to his neck and nibbled at the soft skin, and Eli shivered from the sensation. His partner's gentle kisses were causing chills to develop all over Eli's skin, and he hoped the camera didn't pick up on that. Then Hamish pulled back and looked Eli in the eyes. Hamish's normally deep blue eyes looked almost violet. There was something hidden behind them that Eli hadn't seen when he'd watched his shoots with some of the others. Before Eli could analyze it fully, Hamish slid his hand down and rubbed Eli's tight abs. Eli hissed when Hamish's right hand slid under the waistband of his underwear, peeled back the elastic, and cupped Eli's balls.

Hamish took Eli in hand, squeezed, and slapped Eli's erection against his belly a couple of times. "That's a pretty cock," Hamish said. "How many dicks have you sucked, Cal?"

"That would be two," Eli replied with a chuckle.

"Let's see what you can do, and then I'll show you what I can do."

Hamish leaned back and pulled his underwear down and off, tossing them aside. Eli slid down, rolled onto his side, and rested on his elbow. He took Hamish in hand and slid his fingers up and down his length a couple of times and then lowered his head and wrapped his lips around the large, erect penis. Hamish's skin was soft and warm and Eli suddenly wanted very much to make sure Hamish was enjoying his efforts. He slid his hand away, moved as far down as he could without gagging, and came back up, once again gripping Hamish with his fist. He circled the head with his tongue several times while trying to remember all the things he liked when he got a good blowjob.

Eli felt Hamish's hand gently rubbing little circles on his back, and he sensed his encouragement without Hamish having to say a word. Every now and then, Hamish would whimper and arch his back slightly, which only made Eli want to please him more.

Eli kept the head of Hamish's dick in his mouth and moved his hand up and down in slow, even passes. He literally felt Hamish hardening even more inside his mouth. Hamish raised and lowered his hips in unison with Eli's motions, and the two fell into an easy rhythm. Eli switched his tactics and used his tongue to tickle and tantalize the sensitive skin just under the head of Hamish's penis, which caused a moan to escape Hamish's lips.

Eli saw Royce bring the camera around to the side of the bed, and he let Hamish slip from his mouth. He fisted Hamish with his palm and jerked him off while he stared seductively at the huge cock in front of him, glancing back and forth between the camera and Hamish's member.

This drew a wink from Royce as he backed away and widened the shot once again.

"Cut," Royce said. "Cal, get on your stomach in between Hamish's legs, and Hamish bend one knee and bring that leg up."

Eli did as directed and Royce yelled, "Rolling."

Eli didn't see the camera in his peripheral vision and had this sinking suspicion that Royce was zooming in on his ass. Before he took

Hamish into his mouth again, Eli looked up and their eyes met. Hamish winked and nodded, which warmed Eli to his toes.

Royce then moved the camera to get another side shot and widened the angle once more. Eli repeated all the moves he could remember, taking each one slow and easy, coaxing soft whimpers and moans out of his partner. Needing to see Hamish's face, Eli raised his eyes, and he was not disappointed. He saw one of the most sensual things he'd ever seen. Hamish's head was thrown back and his eyes were closed. He had one hand resting behind his neck and his other hand was rubbing his chest. *Straight or gay, that sight could only be described as beautiful,* Eli thought. Hamish's massive chest, his chiseled features, the way that thick, jet-black, velvety hair reflected the bright camera lights so it looked like a halo floating about his head.

Eli ran his tongue up Hamish's abs to his chest, then back down again, stopping at his balls, licking them and taking them into his mouth one by one. He took Hamish's length into his mouth again, relaxed his throat, and for the first time swallowed a cock to the back of his throat without gagging, which caused a deep, guttural moan to escape Hamish's lips. Hamish moved his hand to the back of Eli's head and gently caressed his hair. Eli had one hand on Hamish's dick as he licked and teased and the other roaming up Hamish's abs and chest, lightly pinching and teasing his nipples.

The next time Eli looked up, Hamish's blue eyes looked almost violet and were staring back down at him with a look that could only be described as desire. *Does he really want me, or is all of this for the camera?* Eli silently asked himself. *I must be queer. The fact that I care if this is real or not is proof of that. But fuck. I want this man right now.*

Eli forced himself to push those thoughts to the far reaches of his mind for later and take advantage of what was in front of him right now. *If Hamish picks up on what I'm feeling, this might be my last opportunity.* At that moment, Royce and the cameras disappeared, and there was no one in the room but him and Hamish.

Eli licked his way up Hamish's torso, placing small kisses in the creases of his neck. He felt Hamish's warm breath on his ear. "Stop overanalyzing and just enjoy this, Eli," Hamish said, using his real name. Eli knew his whisper was far too low for the camera, or even Royce, to pick up, and hearing his given name made it seem more real. "This is good," Hamish added. "Real good."

Eli closed his eyes and let go of his inhibitions. He covered Hamish's lips in a crushing kiss, and Hamish opened to him. They kissed passionately, seemingly lost in each other's embrace. When the kiss ended, Eli once again focused on Hamish's hard cock with his right hand while he ran his left down the inside of Hamish's leg, stopping to kiss the soft spot behind his knee.

As Eli focused all of his attentions on Hamish, he vaguely heard the clicks of Rusty's camera, which quickly reminded him they weren't alone, but he remembered Hamish's words and did the best he could to block it all out and give 'em a good show.

Eli reached down between his legs and felt his penis. He was hard as rock, and the head of his dick was moist with excitement. He gave it a squeeze and release, still wanting to focus on Hamish.

But it appeared Hamish had other ideas. He pulled Eli up to him and kissed him again passionately before moving his lips to Eli's neck. He placed a hand on the other side of Eli's neck and urged him over onto his back, where he looked down at him and smiled.

Hamish was now on his knees between Eli's legs, spreading them wide with his knees while his lips covered Eli's mouth with sensual kisses. Their tongues roamed freely, seeking the pleasure Eli hoped they were both experiencing.

Hamish eventually released Eli's lips and kissed his way down Eli's chest and abs, stopping at the patch of very short hair just above Eli's cock. "I love your scent," he said, brushing his nose over and over the area, inhaling continuously. "God, this is good."

Hamish kissed his way around Eli's dick, brushing it ever so lightly with the day-old beard covering his chin, causing it to jump and a moan to escape Eli's lips. Eli felt tingly all over, and chills were running up and down his spine. When Hamish kissed the inside of his thighs, tickling the soft area with his tongue, Eli instinctively opened his legs wider, giving Hamish better access. Hamish chuckled softly and continued his pursuit, taking Eli's erection in his hand and running his lips up and down each side.

"Jesus," Eli hissed when Hamish took him into his mouth and all the way down the back of his throat. He arched his back, fisted the sheets, and thrashed his head from side to side. When Eli released his grip on the sheets, he grabbed the back of Hamish's neck with one hand and gripped Hamish's right tricep with the other. He moaned and arched as Hamish took him deep and came back up and tantalized the head of his dick with his tongue. Eli felt like he would implode at any moment from all the sensations attacking his body. He'd never experienced this heightened sense of *going over the edge* with any woman, and he simply reveled in the feeling.

After bringing Eli almost to the point of ejaculation on several occasions, Hamish worked his way back up, grabbed Eli by the chin, and covered his lips again. Eli ran his hand lightly up and down Hamish's arms and back, causing him to tremble, which only made him more aggressive. Eli realized that he liked letting go. He liked giving control to Hamish. He'd never relinquished control to another human being in his life, and the feeling was very liberating. In addition, he discovered that he liked feeling the weight of strong muscles on top of him, caressing him, and the hot lips kissing him forcefully. The passion was raw and unforgiving and he wanted more of it.

Hamish rolled Eli over onto his stomach and spread his legs apart. "God. That's a hot ass," Hamish said, kissing Eli's butt cheeks. Hamish worked his way up to Eli's back, shoulders and neck, and lay on top of Eli. Again, Eli wallowed in the feeling of solid, tense muscles and pure, manly weight on top of him.

Hamish continued to nibble at Eli's neck while moving his erection up and down the crack of Eli's ass. The feeling of Hamish's cock brushing against his opening was intoxicating—scary, but intoxicating just the same. He knew what was coming, and he realized he wanted it. Wanted Hamish.

Hamish slid off of Eli and moved behind him. "Show me that hot ass of yours," he said, urging Eli up on his hands and knees. Eli backed his ass up to Hamish's face, and when Hamish split his cheeks and buried his tongue in his ass, Eli saw stars. No one had ever done this to him, and the sensation was like no other. With every stroke of Hamish's tongue against his opening, shock waves were rippling through his body. Wave after wave attacked him until he was backing his ass against Hamish's face, begging for more. "God, Hamish," he said breathlessly. "What are you doing to me?"

Hamish backed off, and Eli almost whimpered for more until he felt Hamish's finger circling his hole. Hamish squeezed some lube onto Eli's ass and Eli felt him spreading it around. Hamish slipped one finger into Eli's ass and Eli stiffened and then relaxed. Hamish moved his finger slowly in and out, giving him time to adjust. When Hamish slid a second finger in, Eli relaxed immediately and pushed through the slight burn.

"Good man," Hamish said. "You're doing great, Cal."

Hamish withdrew, and Eli looked back to see him sliding on a condom. Eli looked forward again and dropped his head in anticipation. Hamish got to his knees and positioned himself at Eli's opening. He gently pushed against the tight muscle, and Eli moaned as the first round of burning consumed him. Hamish paused for a few seconds as Eli adapted to his girth. Hamish pushed again, and when the head of his cock slipped in, Eli grunted as a stabbing pain forced him to lunge forward. His ass was suddenly on fire, but Hamish stayed with him, not allowing himself to slip out.

After a while, Hamish started working his cock into Eli's opening, pulling out a little, then pushing back in a little farther each time. Eli was slowly relaxing around Hamish, but was having a hard time taking the last of Hamish's length. Hamish urged him down onto his stomach and lay over his back to give him more leverage. "Fuck, man!" Eli said when Hamish pushed the last of his erection inside and was seated tightly against Eli's ass.

"That's it," Hamish said. "I'm in all the way."

"Fuck, that hurts," Eli said. "Just hold it there for a few minutes before you start moving again."

"You got it," Hamish assured him. "You tell me when you're ready."

Hamish focused his efforts on Eli's neck and back, kissing his way up and down while he gave Eli time to adjust.

"Give it a shot now," Eli said as he slowly started to relax around Hamish.

Hamish pulled out a little and pushed back in, and Eli felt another stab of pain, but more manageable this time. "You okay?" Hamish asked.

"Yeah," Eli said. "Now move, damn it."

Hamish laughed. "Be careful what you ask for."

"Just shut up and fuck me, Hamish."

Hamish started moving in and out, and it felt like someone was driving a Mack truck up his ass and then backing it out. But as Eli breathed and relaxed, the pain slowly started turning into less pain and then eventually into pleasure. It was an odd sensation, not at all like the dildo. It was warm and giving, bending with Eli's insides. Eli didn't think something so big could fit up his ass and bring him such pleasure at the same time, but damned if it wasn't happening.

Eli started to get into sync with Hamish's thrusts, and before long Hamish was pounding his ass like a piece of meat. Eli was again up on all fours, and although he'd lost his erection during penetration, he was again rock solid. He played with himself and was reminded of the connection between his dick and his ass. Each time Hamish brushed against his prostate, his dick jumped and Eli felt waves of pleasure course through his body.

"I need to see your face," Hamish whispered. "Can you get on your back?"

Eli winced when Hamish pulled out. Then there was an overwhelming feeling of emptiness, and Eli wanted Hamish back in right now. He quickly flipped over onto his back and lay at the corner of the bed with Hamish standing over him. Eli lifted his legs and Hamish grabbed them by the ankles and held them up, resting them on his shoulders. Hamish positioned himself again and pushed in. This time the penetration smarted at best and within seconds was bringing Eli pleasure again.

Eli looked up into Hamish's eyes, and if Hamish wasn't as into this as he was, he deserved an Academy Award because he was one hell of an actor. At that moment, as if reading his thoughts, Hamish leaned down and kissed him forcefully.

When the kiss ended, Hamish rested his cheek against Eli's. "You're beautiful," he whispered, obviously trying to elude the camera microphone. "Absolutely beautiful."

"You too," Eli whispered back. "I'm not going to last long," he added as he stroked his cock in unison with the ass plowing he was getting.

"Nor am I," Hamish said before he rose up again and stood over Eli.

The feeling of Hamish inside of him, the sight of Hamish looking down at him, those blue eyes boring into his, was all too much for Eli to take. "I'm gonna come," Eli cried, throwing his head back and shooting his first round onto his upper chest. "Yes!" he screamed as the second and third rounds landed on his stomach and abs. Eli pumped his dick feverishly as Hamish pounded his ass.

"Oh God!" Hamish cried as he pulled out of Eli and ripped off the condom. Hamish stroked hard as the first round of his release landed almost in Eli's open mouth and the rest mixed with Eli's and puddled on his chest and abs. Hamish dropped down to his knees and gently licked their combined come off Eli's torso. Eli swallowed what had landed in his mouth and Hamish came up and licked the remainder off of his face. Hamish kissed Eli with a mouth full of their combined semen and shared it with him. It was one of the most sensual things Eli had ever experienced.

Eli reached up and cupped the back of Hamish's neck, pulling him closer until their cheeks were once again touching. "That was incredible," he said in a very hushed voice.

Hamish moved his head up and down against Eli's cheek but didn't otherwise respond.

Unwilling to move, the two men lay together, their eyes closed and Eli enjoying Hamish's embrace.

"Cut!" Royce said. "Motherfucker, that was hot!"

Hamish and Eli both opened their eyes and looked at each other as if remembering they weren't alone. They both turned and looked at Royce and Rusty. Royce was white as a ghost, and Rusty's pants were down around his knees and he'd blown a load all over his shorts.

"What the fuck?" Royce mumbled.

Hamish raised his eyebrows. "What do you mean?"

"What just happened?" Royce asked.

"I guess we did our job," Eli said, winking at Hamish.

Royce shook his head. "You did way more than your job."

Hamish stood and offered Eli a hand. "Glad you were pleased, boss," Hamish said, pulling Eli to his feet.

"We agreed that we wanted to give the guys something to talk about," Eli said.

"And, Cal!" Royce said, disbelief in his voice. "I never expected anything like this from you. Especially on your first time."

"Been brushing up on my acting skills," Eli responded, casting a sideways glance and smiling at Hamish.

"You guys get cleaned up while I compose myself so we can do the closing interview," Royce instructed.

When Eli and Hamish got into the bathroom and closed the door behind them, Hamish again covered Eli's lips in a passionate kiss. "You were great out there. God that was hot."

"Hamish, I don't think…." Eli couldn't finish.

"Talk to me, Eli."

Eli tried to compose himself and not blurt out everything currently going through his mind until he had the time to sort through it all. "I just never had so many sensations going through me at one time. It was a bit overwhelming."

Hamish's expression turned to one that could only be described as disappointment. Eli immediately regretted his choice of words, and when Hamish lowered his head and turned away, Eli grabbed him by the arm and stopped him. Eli placed both hands on Hamish's face and kissed him. "That felt incredible, Hamish. I have a lot of shit going through my mind right now, but when I can put it all into words, you'll be the first to know."

Hamish offered Eli a faint smile and a quick peck on the cheek. "I understand. Now we better get cleaned up and get back out there before Mama comes in looking for us."

Minutes later, Eli and Hamish were back in bed, resting against the headboard.

"Rolling," Royce said. "Well, boys. I'm at a loss for words. That was one of the hottest things I've ever had the privilege of shooting, and you know I've been doing this for ten years now."

Eli smiled.

"Glad we could be of service, boss," Hamish said.

"Cal? How was your first time?"

Eli looked at Hamish and winked. He turned back to the camera and flashed his usual smile. "It was real good."

Royce moved the camera around to the side of the bed. "Was it as bad as you thought it was going to be?"

"Not at all," Eli said, meaning it.

"Will we see you again?" Royce asked.

"Oh yeah," Eli said.

"With Hamish?"

"If I have anything to say about it you will," Hamish chimed in.

"I hope so," Eli added.

"Men, I need to go and take a cold shower. As always, thanks for coming."

Eli nodded and winked.

"My pleasure," Hamish said.

"Cut!"

CHAPTER SIX
CONSEQUENCE

FOR THE next couple of weeks Eli did at least two shoots a day. By the end of the second week, all of his videos had been released except for the one with Hamish. Each day, Royce was giving Eli a stack of printed e-mails from adoring fans, and much to Eli's surprise, they were all favorable. On most days he'd receive at least one marriage proposal and a few e-mails with fans spelling out exactly what they'd do to him if they got the chance. And according to Royce, Eli's ratings were among the highest ever on the web site.

He'd now had sex with almost all the guys in the current rotation at least once, some even twice, and they'd done anything from one-on-one to three-ways and even four-ways. He'd racked up a pretty hefty stash of money and was looking forward to the weekend when he thought he would finally look for a new car.

Eli saw Hamish on a daily basis, and their friendship was quickly becoming a bromance and getting stronger by the day. Eli was amazed at how they always seemed to be in sync with each other and the ease with which they interacted. Once their shoots were done for the day, they worked out in the gym, spent time by the pool, or just hung out at Hamish's place or the sports bar in Dumfries. They drank beer, played pool, and even flirted with a few girls, but neither seemed to want to take that any further.

But nine times out of ten, they just talked and laughed. They had long conversations about everything under the sun, and Hamish was always willing to share his views. Eli quickly learned that Hamish was the most nonjudgmental, easygoing, live and let live person he'd ever met, but when he was passionate about something, he would go to the ends of the earth to make his point. Eli was really enjoying getting to know what made the man tick.

Eli was still working through his emotions regarding the gay-for-pay thing, but he was sorting it out little by little and coming to accept his decision as the right one for now. His initial attraction to Hamish stayed with him, flopping around in the back of his head, and it just didn't seem to want to go away. But since their shoot, Hamish had not said another word about their connection or made any attempt to kiss him, take sexual cheap shots at him, or even tease him like he'd done before their shoot.

Eli had gone over the scene in his head so many times, he'd just about convinced himself he'd trumped up the chemistry and chalked it all up to nerves, inexperience, and the fact that Hamish had been the one who'd helped him through the initial experience.

Right before lunch one day, Hamish had picked Eli up and the two men had spent most of the day car shopping, with no luck, and decided that since their video was scheduled to go live at eight o'clock that evening, they were going to watch it together at Hamish's place over dinner.

Eli made lasagna and a salad, and they sat in front of Hamish's laptop and waited for the debut. They were just about through eating when their images appeared on the home page as the week's "Hot Spot."

The scene opened as they had filmed it, the two of them leaning back against the headboard in their underwear. It's what happened from there that had both of their jaws hanging open.

Eli and Hamish watched in silence as the forty-two-minute video streamed across the computer screen in full color. By the time Royce said, "As always, thanks for coming," Eli was hard as a rock and Hamish was openly playing with himself. When Eli looked at Hamish, his eyes were again that deep blue-violet color and full of lust.

Eli stood, now being driven by something other than his brain, dove on top of Hamish, and covered Hamish's lips with his own. Hamish wrapped his arms around Eli, and together they rolled onto the floor with Hamish landing on top. Hamish cupped Eli's face and kissed him desperately, moving his hands from Eli's face to his head and running his fingers through Eli's hair. Hamish dropped down to his neck and nibbled and bit at the tender skin until Eli was moaning uncontrollably.

Hamish eventually stood, pulled Eli up with him, and led Eli to his bedroom. When they reached Hamish's king-size bed, Hamish pulled Eli's shirt over his head and pushed him back onto the bed. Hamish then pulled Eli's sneakers and socks off, unbuttoned Eli's jeans, and dragged them off from the ankles. He stood over Eli and stripped himself until he was naked and then peeled Eli's underwear off and climbed on top of him.

The look Eli saw in Hamish's eyes was indescribable. If he had to put it into words, it would be a mixture of desire and emotion. But the odd thing was that Eli was feeling all the same things. *How can this be? Three weeks! I've been sleeping with men for three weeks.*

"Stop it, Eli. I can see the wheels turning," Hamish said, looking him in the eye. "Do you want me to stop?"

"Hell no!" Eli said, reaching up and taking Hamish's face in his hands. "Please don't stop."

Hamish offered him a seductive smile and once again covered Eli's lips in a passionate kiss.

As Hamish stretched out on top of him, Eli settled in for an unrushed, undirected lovemaking session. Hamish kissed his way down Eli's chin, neck, and shoulders, stopping at his nipples. Eli arched his back and pressed his chest against Hamish's mouth when Hamish bit down gently. Eli sighed and relaxed as Hamish continued down his chest to his stomach and belly button, kissing his way around Eli's abs and sides. When Hamish moved down a little farther and buried his nose in Eli's groin, Eli fought the urge to raise his hips into the simple act.

Moving slowly and deliberately, Hamish took Eli into his mouth and surrounded his length with his warm, wet mouth. He went down and down until his lips were against Eli's skin and Eli was lodged in the back of his throat.

"Jesus," Eli hissed, gripping the sheets to keep his hands from forcing Hamish's head down even farther. Hamish moved, bringing his lips up to the head, and licked and tickled before moving down again. The next time Hamish came up, he let Eli slip from his mouth and focused on Eli's balls and that sensitive little area between his balls and ass. Eli gyrated his hips as Hamish sucked on his balls, tossed them around in his mouth, and gently bit at the skin surrounding them.

Hamish's next move sent Eli into outer space. Hamish pressed against the backs of Eli's thighs and pushed his legs back, exposing his opening and his buttocks. He pressed his lips to Eli's ass cheeks, nibbling and biting until he positioned his tongue at Eli's opening and started licking. Eli took in a deep breath and moved his head from side to side, his nerve endings dancing with the teasing and tantalizing. Hamish darted his tongue in and out and then pushed in farther, bringing Eli up off of the bed.

Eli was rock hard and felt like he was on the verge of exploding with pleasure. Hamish reached over and tore open a foil condom packet and rolled the condom down onto Eli's length, using his mouth. "God, that feels good," Eli said.

Hamish flipped open the top of the lube bottle and coated Eli and himself and then straddled Eli's thighs, slowly impaling himself.

Eli took in another huge breath when Hamish slid down on to him, taking Eli all the way to his core. Eli was surrounded by Hamish's heat, and he felt him all the way to his toes. He looked up and his eyes met Hamish's, and Hamish started to move. Up and down, long unhurried strokes. Hamish tipped his head back and closed his eyes. Eli thought he'd never seen anything so beautiful and sensual in his life.

Hamish again opened his eyes and moved his hands to Eli's nipples, pinching and rubbing as he rode Eli's cock. The combination of all the sensations was sending Eli into mental and physical overload.

"Take me on my back, Eli," Hamish said, easing up and sliding to Eli's side.

Eli got to his knees, positioned himself at Hamish's opening, and pushed in slowly. Hamish readily accepted him, guiding Eli at his thighs, pulling him in closer, tighter against him. Eli opened the lube bottle and covered Hamish's length as he slowly began to move forward and back. He slid his hand up and down Hamish's erection in unison with his thrusts until the two men were moving as one.

Hamish's arms were spread open like wings, his head was tossed back, and he made the most beautiful sounds each time Eli hit his core. "Oh God, Eli," Hamish said. "You feel incredible."

"This is so hot, man," Eli said. "I won't last much longer."

"Fuck me, man," Hamish said. "Hard. Don't be afraid."

Eli picked up his pace and intensity and gave Hamish what he asked for. Minutes later Hamish replaced Eli's hand with his own and stroked frantically. He released a guttural moan when he coated his chest and abs with his release. The look on Hamish's face when he came, combined with the feverish pumping, drove Eli to the brink. When Eli came, he came hard and deep inside of Hamish. Eli pumped until he was sure he'd released every drop and then collapsed on top of Hamish, who wrapped his arms around him and held him tightly.

"That was incredible," Hamish whispered in his ear. "Thank you."

"You're thanking me?" Eli said. "That was indescribable, man. I've never come that hard in my life."

Eli slid to Hamish's side, and Hamish took the opportunity to get up and bring a warm towel to the bed. He cleaned them both off and tossed the dirty towel back into the bathroom. Eli lay on his back with his eyes closed, his arm securely around Hamish, who was resting his head on Eli's chest, drawing little circles on his stomach with his forefinger.

"What just happened here?" Hamish asked, raising his head and resting the bottom of his chin on Eli's chest.

Eli cleared his throat and looked at Hamish. "I don't know, man. I'm really sorry," he said. "One minute we were watching our video and the next thing I knew, I was on top of you."

Hamish chuckled. "No apology needed. I was right there with you. I mean… that video was intense. Not to mention fucking hot."

"How did we not realize that when we were doing it?"

"Are you kidding me? I realized the hell out of it," Hamish said. "And I think you did too, but I don't think you were ready to acknowledge your feelings. Afterwards, you… you seemed very unsure."

"What do you mean 'unsure'?" Eli asked.

Hamish sat up. "In the bathroom, I tried to talk to you about what had just happened between us, but you said you had too many things running through your mind and that when you figured it all out you would let me know. I waited patiently for you to say something, anything, but you didn't. I figured it was one of three things. You needed more time. You'd decided to pretend it hadn't happened, or maybe I imagined it all."

"Shit!" Eli said. "I'm sorry, Hamish. You didn't imagine it. I felt it too, or at least I thought I did, but you seemed different afterward, emotionally distant, so I convinced myself I was imagining it all too."

Hamish lay back down, shoulders just touching Eli's. "Stop apologizing. And for the record, that's called *giving you space*, asshole," he said. "I think that's what you asked for, isn't it?"

"Yeah," Eli whispered. "I guess it is."

They lay there in silence, side by side, for another few minutes.

"Do you know the reason I changed my mind and wanted to do the shoot with you?" Eli asked.

Hamish slowly rolled onto his side again, rested his head in his hand, and cocked an eyebrow. "Wait! I was the one who told you I wanted to do the shoot."

Oops! "Yeah well, you were the one who said it first," Eli admitted. "But I had already decided to ask you to do it before you asked me."

"Fucker," Hamish said, pulling on a little patch of hairs on Eli's stomach.

"Ow!" Eli said, smacking Hamish's hand away. "That hurt."

"Good. I felt like a pervert all day because I thought I was corrupting you. I almost backed out of the shoot at the last minute."

"I wouldn't have allowed that to happen," Eli said, not giving Hamish time to respond. "But what made me want to do it so badly was seeing you with Quaid."

"You saw me with Quaid?" Hamish asked.

"Yeah. And you looked pretty into it."

"It's kinda my job to look that way," Hamish said. "And besides, I was acting. I have no romantic interest in Quaid. He's a happily married man."

"I know, Royce told me. But it wasn't a jealousy thing, like I was jealous because you were having sex with him. It was the way you looked at him and reacted to him. I hadn't seen that in any of your other videos."

Hamish pushed himself up and sat cross-legged facing Eli. "You watched my other videos?"

Eli looked away and then forced himself to meet Hamish's eyes again. "I'm sorry," he said. "But yeah."

Hamish shook his head. "Again with the apologies," he said, rolling his eyes. "Stop it! You don't need to apologize. I'm just surprised."

They were silent again, eyes locked onto each other's until Eli looked away again.

Hamish placed his forefinger under Eli's chin and gently turned his head back so they were face-to-face. "Don't freak out on me, man," Hamish said, taking Eli's hand into his. "This is new to me too."

Eli cocked an eyebrow.

"What?" Hamish said. "You know what I mean. Yes, I've been doing gay porn for a couple of years now, but this is the first time I've had sex with a man and not gotten paid for it. Not to mention in my own bed. I'm a little surprised myself."

Eli swung his legs around, put his feet on the floor, and rested his head in his hands.

Hamish put his hand on Eli's back. "Fuck no, Eli! I'm not letting you run from this again. We already wasted too much time playing cat and mouse. We're gonna settle this here and now."

Eli looked over his shoulder. "Then what in the hell do we do?"

"I say we see what it's all about," Hamish said. "I feel a strong connection to you, and a fuckload of chemistry, but maybe it's just sex. Plain and simple."

Eli had a sneaking suspicion that wasn't the case, and he felt sure Hamish had the same suspicion. They seemed to enjoy each other's company way too much for that and had a great time when they were together, wherever they went. And the sex… well that was just…. Wow!

"I feel the connection, okay," Eli said, suddenly exhausted. "Like there's something bubbling right under the surface. But…."

Hamish chuckled. "But… you're not gay. Right?"

"Cut me a little slack, Hamish," Eli said. "I'm *not* gay. I mean, I was just starting to believe that having sex with a guy for money didn't make a person gay, but what just happened between us pretty much blows that theory all to hell."

"Always with the labels," Hamish said.

"I'm not like you, Hamish. You've had a lot more time to figure all this out." Eli ran his fingers through his hair, stood, and started pacing. "Look, man, I admit it. I still struggle with seeing things black and white. Hell, I started out a straight former Marine who got duped by his parents and needed a way to get back on his feet, and for the last week, I've been having sex with different guys for money to do just that. And... today. Right this minute I just had recreational sex with one of those guys because I wanted to. This shit is blowing my mind."

Hamish climbed out of bed, stood in front of Eli, and placed his hands on Eli's upper arms to stop him from pacing. "Okay I get it. You're not gay. Technically, neither am I, but we can't ignore what just happened. I don't know about you, but I don't think *I* want to."

"So what do we do, man?" Eli asked.

"The way I see it, we have a couple of choices here. We can go out on a limb, regardless of the 'label,' enjoy each other's company, let it run its course, and see where it takes us. Or... we can pretend it didn't happen and let it go because we're simply not gay."

Fuck! I'm not gay, am I? But I don't want to ignore this either! Come on, Eli, it's time to man up!

Hamish must have recognized the turmoil going on behind Eli's eyes because he pulled him closer, wrapping his arms around him and kissing his forehead. "Label or no label, I know what I want," he whispered. "But if you want an easy way out, I'll end it right here and now. I can arrange it with Royce that our paths never cross and we do our shoots at opposite times. It's that easy, man."

But it's not that easy! Eli closed his eyes and rested his forehead against Hamish's chin. He felt drained but oddly secure in Hamish's arms. Gay or straight, he liked the feeling. *Secure!* Eli realized he believed Hamish and knew Hamish would do exactly as he'd said, regardless of his own feelings. No one had ever put him first like that. Suddenly the answer was right in front of him. He surrendered and relaxed into Hamish's embrace. "When you put it that way," he whispered, "I'd be a fool to walk away from you because of a label."

Hamish tightened his hold on Eli. "Good answer," he said, pressing his lips against Eli's.

Nervous and apprehensive, but standing by his decision, Eli let himself get lost in the kiss. He jumped when the ringer of his cell phone sounded from somewhere on the floor at the foot of the bed. "It's Royce's ring," Eli said against Hamish's lips. "Think we should get it? It might be about the video."

"Royce has always had really bad timing," Hamish said.

Eli dug for his phone and accepted the call. "Hey, Royce."

"Is Hamish with you?" Royce asked.

"Yeah, why?"

"Man! You two are blowing up the web site."

"What are you talking about?" Eli asked.

"There are so many people streaming your video that we almost crashed."

Eli smiled and put his hand over the microphone. "Our video just about crashed the site," he whispered to Hamish.

Eli pressed the speaker button so they could both hear Royce.

"This is the most popular video in the site's history, guys."

In complete shock, "Wow!" was all Eli could say.

"And the e-mails are flooding the in-box. Hundreds of them, and everyone loves the chemistry between you guys. Well, almost everyone," Royce added.

"What do you mean 'almost everyone'?" Eli asked.

"Can Hamish hear me?"

"Yeah, I'm here," Hamish said. "Why?"

"Do you by any chance recognize the e-mail address fanofhamish@aol.com?"

"No. But I'm not sure I would. You give us a shitload of fan mail, but I just skim them every now and then. Why?"

"Apparently, one particular fan of yours has no problem watching you have sex with other guys, but does have a problem with Cal. Evidently the chemistry between you two was just too much for him or her to handle, and this person is not happy. They don't want you to do any more scenes with him."

"Really?" Hamish said.

Royce cleared his throat. "It sounds like someone is seriously obsessed with you and seeing you connect so obviously with someone else pissed them off big-time."

"Oh well," Hamish said. "You win some you lose some."

"Anyway, I just wanted to give you guys the great news. But I do want to do another shoot as soon as possible. You know how our viewers like firsts. This time we'll have Eli fuck you, Hamish."

Eli looked at Hamish and mouthed "Firsts?" He put his hand over his mouth and stifled a laugh.

"Will do," Hamish said through a smile.

"When?"

Hamish looked at Eli and shrugged. "How about tomorrow morning?"

"Perfect," Royce said. "Say ten o'clock?"

Eli nodded. "Okay, we'll be there."

"Oh and one more thing. Eli?"

"I'm here."

"It's overwhelming. Everyone wants to see you clean-shaven. Chest, crotch, balls, and asshole. The whole shebang."

"What?" Eli said. "No wayyyy."

"Gotta do what the viewers want," Royce said. "And boys. If this video does as good as the last, there's a serious bonus in it for you both."

"Thanks, Royce," Hamish said. "And don't worry, I'll help Eli with the shaving," he said with a wink.

"Thanks, Hamish. I knew I could count on you," Royce said. "I'll see you when you get home, Eli."

"Uh," Hamish added, "I've had a few drinks tonight so I don't think it a good idea that I drive, so he may just crash here tonight."

"Good idea. Then I'll see you boys in the morning."

"Good night, Royce."

Eli ended the call and threw the phone on the bed.

"I guess we're stars now," Hamish said, taking Eli into his arms and kissing him passionately.

The kiss made Eli weak in the knees, but he also felt certain Hamish wouldn't let him fall. For the first time since he'd left his fellow Marines behind in Afghanistan, Eli felt like someone actually had his back again. The feeling was familiar and comforting, but he also knew as quickly as he'd stumbled upon it, it could be taken away. He said a silent prayer that he was doing the right thing letting Hamish in.

Hamish stepped back and looked him in the eyes. "I hear you thinking again."

"Nope, I'm good," Eli said, pushing those thoughts out of his head. Wanting to change the subject, he said, "But what about this shaving crap?"

Hamish laughed. "It's not bad," he said. "In fact, if you can relax with me using a razor blade around your cock and asshole, I think you'll enjoy it."

"Jesus," Eli said. "I never thought about that part."

"It's best if we do this in the shower," Hamish said. "Come on?"

After about forty minutes in the shower, Hamish stepped out first, dried off, and then held up a large bath sheet from the towel warmer for Eli to step into. Eli dried off and looked at his reflection in the mirror. Except for his head and a little patch above his penis, he was void of any body hair. But to Hamish's credit, he'd been right. The overall process had felt nice, a little odd around his asshole, but otherwise relaxing and pretty damn pleasant. He was sure his asshole was going to be a little raw when the stubble started to grow in, but for now he was as smooth as a baby's bottom.

When Hamish had finished shaving him, Eli had returned the favor and got in a little practice, enjoying doing the shaving almost as much as having it done.

"How do you feel?" Hamish asked.

Eli rubbed his chest and smiled. "Really smooth and extra clean."

"Well," Hamish said. "You look pretty hot. Being hairless really shows off the definition of your muscles."

"Yeah?" Eli said, flexing and posing in the mirror. "You know, I think you're right."

"Oh Lord, I've created a monster." Hamish pulled Eli into his arms. "What do you say we go and try out that new body of yours?"

ELI AND Hamish got to the mansion about nine thirty the next morning, and when they stepped through the front door and into the foyer they were assaulted by loud applause and catcalls. Royce was standing at the foot of the stairs with a huge smile on his face, and the others were standing at various levels on the stairs behind him. "Here are the two guys who almost crashed our web site, boys," Royce said.

The guys yelled louder and whooped and hollered. Royce quieted the crowd. "It's official, men! You got the most hits of any video on the site ever. Not to mention so many e-mails that it'll take a month to answer them all. The viewers loved what they saw, and they want more. So get your asses upstairs, naked, and into bed so we can keep 'em happy."

Eli looked at Hamish and smiled. "Good to know we're loved for who we are and not for how great we are in bed," he teased.

"Tell me about it," Hamish agreed. "I'm feeling like a piece of meat right about now."

"Perfect!" Royce said. "Get said meat upstairs and have it ready to go when I get there."

The guys offered congratulations as they slowly started to disassemble, some heading downstairs and some up, all apparently getting ready for their own shoots.

Eli and Hamish were about to head upstairs when Bristol walked through the front door. "Fuck," he said. "I guess I missed it, huh?"

"Yep, you missed it," Royce said. "Now get your ass downstairs and ready for your shoot."

"Yes, sir," Bristol said, starting down the stairs but stopping. "Oh, I almost forgot. This was taped to the keypad on the front gate," he said, pulling a plain white envelope out of his back pocket, handing it to Royce, and continuing on his way.

"Thanks," Royce said, accepting the envelope and opening it. Royce read the letter, dropped his hand, and sat on the bottom step. Eli instinctively knew something was wrong and ran to Royce's side.

Royce handed the letter to Eli, and he held it so he and Hamish could read it together.

The plain white piece of paper was covered with letters that were apparently cut out of magazines or newspapers and taped to the surface. The note read:

> *How could you Hamish?*
> *No more Cal or else!*

"What the fuck?" Hamish said. "This is crazy."

Royce pulled out his cell phone and held it in his hand. "I wonder if this is the same person who sent the e-mail last night? But how did they find *this* place? This address is nowhere on the site or in any public records. I'm calling the police." He pressed a nine and then a one but Hamish stopped him.

"Come on, Royce. This is just some crazed fan. Let's not jump to any conclusions and wait and see what happens."

"This looks real," Eli said. "I agree with Royce. Why should we take any chances?"

"Eli, think about what you're saying, man. Do you really want to explain to the police what we're doing here unless we absolutely have to?"

"Fuck," Eli said, turning away and punching the palm of his hand. "Good point."

"This will blow over, guys," Hamish said. "You'll see."

"One more of these and I don't care what you say," Royce protested. "I'm calling the police."

"I agree," Eli said.

ROYCE WAVED a hand in the air. "Cut! Another steamy scene! Nice job, men. You guys get cleaned up. I have an idea for the closing interview."

Eli and Hamish went into the bathroom and closed the door behind them.

"You okay?" Hamish asked, pulling Eli into his arms. "You didn't seem yourself out there."

"I'm sorry. I'm just a little preoccupied with the whole *letter* thing."

"Yeah, I know what you mean, but I really do think it's nothing and will blow over soon. Normally these guys move on to their next obsession pretty quickly."

"I hope so," Eli said, kissing Hamish's shoulder. "The whole idea just creeps me out."

The two cleaned up, put their underwear back on, and hopped into bed side by side, with Hamish resting an arm over Eli's shoulder.

"Rolling," Royce said. "Well, boys, I don't know what you're eating, but I sure hope you go back for seconds, because this was amazing. You guys sure know how to sizzle on camera. Hamish? How was it?"

"It was great, man," Hamish said, pulling Eli closer. "Cal is pretty hot, isn't he, guys?" he added, looking right into the camera.

"And speaking of Cal!" Royce said. "Man, you were so comfortable mounting that horse that no one would guess this was your first time fucking Hamish."

Eli looked at Hamish, feeling a little guilty for not being straight with Royce. "*You* know how it is, Royce. You fucked one guy, you've fucked them all," he said, flashing that familiar smile.

"Thanks a lot," Hamish said. "Way to make me feel special."

Eli laid a hand on Hamish's chest. "Toughen up, big guy. You're in the wrong business to be so sensitive."

"You say the sweetest things to me, darling," Hamish said, winking at the camera.

Eli chuckled. "I try, honeybunch."

"Can you guys cut the lovey-dovey crap for a minute so I can talk about something serious?"

"Yes, ma'am," Hamish and Eli said in unison, looking at each other and laughing.

"It's time I let our viewers know that it's official. You two now have the most watched video of all time on hotmilitaryguys.com, not to mention the largest amount of fan correspondence we've ever received."

Eli dropped his arm to his stomach and bowed slightly at the waist while Hamish lifted his hand and flipped a couple of fingers in the air a few times as he bowed his head.

"Seriously, guys. We got so much feedback from people begging for another scene that we just couldn't ignore the onslaught."

Eli thought he knew where Royce was heading with this line of questioning, so he started playing along. "Thank you," Eli said, pointing his fingers at the camera. "The fact that all of you love what we're doing makes all the difference."

Hamish must have clued in as well, because he added, "Cal's right. We all do this for various reasons, but the fact that you love it and support us makes it all worthwhile."

"Well not exactly *all*," Royce said. "We did get one or two negative comments."

"Oh?" Hamish said.

"Yeah. A couple of viewers didn't like the fact that you guys were so into each other, and they asked that I not put you two together again."

"That's not fair to the rest of the viewers," Eli said. "We're straight guys trying to create a fantasy for our viewers."

"Cal's right," Hamish said. "We're just trying to put on a good show."

"Well put," Royce said. "Obviously, since we've done *this* shoot, we've collectively decided to please the overwhelming percentage of our viewers and give them what they want. But for those of you who do not wish to see these two beautiful men together, we understand and support your right to not watch the video. There are hundreds of videos on the site and I'm sure you can find something you like."

Hamish raised a hand. "And this commentary is supported by and does reflect the views of the actors," he added with a wink.

Eli nodded.

"Your support is very much appreciated," Royce said. "And as always. Thanks for coming. Cut!"

"Smart man," Hamish said.

"Yeah, that was brilliant," Eli added.

"I only hope it works," Royce said, lowering the camera and sitting on the end of the bed.

Eli thought Royce looked tired for it being so early in the day, and he realized this was all weighing on him pretty heavily.

"You know," Royce said, running his hand through his hair, "I've often wondered if I've been operating on borrowed time. It's been ten years, and with all the crazies out there, we haven't had one serious incident like this until now. If anything ever happened to any one of you guys, I couldn't live with myself."

"Come on, man," Hamish said, sliding down to the end of the bed. "This is probably nothing. It'll all blow over. You'll see."

"Yeah," Eli said, joining them. "Hamish's right. Let's just sit tight and see what happens."

"Fine! You win," Royce said, slapping his knee and standing. "I don't have time for all this crap anyway. Eli, you're up in fifteen with Logan and Cavanaugh, and then it's Hamish and Bristol immediately following." Royce glanced at his watch on his way out. "We'll use the lower suites to take advantage of the midday lighting. I'm going to load a sneak peek of your session onto the site."

"Go get 'em, tiger," Eli said, jumping up and slipping into his shorts.

When Royce was out of the room, Eli looked at Hamish. "You think he's okay?"

"Yeah," Hamish said. "He's a tough old bird."

"I sure hope so," Eli said, pulling his T-shirt over his head and stepping into his flip-flops. Eli looked around to make sure the coast was clear and gave Hamish a brief peck on the lips. "I think I'm gonna catch a quick shower in my room before my next shoot."

Eli turned to leave but Hamish pulled him back and gave him a crushing kiss. "Meet up after lunch for another round of car shopping?" Hamish asked when he pulled back.

"Sure," Eli said, breathless and feeling well kissed.

ELI WAS in the midst of his shoot with Logan and Cavanaugh when out of the corner of his eye he saw Hamish leaning on the doorjamb, watching the show. Hamish's expression wasn't one that Eli had seen on him before, nor was it one he could identify, and that puzzled him.

When Hamish realized Eli had seen him, he offered a feeble smile, stepped away from the door, and disappeared.

When Eli finished his shoot, he cleaned up again and dressed for the afternoon. He looked at his watch and figured Hamish should be through with his shoot by now and set out to find him. Unfortunately, when he passed the suite three doors down from his, Hamish was on all fours getting his ass plowed by Bristol. Hamish's head was thrown back, and with each thrust he was making little whimpering sounds that were getting Eli instantly hard.

Eli's eyes were glued on Hamish to the point where he had to force himself to look away. Driven by all sorts of sentiments, he turned and leaned against the wall to try to get a hold of his emotions. When Eli looked up, he caught his reflection in the wall mirror across from him and froze. "Fuck no!" he whispered to himself. He recognized his expression immediately as the same one he'd seen on Hamish's face earlier. *No, Eli! You're not gay! You can't be jealous. Let this go.*

Eli was lying on a chaise lounge by the pool with his eyes closed and his fingers linked over his chest when he felt a hand on his shoulder. He jumped and opened his eyes.

"Sorry. Didn't mean to startle you," Hamish said. "You ready?"

"Oh hey," Eli said, laying his head back down and closing his eyes. "Can we make it another day? I'm not really in the mood for car shopping."

Hamish walked around, pushed Eli's legs to one side of his chair, and sat. "Something wrong?"

"Nothing and everything," Eli said.

"You wanna open your eyes and look at me? Maybe I can help."

"Talking won't change anything," Eli said. "I knew at some point the reality of all this was going to hit me."

"Talk to me, Eli."

"Okay. You want to know the truth? I've been lying out here for who knows how long trying to wrap my head around the shit that's happened to me in the last few weeks."

Hamish dropped his head and focused on a spot staining the canvas chair. "Shit being what happens at this place and... me, I suppose?"

Eli regretted his choice of words, but he couldn't deny that Hamish had hit the nail on the head. "Sorry," he said. "Bad choice of words, but yeah."

"What brought all this on?" Hamish asked, looking back up and into Eli's eyes.

"Life. Timing. Reflection. I don't know," Eli said. "Maybe getting jealous when I saw another guy fucking you? Who the fuck knows? I sure don't."

Hamish laid a hand on Eli's leg. "So that's what this is all about?"

"Some of it, maybe, but not all of it."

"The only thing I can say to make this easier on you is—"

Eli cut him off. "Yeah I know. You've all been through the same exact emotions I'm dealing with now. But there's one big difference."

"Me?" Hamish asked.

Eli grabbed the arms of his chair and sat up. "Bingo! You're a great guy, but I don't want to be gay, Hamish. Letting a guy shove his dick up my ass for money is one thing, and a decision I'll have to live with for the rest of my life. But you and I... we crossed the line. I keep telling myself I'm not gay, but when seeing another guy fucking you drives me insane with jealousy, well that just says otherwise."

The concerned expression Hamish had when he sat down turned to one of hurt. Then all expression quickly disappeared, and Eli knew Hamish was trying to put up a good front. But he also knew Hamish well enough now to know a cover-up when he saw one.

"I get it, man," Hamish said. "We had some fun and it was good, but just take me out of the equation, then. That should make things a lot easier on you."

Eli was struck with a sense of relief and sadness all at the same time. "But what about you?" he asked.

Hamish stood. "I don't really matter, Eli," he said, looking down at him.

With the sun shining on his face, Eli could see Hamish's normally bright blue eyes were suddenly gray and dull. The flash of pain that Eli had seen earlier was again very obvious, even though he knew Hamish was trying to play it cool for his sake.

"Don't worry about me," Hamish told him. "I'm a big boy and can take care of myself. Oh, and don't worry about our shoots either. I'll tell Royce that I've decided to not push the envelope with the crazy person, and after the current video airs, we don't want to do another one. I'll also tell him to switch my shoots to the afternoon so we won't run into one another." With that Hamish turned and walked away.

"Fuck!" Eli cursed, slamming his hands down on the arms of the chair. "Way to fucking go, dipshit."

Eli remained by the pool feeling sorry for himself until his face started burning from the effects of the afternoon sun. He'd not felt so alone since he left his buddies in Afghanistan, and being away from town and not having a vehicle made him feel even more isolated. He decided he needed to get away from the mansion for a while, so he bit the bullet and took a cab into town to look for a car after all.

Eli ended up at the local CarMax, found a 2011 Ford Fusion that was in great shape, and paid cash for it on the spot. It was no BMW like Hamish's, but it got great gas mileage and would do just fine for the time being. Eli signed up for insurance before he left the lot and felt a little lighter for having taken a step forward. After all, he was doing this to get back on his feet, and having a vehicle for the first time since he'd been stateside was a step in the right direction. Wasn't it? At least now he had something to show for his sacrifice.

By the time Eli left the used car lot, it was six o'clock, and having had no lunch, he was starving. He pulled into the sports bar parking lot and looked around to make sure Hamish wasn't there. It's not that he didn't want to see Hamish. He felt badly about how the afternoon had gone down and wanted to try and explain his feelings better, but he didn't think Hamish wanted to see him.

Eli walked into the bar and was instantly overwhelmed with memories of Hamish. He glanced at the spot at the end of the bar where they always sat and quickly decided on a table in the corner. He ordered a beer and a burger and stared up at the wide-screen in front of him. EPSN was airing a soccer game, and although he knew nothing about soccer, it was a great diversion from dealing with what was truly nagging at him.

On the way back to the mansion, Eli cranked up the volume on the radio when he heard John Mayer singing "Heartbreak Warfare." It was so loud the entire car was vibrating, but he wanted—no, needed—the distraction. He turned off the main road and followed the lake until he came to the mansion's driveway.

Eli reached over and shut the radio off immediately, hand trembling, when he saw the plain white envelope taped to the security keypad. Eli peeled off the envelope, entered the security code, and waited until the gate opened. He drove through and stopped to make sure the gate closed behind him before he proceeded.

"Royce!" Eli yelled at the top of his lungs as he entered the foyer. "Royce? Where are you?"

"In here," Royce yelled from the back of the house.

Eli followed his voice and found him in the kitchen stirring something on the stove.

"You hungry?" Royce asked. "I made chili."

Eli held up the white envelope and watched the blood drain out of Royce's face.

"When? Where?" Royce asked.

"Just now. It was taped in the same place as the last one."

"What does it say?"

Eli handed the envelope to Royce. "I don't know. I didn't open it."

Royce accepted the envelope and opened it with shaky hands.

I saw your little sneak peek.
So disappointed Dawes Turner!
Someone will have to pay!

"That does it!" Royce said. "I'm calling the police. You call Hamish and get him over here."

"But—" Eli said.

"Now!" Royce insisted.

Eli walked onto the patio and dialed Hamish's number.

"What's up, Eli?" Hamish said.

Surprised that Hamish had even answered his call, Eli stuttered. "L-look, man, I know I'm the last person you want to hear from but...."

"What's wrong, Eli?"

Eli was amazed how well Hamish could get a read on him so quickly. "We got another letter."

"What? When?"

"A little while ago. The same place as the last one," Eli explained. "Royce is on the phone with the police now, but he wants you to get over here."

"Shit," Hamish said. "I'll be right there."

The line went dead. Eli put his phone back in his pocket and went inside.

Royce was just hanging up as well. "They're on the way," he said.

Eli nodded. "So is Hamish."

"Look I'm sorry, Eli, but we're gonna have to be honest with the police."

"It's okay," Eli said. Then he surprised himself with his next statement. "I'll do whatever it takes to keep Hamish safe."

Royce gave him a knowing glance.

"I mean… this could be some crazed lunatic."

"Cut the crap, Eli," Royce snapped. "I've been watching the two of you interact over the last few weeks, and whether you know it or not, there is something definitely going on between you. And don't tell me you're just good friends."

Eli took a step back and felt his mouth hanging open. *How could he know?*

He opened his mouth to deny it, but then stopped.

"Come on, man. Give me a little credit. I've been doing what I do for a very long time, and the scenes you guys have pulled off? Well let's just say they go way beyond going through the motions. I can see it and apparently so can a couple of our viewers."

"You're right. There *was* something," Eli admitted. "But not anymore."

"Bullshit!" Royce said. "Whatever it was is still there and you know it. You may not want to acknowledge it, but trust me, Elijah, it's still very much there. What I witnessed between you doesn't go away overnight."

Busted! Eli was about to speak when he heard the front door slam shut, giving him a momentary reprieve.

"Royce?"

"We'll talk about this later," Royce said. He raised his voice. "In the kitchen, Hamish."

"Let me see the letter" was all Hamish said when he rounded the corner.

Eli thought the glow Hamish always wore was gone. He looked tired and stressed out, and Eli felt responsible for it all.

Eli watched him unfold the note and read it out loud. "I saw your little sneak peek. So disappointed, Dawes Turner! Someone will pay!"

"Someone will have to pay!" he repeated, looking directly at Eli. Eli recognized Hamish's look immediately as one of concern. He'd seen the same look before when Hamish had come to his emotional rescue. *He's worried about me. This person has threatened him, now knows his real name, and he's still worried about my safety.*

"What did the police say?" Hamish asked, looking at Royce.

"Nothing yet," Royce said. "But they should be here any minute."

Eli walked up to Hamish. "How did they get your real name?" he asked, laying a hand on Hamish's forearm.

Hamish flinched and Eli removed his hand. "Who knows? They could have found a match by doing a photo search online, or since they know where this place is, maybe they followed me home one day and got my address and looked it up that way."

The hairs stood up on the back of Eli's neck. "Then that means they could very well know where you live."

"Maybe," Hamish said. "But then, why didn't they put the note in my mailbox?"

"That's a good point," Eli said, feeling slightly better.

The intercom on Royce's house sounded three beeps, alerting him that someone was at the gate. "Hello," Royce said, pressing the intercom button.

"This is Detective Shane O'Hennesey with the Dumfries Police Department. Our department received a call from a Royce Mackey regarding a possible stalking case."

"I'm Royce Mackey. Hold on and I'll open the security gate." Royce pressed and held the star key on the phone, the shriek sound reverberating through all the phones in the house.

"Thank you, sir," the detective said. "I'll be right up."

Royce left the room, apparently heading to the front door, and Eli wanted to take this opportunity to try to talk to Hamish, but he really didn't know what to say. He looked Hamish in the eye and started with "This is all my fault."

Hamish shook his head. "Not everything is about you, Eli," he said.

Ouch! That stung, but Eli knew its origin. "If I hadn't joined the group and we hadn't connected like we did, this wouldn't be happening."

"Connected?" Hamish chuckled. "What connection? You couldn't have connected with me. You're not gay, remember."

Ouch again! Eli could hear the pain in Hamish's voice, and he hated that he'd put it there. "Fuck, Hamish! Yeah, I deserved that and probably a lot more, but can we put that shit aside for a second and deal with this issue right now? And I promise you, after we get done, you can hurl all the insults you want at me, and I'll take them like a man."

Before either could say anything else, Eli heard voices. Shortly after, Royce appeared with a portly police officer. "Guys, this is Detective Shane O'Hennesey with the Dumfries Police Department."

Eli and Hamish introduced themselves and exchanged handshakes with the detective. They all sat at the bar, and Royce opened a drawer and removed the first letter and a copy of the e-mail he'd received. He laid everything on the counter and looked at the detective. "This is what we're dealing with."

Detective O'Hennesey read the e-mail and then the two letters. "Okay, if I remember correctly from introductions, you're Eli," he said, looking at Eli. "Who is Dawes Turner?"

Hamish raised his hand. "That would be me. It's my given name, but everyone calls me Hamish."

"So I'll assume you are the gentlemen to whom this is all referring?"

"They are," Royce said, taking it upon himself to explain what his business was all about.

Shortly after Royce began his explanation, the detective held up his hand. "We are very aware of what you do here, Mr. Mackey. In fact we've had a couple of complaints from Quantico about you."

A surprised look appeared on Royce's face. "No one ever contacted me about any complaints."

"That's because we determined you weren't doing anything illegal," Detective O'Hennesey explained. "We did a preliminary investigation of you and your site, made sure you had no warrants out for your arrest or any prior convictions prohibiting you from operating this type of business, made sure the corporation to which you referred on your web site was legitimate, your corporate income taxes were filed appropriately and paid in a timely manner, and so forth and so on. We found nothing out of line and therefore we had no grounds for any further steps."

"It sure would have been nice to know all this was going on," Royce said.

"You would have been notified immediately had we found any incriminating evidence that could have possibly led to an indictment."

"I don't believe this," Royce hissed, shaking his head.

"Let it go, Royce," Hamish said, laying a hand on his shoulder. "They did their job and found nothing."

"Of course they found nothing," Royce snapped. "There is nothing to find. But it sure would have been nice to know all this was going on."

"Relax, Mr. Mackey," Detective O'Hennesey said. "We get tons of calls like this, and we followed standard procedure."

"Okay, fine. I'll relax, but I want this lunatic stopped."

"Stalker is the term we prefer to use," Detective O'Hennesey said. "Tell me everything you know."

Royce, Hamish, and Eli filled the detective in while he took notes.

"Since he found the first note, I'll need to talk to this... uh...." Detective O'Hennesey flipped back through his notes. "Bristol as soon as possible. But we'll start with a fingerprint check on the letters to see if we can pick up anything there, and it should be pretty easy to run a trace on fanofhamish@aol.com and its origin."

Royce nodded. "How long does all this take?"

"Not long. I can probably have the fingerprint check by tomorrow. The e-mail will be easier to trace, and I can probably have an answer on that by the end of the day. Uh... do you happen to have a camera at your gate as part of your security system?"

"No," Royce said. "The only reason that gate is there is because it came with the house. I have nothing to hide."

"I understand. Just checking," the detective said. "But I'd consider it if I were you."

"I'll take care of it first thing tomorrow morning," Royce said. "But how should I proceed with my business?"

"I'd say hold off on posting any other videos of these gentlemen until I can get my preliminary investigation complete. It may be as easy as tracing the e-mail back to the sender and nabbing our suspect. But...," the detective said, "I have a hunch that the e-mail and the letters are two totally separate incidents."

"Oh Christ," Royce said. "Now we have two lunatics on our hands? I have a snippet of the latest video live now as a tease. Do I take that down?"

"No. I think I'd leave it there," the detective said. "At least one of the perpetrators, if there are two, has already seen it, so I don't want to send up any red flags by altering the way you do business."

"Why do you say you think there are two stalkers?" Eli asked the detective.

"In my experience, a stalker wouldn't send an e-mail and then follow up with anonymous letters. My gut tells me the e-mail comes from a harmless, disgruntled viewer who just wanted to be heard. He didn't threaten anyone and hasn't sent another e-mail. But the letters... that's a totally different animal altogether."

"I see," Eli responded. "How should Hamish and I proceed?"

"Just for the time being, I would be cautious and have each other's backs." The detective's face suddenly turned red, and he stuttered his next words. "I... I mean just look out for one another and stay on your guard. Most times these things blow over, but you can never be too careful."

The detective fumbled with his notebook and gathered the letters and e-mail. "I'll be in touch as soon as I have any information to share."

"Thank you, detective," Royce said. "I'll show you out."

"No need," Detective O'Hennesey said. "I can find my way out."

Royce nodded. When he heard the front door close he looked at Hamish. "Take Eli with you and go get some things. You're gonna stay here until all this blows over."

"Like hell I am," Hamish said. "I'm not letting this crazed lunatic—oh, excuse me— *stalker*," he corrected, "dictate my life."

"Come on, Hamish," Royce said. "You heard the detective. Until we know what we're dealing with, please just humor me."

"Royce is right," Eli said. "You'd be much safer here."

Hamish looked at Eli with a scathing expression. "Your overwhelming concern for my well-being is very touching, but not needed," he said. "I can take care of myself. Now. If you'll excuse me, I'm going home. Call me if you hear anything I should know about."

With that, Hamish turned and walked out of the kitchen.

"Please be careful," Royce yelled.

"I will," Hamish yelled back right before he slammed the front door.

Eli jumped when the heavy wooden door made contact with the casing and the sound echoed through the entire house. "I guess that says it all," Eli said.

"Eli?" Royce begged. "I don't know what in the hell is going on between you two, but please go after him. And if he won't come back here, stay with him until this blows over. The thought of him being over there alone scares the hell out of me."

"Trust me," Eli said, "he won't want me there."

"After the way I saw him act toward you just now, I beg to differ," Royce said. "The man has feelings for you, and I'd bet my life he'd welcome you there."

"That's the problem, Royce," Eli said. "I think he does have feelings for me, but I can't return those feelings. I'm not gay."

"What the fuck does being gay have to do with anything?" Royce asked. "Do you care about him?"

"Of course I care."

"Then help me keep him safe."

Eli hung his head but didn't respond. He ran the different scenarios through his mind. He knew Hamish didn't want him there, but if this crazy person did know where he lived, anything could happen. He surely didn't want to see Hamish there alone. Hell, someone could be following him right now.

Royce walked up to him and put his hands on Eli's shoulders. "Look at me, boy."

Eli looked up and met Royce's gaze.

"Do *you* have any feelings for *him*? And don't lie because I saw the way you guys connected in your shoots."

"No! I mean, yes!" Eli covered his face with his hands. "I don't know anything anymore, Royce."

"Go to him," Royce said. "Figure this out or don't figure this out, I don't care. But make sure he's safe."

Eli dropped his shoulders in defeat. "I will."

"Thank you, Eli. I won't forget this."

Eli went to his room, put some things in one of his duffel bags, and got his .45 out from the top of the closet. He ejected the magazine to make sure it was loaded, popped it back in, and threw it in the bag as well.

When he got back to the kitchen, Royce was waiting for him. "Call me when you get there, and please take every precaution." Royce threw his arms around Eli's neck and whispered, "I'll call as soon as I hear anything from O'Hennesey."

"Thanks," Eli said, returning the embrace.

Eli drove down the long driveway to the main road, his mind calculating all sorts of ideas about the way this was going to play out. But as soon as he turned on to the highway, his military training and years of experience in Afghanistan kicked in, and he became very diligent. He took the long way around the lake, making a few extra turns here and there, checking his rearview mirror frequently, composing mental notes of the different cars that followed him and for how long. He scanned the roads on both sides of the highway, looking for any suspicious cars or trucks, and when he finally turned into Hamish's driveway, he felt certain he hadn't been followed.

Eli rang the doorbell and stood with his duffel bag in hand, nervously bouncing from foot to foot. He heard footsteps in the distance, and they got louder and louder until he saw the doorknob turn.

When the door finally opened and Eli saw the look of distress on Hamish's face, he said the first thing that came to his mind. "Do you have a relationship with Jesus?"

It looked like Hamish was fighting back a grin, but he caught himself just in time. "I'm an atheist," he said, attempting to close the door in Eli's face. "You'd have better luck converting the Goldbergs across the street."

"Oy vey," Eli said, pushing his way into the foyer. "No thanks. The Jews are a tough sell."

"What are you doing here?" Hamish asked, slamming the door shut.

"You wouldn't stay at the mansion and allow me to protect you there, so I'm protecting you here."

"I really don't need your protection," Hamish said. "I told you both I would be careful."

Eli dropped his bag in the foyer and walked right past Hamish and into the living room, Hamish on his heels.

"Were you being careful when you opened the door without asking who it was?" Eli asked.

"Oh, stupid me," Hamish said, slapping himself in the forehead. "Whoooo issss itttt? It's your stalker, Hamish. Open up so I can rape or kill you. Or both."

"Good point," Eli said. "But you should have at least looked through the window."

"How do you know I didn't?"

Eli gave Hamish a very disappointed look. "Because I followed the sound of your footsteps, and you walked from the living room to the foyer without stopping. And you can't see the front door from the living room."

"Thank you very much, Sherlock Holmes. I'll remember that."

Eli kicked off his shoes, picked up the remote, and plopped down on the couch. "There must be a game or something on we can watch."

"Eli, go home," Hamish said in a defeated tone. "I'm really not up for any of this."

Eli thought it was time for a different tactic. He got up, walked over to Hamish, and stood in front of him. "Look, man. I know I'm a confused asshole, and you have every right to be frustrated with me—"

"Frustrated?" Hamish interrupted. "Really?"

"Okay," Eli said, putting both hands on Hamish's forearms. "Angry. Foolish. Hurt. Royally pissed off. Whatever you want to call it, but this is serious stuff. We could both be in danger, and frankly, I'm a little unnerved."

"The big bad Marine?" Hamish asked.

"Look. I'll fight anything I can see, and nine times out of ten, I'll win, but this I can't see."

Hamish finally made an expression like he knew what Eli was talking about.

"Come on, man, you remember Afghanistan," Eli said, waving the remote through the air and trying to appeal to the Marine in Hamish. "It's lurking out there like the Taliban, and that creeps me out. Besides, I sort of feel responsible."

Hamish rolled his eyes, and Eli knew the man was allowing himself to be played.

"Okay, you can stay, but you're sleeping in the guest room."

"Deal," Eli said. He plopped back down on the couch, put his feet up on the coffee table, and looked at Hamish. "What's for dinner? I'm starved."

Hamish just stared at him with a lopsided grin and shook his head.

Now that Eli was really paying attention, Hamish looked extremely tired. Exhausted even. Eli quickly realized that between his crazy issues and this stalker business, it was all starting to take its toll on him. He felt this strong need to go over and wrap his arms around Hamish and tell him it was all going to be all right, but he feared Hamish wouldn't take kindly to that, so he sat tight and waited for his answer.

When the response finally came, Eli had to smile. "I have no fucking idea. It's your turn to cook anyway."

Eli jumped to his feet. "Then I guess I better scout around that kitchen of yours and see what I can whip up."

"Fine," Hamish said. "I'm going to take a shower."

While Eli rummaged through the kitchen, he called Royce. He told him he'd made it there without incident, that everything was okay, and that he'd call him again in the morning.

"Bingo!" Eli said to himself when he found fresh ground sirloin in the refrigerator and all the other ingredients for his grandmother's special meatloaf and mashed potatoes. What little he knew about cooking he'd learned from her when he'd visited every year during summer vacation. She'd been the only real role model in his life and died while he'd been in Afghanistan. His parents hadn't even bothered to tell him and buried her three days later, he assumed to get their hands on what little money she'd had.

After he combined the ingredients, he kneaded the mixture and fondly thought of her and remembered the day on his way to Quantico when he'd stopped in South Carolina, knelt at her grave, and said his final good-byes.

With the meatloaf in the oven and the potatoes boiling, Eli reached into the freezer and grabbed two frozen mugs. He poured himself a beer and one for Hamish. *He's got to be out of the shower by now.*

Eli padded down the hall in his sock feet, carrying two cold beers, and used the tip of his big toe to knock on Hamish's bedroom door. The door was slightly ajar, and the force of Eli's kick opened it a good bit more to where he could see into the bathroom. Hamish was still in the shower, and although Eli knew he should retreat, the sight of Hamish's muscular body standing under the spray, his strong hands caressing his skin, held him firmly in place. He was instantly hard and fought the sudden urge to strip down and join Hamish, invitation or not.

Mine! was his first thought. Quickly followed by, *What the fuck? No! Not yours, Eli. You saw to that earlier today.* He turned and made a beeline for the kitchen, downing his beer on the way and starting on Hamish's while trying to get the image of Hamish in the shower out of his mind.

Eli busied himself mashing and seasoning the potatoes and lowering the heat to keep them warm. He opened a couple of cans of green peas, adding a little butter and putting the pot on the stove to simmer while he cleaned up after himself.

Damn if his mind didn't keep going back to Hamish and his jet-black hair, wet and slicked back on his head. Those muscular shoulders and back, not to mention his round ass and beefy thighs and calves, filled his mind's eye. "You need to make up your mind, Eli," he said to himself. "You want Hamish or you don't. You can't have it both ways."

Around that time Hamish walked into the kitchen wearing a dark blue V-neck T-shirt tucked into blue jeans that were perfectly fitted and riding low on his hips. His hair was still slicked back and glistening but starting to dry, and he looked considerably more relaxed than when he'd left. Eli wanted to comment on how good he looked but knew that was the last thing Hamish wanted to hear.

"Smells good in here," Hamish said. "What are we having?"

"My granny's special South Carolina meatloaf, mashed potatoes, and green peas."

Hamish nodded, walking to the stove and peeking into the pot of potatoes. He picked up a spoon, filled the tip, and took a taste.

"Really good," he said, banging the spoon on the edge of the pot before covering it again. A splash of potatoes landed on Hamish's finger, and Eli instinctively grabbed Hamish's hand, brought it to his mouth, and licked off the potatoes.

Eli froze when he realized what he'd done. He released Hamish's hand. "Sorry. I shouldn't have done that."

"No, you shouldn't have," Hamish replied with a cold tone in his voice.

"It won't happen again," Eli promised.

Desperately wanting to make up for his lack of judgment, Eli said the first thing that came to his mind. "How about a beer?"

"Sure. How long until dinner?"

Eli looked at his watch and the timer on the stove. "Oh, about twenty minutes."

"That means I have time for a smoke, right?"

"I think so."

Hamish walked up to the humidor and pulled out a half-smoked cigar, cut the tip, and headed outside with the lighter.

Eli waited for an invitation that never came and decided he had no choice but to give Hamish the space he needed. On some level he understood why Hamish was acting like he was, but on another level it still hurt like hell. Hamish had become Eli's best friend, among other things, and the distance that was now suddenly between them was a hard pill to swallow.

With nothing else to do, Eli again stirred the potatoes, but kept his eye on Hamish leaning on the rail and smoking his cigar, seemingly very preoccupied. He turned the peas off and a few minutes later took the meatloaf out of the oven. He mixed ketchup and brown sugar together and iced the top of the meatloaf and popped it back in the oven. When Eli turned, Hamish was leaning back against the railing with his bare feet crossed at the ankles, one hand on the cigar and the other in his pocket. He was staring at Eli, the tip of the cigar glowing brightly in the dusk. Their eyes locked and Eli held his gaze. Neither flinched until the timer on the stove went off and Eli looked away quickly and then back. When their eyes met again, Hamish was smiling slightly with an *I win* look on his face.

Eli flipped him the bird, and Hamish's smile broadened.

They ate dinner almost in silence, Hamish commenting on how good everything was from time to time. Eli hated the distance that now filled the once small space between them, but it was obvious that neither was quite ready to acknowledge the elephant in the room. After dinner Eli cleaned the kitchen and eventually joined Hamish in the living room.

Hamish was watching the Pittsburg Steelers and the Miami Dolphins while sipping on something in a small glass.

"Mind if I join you?" Eli asked.

"Suit yourself," Hamish said. "I've opened a bottle of port if you're interested."

"I've never had port. What is it?"

"It's a red after-dinner wine made in Portugal," Hamish explained. "This particular vintage is quite dry and pretty good."

Eli picked up the small glass that Hamish had obviously put out for him and poured a little into the bottom. He took a small sip and savored the flavor as the smooth liquid slid down his throat extremely easily. "This is good," he said, pouring more into his glass. "Who's winning?"

"The Dolphins, ten to three."

"Yesss!" Eli said. "I love the Dolphins."

"I hate the Dolphins. I'm pulling for the Steelers."

"Go figure," Eli said.

Hamish smiled but didn't say a word. Eli realized that he kind of liked the cat and mouse game they were playing and settled down for the long haul, putting his feet up on the table and sipping his port.

During the third quarter, the Steelers scored and tied the game. By the last few minutes, the two men were up on their feet yelling at the television, cursing like sailors. When the Dolphins scored the final touchdown, Eli wrapped his arms around Hamish and kissed him right on the lips. When he realized what he'd done, instead of pulling back, he pressed his tongue against Hamish's lips, and Hamish opened. Eli raised his hand and gripped the back of Hamish's neck and held him securely in place as he explored the inside of his mouth. Hamish tasted so good, a mixture of cigar and port that went straight to Eli's dick.

Eli brought his other hand up and positioned it at the small of Hamish's back and pulled him in closer, but Hamish suddenly pulled away. "This is not happening," he said.

Eli was left breathless and hard. In his heart he understood why, but his cock was something else altogether.

"No. I understand," Eli said. "I had no right."

"Damned straight," Hamish said. "You gave away that right."

Eli hung his head.

"I'm going to bed," Hamish said. "I'm sure you can find the guest room on your own."

Eli stood in the living room, alone and confused. His first thought was to chase Hamish into his bedroom and fuck the hell out of him, or better yet, have Hamish fuck the hell out of him. But that didn't seem like the right thing to do. He needed to get his shit straight before he hurt Hamish any more.

Eli turned off the television, curled up on the couch, and tried to sleep, not able to bring himself to sleep alone in the guest room. After a few hours of tossing and turning, he finally dozed off and vaguely remembered waking up a bit later shivering from the cold. The next time he woke, he had a warm blanket surrounding him and went right back to sleep knowing Hamish cared at least enough to cover him up.

The smell of fresh-brewed coffee woke him, and he opened his eyes to the bright sunlight streaming in through the living room windows. He wrapped the blanket around himself, went into the kitchen, and froze in his tracks when he saw a note from Hamish next to the coffee pot.

"Going for a run" was all it said.

"Fuck!" Eli said to himself. "Come on, Hamish. Work with me here." Eli looked at his watch; it was nine fifty-five in the morning. *What time did he leave? How long has he been gone? Which route did he take?*

Eli dropped the blanket on the kitchen floor and ran back into the living room. He pulled on his sneakers, dug a ball cap and sweatshirt out of his bag, and slipped his .45 in the waistband of his jeans at the small of his back. He pulled the sweatshirt over his head, slapped on the ball cap, and opened the front door.

He froze when he found Hamish standing on the front porch with his key in his hand.

"Jesus," Eli said, wrapping his arms around Hamish's sweaty body and drawing him close. Then Eli suddenly pushed him away. "Don't ever do that crap to me again," he said, turning and walking back into the house.

Hamish followed him in, closing the door behind them. Eli sat on the couch, covered his face with his hands, and tried to calm his racing heart. He leaned forward and pulled the gun from his back and laid it on the table in front of him.

"Shit," Hamish said with a surprised tone in his voice. "You were gonna kill me because I went for a run?"

"No, you ass," Eli yelled, his voice shaky. "I was gonna kill anyone who tried to hurt you."

Hamish sat down next to Eli and rested a hand on his knee. "I left you a note."

"Thanks a lot," Eli said, trying to steady his voice. "And a lot of good that did me. It didn't say when you left, how long you would be gone, or which route you were going to take. Tell me, Hamish. How does that help me?"

"You're right, Eli. I'm sorry," Hamish conceded. "I'm just so pissed off at you right now I'm not thinking straight."

"I get that. I do, Hamish," Eli said, taking Hamish's hand in his. "Be pissed off at me all you want, but don't be stupid. I'm trying to figure out my shit where we're concerned, but I can't do that if I'm constantly worried about you."

"Okay," Hamish conceded. "I won't go out without you until this stalker crap is behind us."

Eli's hands were still trembling, but he brought Hamish's hand to his mouth and placed a gentle kiss on it. "Thank you."

Hamish wrapped his other arm around Eli's shoulder and held him until he calmed down. "I'm okay," Hamish said. "Nothing happened to me."

Eli buried his head against Hamish's chest and closed his eyes. Eli again felt safe and secure in Hamish's arms and secretly cursed himself for hurting this man.

LATER THAT afternoon, Eli was bored to tears and watching the Maury show when his phone rang. He checked the caller ID and saw it was Royce. He called to Hamish and answered the call. "Hey, Royce."

"I've got some news," Royce said. "I'm sorry I didn't call earlier, but the security guy was showing me how to operate the new camera at the gate."

"No problem," Eli said as Hamish joined him on the couch. Eli pressed the speaker button. "We're both here," he said.

"Okay. Detective O'Hennesey called about an hour ago, and they traced the e-mail, got a source and a search warrant, and paid the guy a visit."

"Really? That quick?" Eli said.

"And?" Hamish added.

"The detective's hunch was right," Royce explained. "The guy was a homebound, four-hundred-pound recluse living in the DC area who admitted to being in love with Hamish. After a little questioning, the guy confessed and told O'Hennesey he was just so upset when he saw the way you interacted with Eli that he just couldn't handle it."

"No shit," Hamish said.

"The problem is," Royce continued, "the guy swears he didn't send the letters, and a thorough search of his house shows nothing to the contrary. The detective thinks he's telling the truth."

"So where does that leave us with the letters?" Eli asked.

"According to Detective O'Hennesey, the two letters are proving to be a bit more complicated," Royce explained. "Oh, by the way, if you see an unmarked car outside your house, don't get alarmed. O'Hennesey is putting a detail on your house."

"Thanks for the warning."

"Don't mention it," Royce said. "Where were we? Oh yeah, the letters. It appears that there were no fingerprints on either of the two letters, other than ours, and the same on the envelopes, except one of them had a match to Bristol. That tells the authorities the perpetrator is somewhat intelligent and is being very careful. Furthermore, the analysis of the cut-out letters showed an exact match to the paper used by the Stafford County Sun, so we believe the perpetrator to be local or at least staying in the area now."

"Is that a good or a bad thing?" Eli asked.

"The detective seems to think this really narrows things down and is in our favor."

"What about how the letters got attached to the security gate keypad?" Hamish asked.

"The police are interviewing the neighbors to see if anyone saw anything suspicious, or more specifically, anyone adhering the envelopes to the keypad. Based on the information and timeline we provided, they have narrowed down windows of time when the letters were probably delivered and are checking the intersection traffic cameras at the neighborhood entrance and on all major intersections nearby to see if they recognize the same vehicle on both days during those designated times. And that's about all I have…. But, guys?"

"Yeah," Eli said, looking at Hamish.

"He thinks this is more serious than he first thought and suggested that you guys be really careful."

"I'm on this, Royce," Eli said. "I won't let him out of my sight."

Hamish rolled his eyes. "Can you not talk about me like I'm not sitting right here."

"Sorry," Eli said. "You're right."

"How in the hell long will we have to deal with this?" Hamish asked, shaking his head.

"Not too long, it seems," Royce said. "Detective O'Hennesey indicated that if the perpetrator doesn't make another move in the next couple of days, he wants us to air the next video."

"No fucking way!" Eli said, jumping to his feet. "They are not using Hamish as bait. That's way too dangerous."

"Calm down, Eli," Royce said. "I agree with you, but O'Hennesey assures me that Hamish will never be in any danger. As I said, they're putting a full-time unmarked guard in front of Hamish's house and one here as well, and they will monitor the areas around both houses 24/7. They fear the longer the perp stews, the more worked up or violent he or she might become."

"I still think it's too dangerous," Eli said.

"Do I have any say in this?" Hamish asked.

"Of course you do," Royce said.

"Then I say let's do it and get this crap over with."

Eli turned his head away and cursed under his breath. "Just please keep us in the loop," he asked.

"I will, and, Eli?" Royce cleared his throat. "I pushed back tomorrow afternoon's shoot with Cavanaugh until the following morning at nine o'clock."

"Can we please postpone that until this is all over?"

"Unfortunately not," Royce answered. "Cavanaugh is only here two more days, and then he's heading back to the West Coast."

"Fuck, Royce. Come on, man."

"I know and I'm sorry, but I'll make the shoot as quick as we can."

"Stop it, you two," Hamish chimed in. "I'll be fine. I'll either come with Eli, or I'll lock myself in the house. Maybe it'll all be over by then."

"Okay. We'll decide when the time comes," Eli said.

"Is that it, Royce?"

"That's all I have so far."

"Thanks, man," Hamish said.

"Take care, boys."

THE REST of the day and the next went by without incident. Eli and Hamish were both putting forth a conscious effort to make the best of an awkward situation, and it was going okay. When they weren't sleeping, they watched ESPN continuously, played cards, drank, and ate everything in sight.

They had finished dinner, and Eli had been feeling uneasy all day about his shoot the next morning. He knew Hamish was going to go all macho on him and make light of being left alone, but Eli was determined to not let that happen. He wanted Hamish safe, and he was prepared for a fight to get what he wanted.

Before Eli could bring up the topic, the doorbell rang. Eli walked into the dining room, pulled the drapery back, and looked through the window. There was a tall, slim, and very good-looking guy standing at the door wearing black jeans and a black T-shirt with *DPD* on the left pocket, which Eli took for Dumfries Police Department. But Eli didn't need the *DPD* to know this guy was a cop—based on his stance alone, Eli could have picked him out of a lineup. The only thing that might have thrown Eli off was the guy's age; he didn't look a day older than twenty-five. The guy saw him and flashed a badge, and Eli nodded. He walked to the door and opened it. The security detail introduced himself as Sergeant Todd Eldridge and gave Eli a card with his cell number on it just in case they needed anything at all.

After saying good night to the officer, Eli joined Hamish out on the deck, where they sipped port and passed a Bolivar back and forth between them.

Eli had been trying all day to figure out a way to broach the subject of tomorrow without pissing Hamish off, and he'd come up with nothing.

"What?" Hamish said. "You've been staring at me for the last hour."

"Have not," Eli said defensively.

"Have too," Hamish retorted, handing back the cigar.

Eli took a draw and exhaled. "Fine. If you must know, I've been trying to find a way to ask you to come with me tomorrow morning for my shoot so I won't have to worry about leaving you here alone."

"I'm sorry to ruin your night, but I've decided to stay here," Hamish said.

"Please, Hamish? I'm prepared to get on my knees and beg if I have to."

"Not that I wouldn't mind seeing that," Hamish teased. "But I just can't, Eli."

"Why?" Eli asked, passing the cigar back to Hamish.

"I've got my reasons. Okay?"

"That's not fair," Eli whined. "I've been honest with you about everything I've been going through, and now you're keeping things from me?"

Hamish took a draw and tilted his head back and exhaled the sweet, smooth smoke. "I think things were a little different when you were pouring your heart out to me."

"Fuck, Hamish! I care about you, okay?"

"But you're not gay, remember?" Hamish said, calmly taking a sip of his port.

"No!" Eli said. "I'm not gay, but I'm struggling with my feelings for you. Can't you just cut me a little slack and give me some time to sort this all out?"

"You've got all the time in the world, Eli. I'm just not going to waste mine waiting."

Eli slid out of his chair, dropped down to one knee, and took Hamish's hand. "Please come to the shoot with me tomorrow."

Hamish looked Eli in the eye. "I can't."

"At least tell me why, then?" Eli asked.

"If you must know," Hamish said in a huff, "I don't want to be in that house while you're fucking another guy or, even worse, some other guy is fucking you. Okay?"

"But—"

"No buts about it," Hamish said. "You think you corner the market on jealousy? I watched part of your shoot with Logan and Cavanaugh, and I wanted to wrap my fingers around each of their necks until they turned purple."

"I know," Eli said. "I saw you in the doorway, and you had this weird expression on your face. The funny thing is, I didn't recognize the look until I saw my own reflection in the mirror after I saw you getting plowed by Bristol. Funny, then I knew right away it was jealousy."

"So you know how I feel, then?" Hamish asked.

"Yeah. I hate it but I understand."

"Look, Eli," Hamish said softly, almost inaudibly. "I care about you too, okay? But I just can't do this." He moved his hand back and forth between the two of them. "I've been thinking a lot, and I've decided to give up the biz, move closer to Josh, and try and start my life over again."

"No!" Eli protested, still on his knees. "You can't go. You have Josh to worry about. You said you needed one more year."

"Things change," Hamish said. "I can't stay here now. I can't watch you day after day having sex with other men. I thought I could handle it, but I was wrong."

Eli got to his feet and looked out over the lake. "This is all my fault. I should have never—"

"Stop it, Eli," Hamish interrupted, joining him at the railing. "This is not your fault. We"— he gestured between them again—"did this to each other. Neither of us planned it, it just happened. That's what was so magical about it for me. We were just two people who connected. Not straight, not gay, just two people who let their barriers down and connected."

Eli felt a tear slide down his cheek. "If one of us has to go, it'll be me," he said. "You have Josh to take care of. I only have me to worry about, and I've got enough money saved now to get a new start somewhere. As soon as this shit with the letters is over, I'll go."

Eli turned to meet Hamish's gaze, his heart breaking. "Please don't ask me to go when I know you're still in danger. That would kill me."

"I won't ask that of you," Hamish said, leaning in and pressing his lips against Eli's. Eli closed his eyes and lost himself in the tenderness of the kiss.

They sat side by side for hours, holding hands and not saying a single word. When the dampness of the night air became too much to bear, Hamish suggested they turn in. "You have an early day tomorrow," he whispered. "We better get some sleep."

Eli stood but didn't respond. He followed Hamish into the house and locked the door behind them. "Good night," he said, taking his spot on the couch.

Hamish held out his hand, and Eli stood. "Just sleep. Nothing more."

Eli nodded and followed Hamish to his bedroom.

Eli spent the night with his head on Hamish's chest, wrapped tightly in his strong arms. He didn't sleep a wink for fear of missing a single moment of the serenity and security he felt during those moments. The feelings were some he'd never experienced until he met the dark-haired man, and he was sure he would never experience them again. He briefly wondered why life kept doing this to him. Giving him people to love and then taking them away. His pitiful excuse for parents, his grandmother, his best friends in Afghanistan, and now Hamish and Royce. He figured that somewhere, sometime, he must have done something really bad to deserve this kind of heartbreak.

Eli didn't realize he'd been crying until Hamish brushed away the tears with his thumb and held him tighter. That simple act of kindness pushed Eli over the edge, and he let go of emotions he'd been holding back for a long time, probably since childhood. His silent crying led to sobs, which lasted for hours. He cried for every lousy thing his parents had done to him throughout his life and for not being there for his grandmother's passing. He cried for the fellow Marines he'd lost in combat and for the buddies he'd left behind. But mostly he cried for the loss of love, something he'd never allowed himself to do before.

Eli had always taken his life in stride, the good along with the bad, and figured whatever came his way was his due. But now he was second-guessing everything he'd ever believed in. What had his life become?

When his sobs eventually turned to whimpers and finally stopped, Eli lay there listening to Hamish's breathing. He'd known the minute Hamish had finally allowed himself to sleep by the way his breathing slowed to a steady in and out.

Eli stared at the window as the lonely darkness of the night transitioned to a bright sunny morning. His grandmother had always told him that with each new sunrise came new hope, but hope seemed to elude him this morning.

Somewhere around seven, Eli forced himself to release Hamish, both physically and emotionally. He slipped out of bed and tiptoed to the door, stopped, turned, and watched Hamish in his slumber for the longest time. He was lying on his side, his hair falling softly across his face, and even in his sleep, Hamish's sadness was obvious. Eli silently cursed himself for causing him pain.

Feeling forlorn and exhausted, Eli dressed, made a pot of coffee, and sat at the breakfast bar contemplating his future while he sipped. With no real answers in sight, Eli laid his .45 on the counter and wrote a note.

> *Good Morning, Hamish,*
>
> *I really apologize for my meltdown. It appears that years of holding back does come with a price, and unfortunately you had to pay the piper. I'll be back as soon as I can, hopefully before lunch. You're a Marine, I know you won't be afraid to use this if you need it. It's loaded and ready to go, so be careful. Please stay safe and call the detail immediately and then me if there's any trouble. I'm sorry for everything.*
>
> *Eli*

He poured a to-go cup and slipped out the front door, locking it behind him. He walked over to the black car across the street, tapped on the window, and when the tinted window came down, he handed the officer a steaming cup of coffee. "All's well inside. I'll be back around lunchtime."

When he got to the mansion, he found Royce busying himself in the kitchen. Royce took a good look at him when he walked in. "You look like hell," he said.

"Good morning to you too," Eli responded. "It was a rough night, and please leave it at that."

"The stalker?" Royce asked with panic in his voice.

"No, sorry. Nothing like that," Eli said. "Just exorcising some demons is all. Is Cavanaugh here yet?"

"Yeah," Royce said. "He's upstairs waiting for you."

"Let's get this show on the road so I can get back to Hamish."

They did the shoot, and Eli did his best to be cordial and look like he was into the scene, but it took every bit of skill he could muster. All he could think about was Hamish and how much he wanted to be there.

When the shoot was over, Eli ran down to his room, showered, and grabbed more clothes. Anxious to get back, he took the stairs two at a time. When he reached the foyer, Royce was standing there, ghostly white and holding a white envelope in one hand and a letter in the other.

CHAPTER SEVEN
DESPERATION

ELI FROZE and his heart sank to his feet. "Fuck!" he hissed. "Let me see."

"It came in the mail," Royce said, shakily handing the letter to Eli.

> *Dawes Turner and Elijah Preston!*
> *I hope you enjoyed your lakeside love nest!*
> *Betrayal comes with a price!*

Eli bolted for the front door. "Call O'Hennesey!" he yelled. "He knows where Hamish lives."

Eli slammed the door behind him, not waiting for a response from Royce. He jumped in his car and sped down the long driveway to the main road. Trying Hamish's cell over and over again, Eli finally threw it on the seat when every call went right to voice mail. Then he remembered the security detail. "Fuck!" He'd left the card with Todd's number on the counter for Hamish. Eli slammed his fist on the dashboard and cursed himself. "You're a fucking idiot."

The drive seemed like hours instead of minutes. Eli ran every red light and took all the corners at full speed. He sighed in relief when he saw the black car right where it had been when he'd left that morning. Pulling up to the car and jumping out, he tapped on the window, but the window didn't come down, as it had this morning. He tapped again frantically. Finally he tried the door handle, and the car was locked.

The house, Eli thought.

After bolting across the lawn and up the steps to the porch, Eli stopped when he noticed the front door was ajar. He knew he'd locked it when he'd left this morning, and the hairs stood up on the back of his neck. His instincts told him something was terribly wrong. Survival mode kicked in, and he reached for his gun, suddenly remembering he'd left it on the counter for Hamish. His heart raced as he pushed the door open slowly and eased his way into the foyer. He stopped and listened for any signs of life, but he heard nothing. He moved farther into the house, stopping at the edge of the foyer and looking into the living room, but still no Hamish.

There were no signs of a struggle, and everything seemed to be in perfect order, so he kept going. He slipped into the kitchen and saw his gun on the counter, sitting next to the note he'd left and Todd's card. He made his way quietly to his gun, lifted it, and checked the magazine. It was still loaded. Holding it out in front of him, he was about to make his way to the other side of the house when he heard Hamish's voice. He shoved the gun in the back of his jeans and ran toward the sound, his heart soaring with hope.

Eli found Hamish alive and standing in the foyer. He ran to him and wrapped his arms around his waist, burying his head in Hamish's neck. "Thank God, Hamish. You're alive," he cried. "We got another letter this morning. They know where you live, and they said someone was going to pay. I raced back here. The security detail was missing, and I couldn't find you. The front door was open, and Jesus, I thought they'd taken you."

Right about then Todd popped in the front door all sweaty and trying desperately to catch his breath. "You're one hell of a run—"

He stopped when he saw the look of relief on Eli's face and his arms tightly around Hamish.

"What? Is everything okay?" Todd asked.

Before Eli could answer, Hamish said, "I'm okay, Eli. We just went for a run."

Eli heard what Hamish said, but the words didn't register right away. Then the reality of the situation slowly started to sink in. His muscles tensed, his spine straightened, and he stepped away from Hamish. *He went for a fucking run after he told me he wouldn't go out without me until this stalker crap was behind us.*

Eli felt the anger rising from his toes. "You selfish son of a bitch! You went for a fucking run?"

Before Hamish could answer him, Eli drew back and nailed Hamish right in the jaw. Hamish stumbled back and hit the wall. He grabbed his jaw, slid down the wall, and landed on his ass, looking up at Eli with a shocked expression on his face.

Eli bent over and put his finger in Hamish's face. "If you have so little fucking regard for your own life, why am I fighting so hard to keep you safe?"

He looked over at Todd, who was frozen in place. "He's your responsibility now. I'm outta here."

Eli stormed down the hall to Hamish's bedroom, picked up his duffel bag from the corner of the room, gathered his dirty clothes, and stuffed them in. His next stop was the bathroom, where he gathered the few things he had there and headed back to the front door.

ELI WAS so focused on getting his things and getting outta there that he didn't see the eight-by-ten picture of himself in the middle of the bed with a dagger shoved right through his face.

ELI MADE it to the foyer, where Royce and Detective O'Hennesey had now joined Todd and Hamish. Royce was holding an ice pack on Hamish's jaw, and Hamish was staring blankly at the wall in front of him.

"Royce, I've had enough of all of this," Eli said. "I thank you for all you've done for me, but this is the end of the road."

"Eli, please," Royce said.

Eli raised a hand. "No, man, I've had enough. I can't stay and there's really no need to anymore. Do you mind if I go back to the house to get the rest of my things?"

"Of course not, but...."

"Thanks. Good luck with all this," he said, waving his hand in the air.

Eli took one last look at Hamish, who now had tears in his eyes, and no matter how much he hated him right now, he immediately regretted hitting him. Eli admitted to himself right then and there what he'd been fighting for the last few weeks. He'd fallen in love with the guy.

Without another word, Eli turned and walked out of the house, down the stairs, across the street, and got in his car without looking back. He was too afraid that if he looked back, he might not be able to leave, and he knew there was no other solution. He opened his car door, tossed his bag in the passenger seat, and slid in behind the wheel.

As he drove around the lake, Eli took one last look at the shimmering water he and Hamish had gazed upon so many times. Then he turned onto the main road, leaving the lake and his memories behind. He pulled up to an intersection and rested his head on the steering wheel while he waited for the traffic light to turn green. "You're doing the right thing," he said out loud.

Eli jumped when he heard a voice from the backseat. "You certainly are." Instinctively Eli looked in the rearview mirror, but he saw nothing. His entire body stiffened when he felt something cold against the left side of his neck.

"No sudden moves. I'm not afraid to use this. And just so you know I'm not bluffing...." Eli heard the gun being cocked.

"I get it," he said. "You're not bluffing."

Eli thought the voice was female and sounded vaguely familiar, but he couldn't for the life of him figure out from where. "What now?" he asked, wanting to hear more so he could try and identify the voice.

"This is all going to end where it began," the voice said.

Began? Began? Began? He tried to think. Then it hit him. "The Seasons Motel?" he asked.

"I'm impressed. Too bad you weren't that smart when you were warned to stay away from Hamish."

Eli knew exactly where he was going, so he drove on autopilot while he contemplated his options. He first ran a red light, trying to get the attention of the cops, but just his luck, none were in sight. "Do that again and you're a dead man," the voice from the backseat said.

He tried speeding and got called down for that as well. *I'm a fucking Marine. I'm not just going to accept my fate.*

Eli had his gun, but there was no way he could use it in the car without chancing getting shot himself. He didn't know how crazy this person was and wasn't about to chance it. But he also knew that when he got out of the car, depending on who got out first, the gun was going to be very visible.

Before he could come up with any other ideas, they arrived at their final destination.

"Pull in over there," the voice said, pointing to a room that was, coincidentally or not, right next to Eli's old room.

Eli did as he was told and put the car in park. "Now shut the engine off and give me the keys."

He followed instructions again, and when he handed over the keys, he was given a room key. "Listen to me very carefully," the voice said. "We're going to get out of the car very calmly at the same time, and you are going to walk in front of me, straight to the door, unlock it, and let us both in. Got it?"

Eli nodded, scanning the area to see if there were any other people nearby, but no such luck.

"Now," the voice said.

By this time, Eli was fairly convinced his captor was a woman and figured he could take her if he got the chance. He was already planning his escape as he opened his door and stopped, waiting for the back door to open as well. He slid out of the car, trying to keep his gun hidden, and stood motionless. Out of the corner of his eye, he saw the form of a person about his height, but much thinner, slipping out of the backseat. His captor was wearing all black with a hoodie and dark, nondescript glasses. *This has got to be a woman.*

His captor pressed the gun into the small of his back and stopped him. "Freeze!"

"Fuck!" Eli said under his breath.

He felt a hand rip the gun out of his belt. "Now go."

Eli walked up to the room as instructed, slid the key into the lock, and opened the door. He stepped in with the barrel of his captor's gun still pressing against his back. As soon as the door was closed behind him he made his move.

He spun around in a flash, grabbed both his captor's wrists, and with all his might raised them over his head and held them against the back of the door. In some kind of martial arts move, his captor brought up a knee and caught him in the groin hard enough to send him to *his* knees in agony. The last thing he saw was long blonde hair coming out of the hoodie before he took a boot to the face and everything faded to black.

When he came to, he was lying on his back, disoriented and confused. The minute he heard her voice, it all came flooding back to him. He panicked and tried to struggle to his feet but found his hands were duct taped to the bedposts and his ankles were held to the bed with the duct tape running completely around and underneath the mattress and springs. And… he was naked.

"Try anything again and you're a dead man," the blonde said. He tried to focus and racked his brain to remember where he'd seen his captor before. Suddenly it came to him: *Bambi from the sex store.*

"Bambi?" he said.

"Good memory, Eli."

"You don't want to do this," Eli said softly.

"Oh hell yeah, I do," Bambi said. "Hamish is mine. And the only reason I haven't killed you yet is because I want him to be here to witness it."

"Hamish has no idea I'm even missing, nor does he have any idea where I am," Eli explained. "He's not coming here, honey."

Bambi backhanded Eli across the cheek. "Don't call me honey." Eli ran his tongue across his lip and tasted blood. "He has no idea where you are now, but he'll know as soon as you call him."

"Bambi, you're just gonna have to kill me now because I'm not calling Hamish."

"Oh yes you are," she said. "Because if you don't, the very next thing on my agenda is a road trip to get to know one Joshua Turner."

Eli closed his eyes. *Fuck! This bitch is insane. And… did her homework. Now what do I do? If I call Hamish, I put him in danger. If I don't, Josh is in danger, and Hamish would never forgive me for that. Maybe Hamish can talk her out of whatever she has planned. He's Josh's only hope and mine. God, please let me be doing the right thing.*

"Okay," Eli said. "I'll do it. But I can't call him with my hands bound."

"Good try," Bambi said. "How stupid do you think I am? But… no worries, I've got your phone, and how sweet. Hamish is on speed dial."

Bambi pressed the speed dial button for Hamish and put the phone to Eli's ear.

"Remember," Bambi said, waving the gun in his face. "I'm listening, and one wrong word and you're both gonna be dead men."

Hamish answered on the first ring. "Eli! Are you all right? We know someone has you."

Wondering how they already knew he'd been abducted, Eli said, "I've been better."

"Where are you?" Hamish asked.

"I'm at the Seasons Motel. Room ten."

"O'Hennesey already has a plan. We're on our way. Eli, I'm so sorry. This is all my fault."

Eli could hear the guilt, concern, and stress in Hamish's voice, and all he wanted to do was make it better. *What can I say to warn him?*

Bambi was making signals for him to wrap it up. "I need to see you," Eli said. "But come alone."

"Alone?" Hamish asked.

"No!" Eli said.

"I don't understa—wait. Is someone telling you what to say?"

"Yes," Eli said, relieved. "I'll see you in a few, then."

"We're on our way. I… I love you, Eli."

Before Eli could respond, Bambi took the phone away from Eli's face and ended the call.

"He's on his way," Eli said, closing his eyes and hoping he'd done the right thing.

Bambi sat on the end of the bed and stared at Eli for a few minutes. "You're good-looking and all, but for the life of me I can't see what Hamish saw in you."

"Neither can I," Eli said. "He told me he liked you a lot when he got in the car after we left the sex store that night."

"He did?" she asked, her eyes lighting up.

"Yeah," Eli continued. "I know he kissed you that night too."

Bambi brushed her fingers over her lips as though she'd forgotten somehow. "Yeah. It was nice."

"If you're so convinced he's so in love with me, why was he kissing you?"

"Good question," Bambi said. "He told me once he wasn't gay and was only doing this for the money."

"He told me that too," Eli said.

"Then why—"

There was a knock on the door and Bambi jumped up. She stepped up to the door and peeked through the peephole. "It's him! He came!" She opened the door and stood behind it.

Hamish's eyes widened when he saw Eli. Hamish ran for him, stopping in his tracks when Eli gestured with his eyes to the door. Bambi slammed the door closed, and Hamish froze when he heard the sound behind him. When he turned, he locked eyes with Bambi. "Bambi?"

"Hello, sweet cakes," she said. "Came to see your man take his last breath?"

Hamish turned away from Bambi, ran to Eli, and started removing the tape from his hands. "Stop," she said. "No, Hamish."

Hamish didn't stop.

"I'll shoot," Bambi said.

"She's not joking," Eli said. "I'm okay. I don't want you to get hurt."

Hamish stepped away from the bed and turned to Bambi. "What in the fuck do you want?"

"Before *you* die," Bambi said, "I want you to watch your man take a bullet and slowly fade away just like our love did."

"No!" Eli said. "You only wanted me, remember? He loves you, and you say you love him. What kind of woman kills the man she loves? What will you have left?"

Bambi looked like she was thinking about what Eli said. "Do you love me?" she asked Hamish.

Hamish looked at Eli and Eli pleaded with his eyes for Hamish to say yes. "Yes, I love you, Bambi. I always have. I told you I'm not gay, and I only do this for money."

Bambi lifted the gun and pointed it at Eli. "Then if you love me, you won't care if I kill him?"

"Nooo!" Eli yelled when he saw Hamish lunge in his direction. The gun went off and the next thing he knew, Hamish was lying on top of him not moving. Bambi dropped the gun, screamed Hamish's name, and threw herself on top of Hamish. At the same time, the door was kicked open and O'Hennesey, Eldridge, and three other uniformed policemen entered the room with guns drawn. O'Hennesey cuffed Bambi and pulled her kicking and screaming out of the room.

"Oh God, Hamish. Somebody call 9-1-1," Eli screamed.

Eli fought frantically to escape his bindings, but nothing gave way. "I've got to get free," he yelled. Eldridge pulled out a pocketknife and ripped Eli's bindings, and Eli rolled Hamish over. Hamish moaned very loudly.

"It's okay, baby, I've got you," Eli said, tears streaming down his face. "The EMTs are on the way. Just hang on."

Hamish opened his eyes and tried to mumble something.

"Save your energy, man. I'm here."

Hamish opened his mouth again. "Don't leave me, Eli. Promise me you'll never leave me," Hamish begged.

"I promise," Eli said, laying his head on Hamish's chest. "Just hold on."

Hamish rolled over and got to his knees.

"Don't move," Eli screamed, trying to keep Hamish down.

"God, I'll bet that's gonna leave a mark."

Eli felt his eyes widen. "What the fuck?"

"I'm wearing a bulletproof vest," Hamish said through a half smile.

"You son of a bitch," Eli said as he threw his arms around Hamish and kissed him right in front of Eldridge and the others.

"Get a room and put some clothes on," Royce said as he walked into the room. "You're scaring the poor policemen."

Eli and Hamish burst into uncontrollable laughter.

"Remember," Hamish said when he could catch his breath. "You promised you would never leave me."

"And I meant it," Eli said, pulling on his pants. "But how did you know I was in trouble before I called you?"

"O'Hennesey," Hamish said. "Right after you stormed off, I found a picture of you on my bed with a knife stuck through it. O'Hennesey accessed the traffic cams and saw your car at the entrance to the neighborhood. When he zoomed in, he saw someone holding you at gunpoint. But after that we lost you."

Eli nodded and looked over at O'Hennesey. "Thanks, man."

"Just doing my job," O'Hennesey said. "It's a good thing you called, though. I have no idea how long it would have taken for us to find you."

Eli shook his head. "I didn't want to call and put Hamish in danger, but she threatened his brother Joshua."

"Joshua?" Hamish asked in surprise.

"This woman did her homework, Hamish, and she had it bad," Eli said. "I have no idea how she found out about him, but she did. She told me that if I didn't call you, she was going to kill me and then find Josh and take care of him."

Hamish wrapped his arms around Eli again. "I'm so glad this is all over."

"Me too," Eli agreed. "But you know we're still facing the same issues we were facing before all this happened."

"No we're not," Hamish said. "I have it all figured out."

Eli raised an eyebrow. "Oh?"

"I had a long talk with Royce and told him that if he still wanted us, he would have to cast us only in scenes with each other and maybe, just maybe, an occasional third person—only if we both agree. And in return, I agreed to one more year for both of us."

Eli looked at Royce for confirmation, and he nodded.

"I can do that," Eli said, then took Hamish in his arms again. "I have no idea what the fuck is going on, but damn I love you, man," he said. "Label or no fucking label."

SCOTTY CADE left Corporate America and twenty-five years of marketing and public relations behind to buy an inn & restaurant on the island of Martha's Vineyard with his partner of sixteen years, husband of six months.

He started writing stories as soon as he could read, but only recently for publication. When not at the inn, you can find him on the bow of his boat writing romance novels with his Shetland sheepdog, Mavis, at his side. Being from the South and a lover of commitment and fidelity, most of his characters find their way to long, healthy relationships, however long it takes them to get there. He believes that, in the end, the boy should always get the boy.

Scotty and his partner are avid boaters and live aboard their boat, spending the summers on Martha's Vineyard and winters in Charleston, SC, and Savannah, GA.

Visit Scotty at http://www.scottycade.com and Scotty Cade on Facebook and Twitter. You can contact him at scotty@scottycade.com.

Love Series

Bounty
of Love

SCOTTY CADE

http://www.dreamspinnerpress.com

Foundation of Love

SCOTTY CADE
and Z.B. MARSHALL

http://www.dreamspinnerpress.com

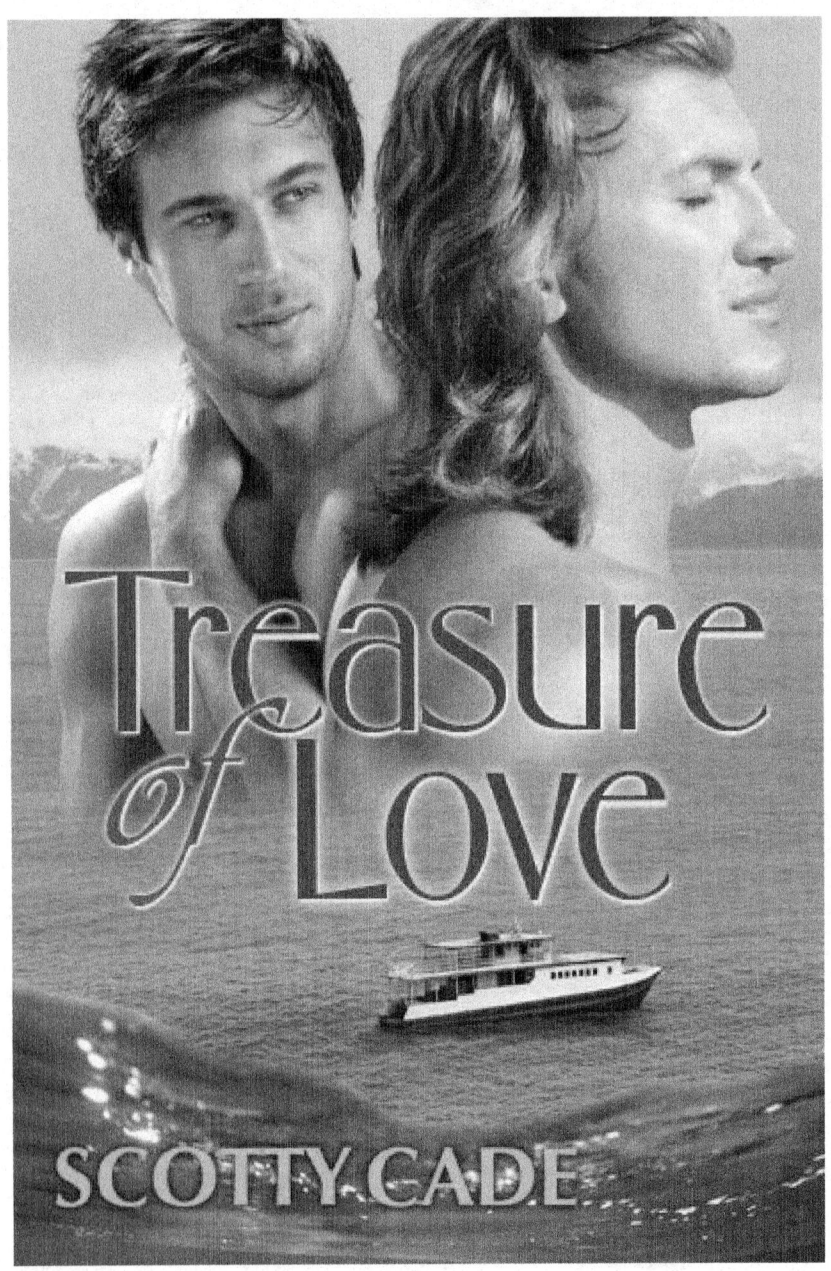

Love Series

Treasure of Love

SCOTTY CADE

http://www.dreamspinnerpress.com

Love Series

Wings
of Love

SCOTTY CADE

http://www.dreamspinnerpress.com

SCOTTY CADE

SUNRISE
OVER
SAVANNAH

http://www.dreamspinnerpress.com

SCOTTY CADE

CHASING
THE
HORIZON

http://www.dreamspinnerpress.com

AN
*Un*CONVENTIONAL
COURTSHIP

Scotty Cade

http://www.dreamspinnerpress.com

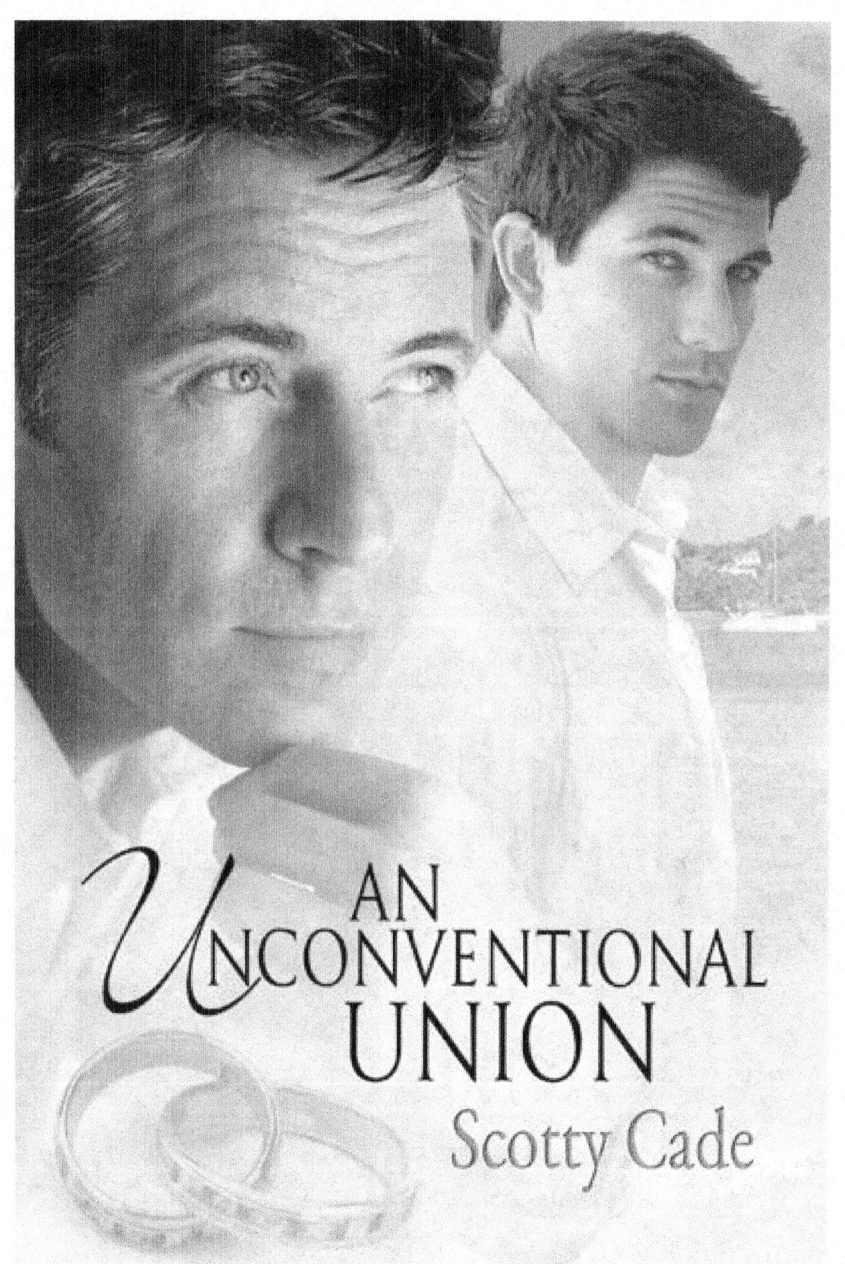

AN
UNCONVENTIONAL
UNION

Scotty Cade

http://www.dreamspinnerpress.com

FINAL ENCORE

Scotty Cade

http://www.dreamspinnerpress.com

THE *Mystery* OF
RUBY LODE

SCOTTY CADE

http://www.dreamspinnerpress.com